Tide Road

TIDE ROAD

a novel

Valerie Compton

GOOSE LANE

Edited by Bethany Gibson.
Cover background: shutterstock.com; figures courtesy of David Routh.
Cover and page design by Jaye Haworth.
Art direction by Julie Scriver.
Printed in Canada.
10 9 8 7 6 5 4 3 2 1

Library and Archives Canada Cataloguing in Publication

Compton, Valerie, 1963-
Tide Road / Valerie Compton.

ISBN 978-0-86492-635-7

I. Title.

PS8605.O5458T54 2011   C813'.6   C2010-907059-3

Goose Lane Editions acknowledges the financial support of the Canada Council for the Arts, the Government of Canada through the Book Publishing Industry Development Program (BPIDP), and the New Brunswick Department of Wellness, Culture, and Sport for its publishing activities.

Goose Lane Editions
Suite 330, 500 Beaverbrook Court
Fredericton, New Brunswick
CANADA E3B 5X4
www.gooselane.com

FSC
Mixed Sources
Cert no. SW-COC-000952
© 1996 FSC

For my parents, for Anne,
and for my sons, Jesse and Liam

A few of these islands are high and wide, with extensive dune fields and well-established maritime forests. Others are narrow with low and irregular dunes and few trees. Still others are little more than strips of sand with poorly developed dunes. When these barrier islands are attacked by rising seas, their natural response is to back out of the way. Storm waves wash over them, carrying sand to the back side in overwash fans of sediment. Marsh plants colonize these sand deposits and trap still more sand. As the islands erode on the ocean side, they grow on the sound side, maintaining their overall shape as they shift inland to higher ground.

Cornelia Dean, *Against the Tide*

ONE

January 1965. Prospect, Prince Edward Island.

He came through the door like a thunderclap, like a breeze. Hey! he yelled. Or, Hey, he said. He let the door slam. He eased it shut.

Which way had it gone? She couldn't be sure. She was tired, not paying attention.

To walk right in was normal for Evvie, to roar, to not care.

But something was different this time. Something was wrong. You could see by the look on his face.

She saw — she understood what she saw — and then she could no longer hear.

Woooooor, he said. Whirrrr, whooaar. As if they were underwater. As if the words he'd spoken had travelled through a mile of sea.

In some part of her brain, alarm bells rang and panic set in. But the words themselves eluded sense.

Stella's gone.

What did it mean?

Frances grasped her arm. "Mum! *Mum, please*—" Then Frances too disintegrated into underwater roar.

The room spun.

Someone led her to the cot and sat her down.

Inexplicably, she heard a baby cry.

Dan and Rose took charge and Frances stayed by her side, forced to remain at home minding her inept mother while everyone else in the community searched for Stella.

Later, that's how Sonia thought of it.

To Sonia, it seemed everything was connected to that moment — or contained within it, like the tree inside a seed.

But even in retrospect she could not make sense of the welter of contradictory impressions that washed over her.

Had she imagined Evvie into being? Was it possible she'd brought this all on, somehow?

TWO

Surely she could make sense of everything that happened if she tried. If she went back to the beginning.

She'd been working at the stove: frying fish cakes, making tea, taking beans out of the oven, adding wood to the fire, putting biscuits in to bake.

Frances came up beside her, dropped an armload of kindling into the woodbox, and stretched across the stove to inhale the seductive aroma of fish cakes browned in butter, biscuits puffing in the oven, beans enriched with bacon. She clapped the wood dust from her hands, slid into the rocker and closed her eyes.

Sonia had also been outside for hours, and she was hungry too. But she was not floating on a reverie of food, as her perpetually famished sixteen-year-old daughter seemed to be. She was caught in a replay of the walk she'd taken that afternoon, along the tamped-down path Rob had made with Dan's snowshoes through the woods behind their house.

She felt the heat of the stove against her hip. At the same time, she was in the woods, below the pastel sky and naked trees, surrounded by the bubbling voices of tiny acrobatic birds she'd never seen before and the intoxicating, hope-inducing smell of spring rising from the evanescent snow. *Borrowed day,* she thought, her mind lighting on the phrase Islanders used to describe the unexpected arrival of a springlike day in winter.

It had been a hard winter, a hard few years. But she felt satisfied that she had made the most of this one borrowed day. Now she would eat a good supper and she and her children would bask in the pleasure of relaxation after their busy day.

But then Frances stopped rocking. "Mum?" she said.

And Rose broke in. Nineteen-year-old Rose speaking in a child's fearful voice, not her usual, impatient one—gasping—shrieking— *"What! What do you mean?"*

Sonia turned, and there was Evvie in the doorway, holding Kate against his chest.

It was all wrong, Evvie holding Kate like that. *Funny thing*, he said. Casual as anything. *Stella isn't home.* Then Kate slithering out of her father's arms and Rose and Frances shouting and everything going silent and screaming noise at the same time. The spatula falling from her hand and its silent clattering across the lino floor.

Kate crying.

Evvie going on.

Funny thing. He thought he saw her coming toward him on the ice, but when he turned to look, she wasn't there. First he thought she was a vision. Then he thought she was bringing him his lunch.

There was a soft spot covered over with slob ice, he said, what the fishermen called lolly. He'd walked around that spot himself.

How she remembers that moment depends on how far back she travels. Her focus changes depending on whether she is re-experiencing the instant of knowing, or remembering what preceded it, or trying to make sense of all that happened later.

Memory changes, as the events of history never do.

Scrap that.

She is determined to make the ending come out a different way.

THREE

Because memory is pliable, isn't it? It depends on where you start, on the details you attend to, and on the ones you let slip away.

The way it began: there was an ice fog in the night, and she woke to a silver thaw.

Every tiny twig on every branch was glazed—every bud at the tip of every twig. It was as though the world had been dipped into liquid glass.

It was a liar, that stunning day. Trust me, it said. Revel in my beauty. Who imagines betrayal behind such glittering, extraordinary promise?

She went out after breakfast with suet and bread crusts for the birds, but only the blue jays took the food. The smaller birds that like to wait nearby couldn't get a grip on the coated branches. She tried to coax them, holding bread in her hand and calling, *chickadee-dee-dee*, but they wouldn't land. They fluttered all around then flew off, leaving her alone in the sparkling world.

Of course, it was a temporary state. By nine o'clock the tips of twigs had begun to drip, and by ten the sun had melted most of it away.

The weather had been strange all winter. Days of odd phenomena, days that started off super cold and heated up so rapidly that ice was melting off the roof at noon, days of whipping winds and massive quantities of snow. Recently, days that seemed too warm for winter. There had never been so much snow, and no one had ever seen it melt away so fast.

The melting seemed a blessing. The sun was out for the first time in a week, and everyone was outside to enjoy it. As soon as Rob and Frances got home from school, they went outside. Sound expanded with the warmth of the day. Sonia could hear their conversation, the chatter of the small birds in the trees, and over that, Dan singing to himself.

Every now and then there was a rash of banging. Dan was doing something complicated underneath the hood of their old truck. Evvie had called in to borrow Dan's auger and was on the river fishing smelts. Rose was hanging clothes out on the line. Rob was down to shirt sleeves, shovelling through a snowbank in the blazing sun. And Frances cleared a path from the woodshed to the woodpile behind the granary.

Sonia spent hours tromping through the woods. She lost track of time, her muscles ached deliciously, and she felt inexpressibly alive.

Then it was suppertime. She shaped and fried the fish cakes. Frances brought the kindling in. Evvie came through the door.

After Sonia screamed and dropped the spatula, Rose said, "Now, let's think," in her authoritative voice and everyone went quiet. "Where could she be?" Rose said. "She could have gone down to the root cellar or out to the woodshed. She could have gone to Cece and Mae's."

Stella and Evvie's house was half a mile away. Cece and Mae's was in between.

Evvie said, "I checked the cellar and the shed. I'll call in at Cece and Mae's." And he turned and was gone, leaving Kate.

Rose made up packages of food and Dan got on the phone and organized a search. Rob found two flashlights and filled all the oil lanterns. When Evvie didn't come back, Frances went to Cece and Mae's. Evvie was sitting down to supper, she reported when she returned. He hadn't told them Stella was missing.

Evvie often ate at other people's houses. He had a knack for walking in on meals. Stella doesn't feed me enough, he'd complain, and laugh.

It was a moonless night, cold and very dark. Dan built a fire in a barrel on the riverbank, a light to see by and a beacon for Stella, wherever she had gone.

The wind whipped that fire like a flag.

Neighbours came. Cece Ladner and his lame brother Jim, Lyman Cray, who went to school with Frances, Grover Hurry, Eddie Mack, a dozen farmers from all around. For the first few hours they were calm, hopeful maybe, or soothed by the rhythm of the work, as men are who work in fields or woods together, in the familiar comfort of each other's company.

They searched steadily and systematically, walking in parallel lines, calling Stella's name, beating the dark brush at the river's edge with sticks.

Mae Ladner and Marina Cray sent over sandwiches and squares and bottles of tea, and Rose took them down to the men.

At midnight, intending to relieve Rose, Sonia went down with hot baked beans in a pan and a fistful of spoons. "Go home and sleep," she said, but Rose would not leave. Her eyes were wild. They seemed to reflect both Dan's ferocity and Evvie's strange intensity. Someone had taken out a flask and it was going around from hand to hand. Sonia watched Dan wave it off. "We have to look farther out," he said.

Now the bean pan was coming back, scraped clean. Sonia took it in her hand. The dented metal already cold.

Eddie Mack whispered something to Rose, then came up beside Sonia. "Go on back, dear." He put an arm around her shoulder and pulled her body into the curve of his own. "Take your daughter home. Look after her." Then he released her.

Sonia stumbled up the bank, Rose already yards ahead, stepping mechanically through tracks created by the men, whose strides were so much longer than her own.

Sonia watched her daughter walk ahead, alone into the dark.

Later, she would wonder what Rose's experience of that moment was. She would try to fathom how Rose could bear the terrible uncertainty of not knowing what had happened to her older sister and when, or indeed if, she would turn up.

Sonia hadn't known how to help.

Later, she would hear Rose say, Mum is somewhere else.

This certainly seemed true. In retrospect, there were so many moments in which Sonia herself did not know where she had gone.

FOUR

Stella ran away.

Sonia said it, and her conviction grew.

In some part of her mind, she had always known this would happen. It was her fault, her punishment. The mistakes we make have consequences we cannot predict.

How far back would she have to go to change what happened? Sonia thought about Stella leaving home; Stella's accident, in which she lost the sight in one eye, when she was thirteen; Stella with Max and the other kids; Stella playing alone at three. She thought about Stella being born, a winter baby. She wrapped her arms around that sad, lost child. She smoothed her hair. And then she was on a beach, under a barely overcast, inscrutable sky.

June 1941. Surplus Island, Malpeque Bay, Prince Edward Island.

They walked, and it seemed to Sonia she had never walked before.

The surf rolled slowly up to the wrack-lined beach, stalled, and rolled slowly back, leaving in its wake a distasteful foamy lacework she stepped over automatically, other days. Today, the same pinkish seafoam called up the frilled edge of a dainty chiffon skirt.

"My dear—"

He looked at her, and she wanted to scream out the queer feeling of excess that filled her chest. Exhaling did nothing to dispel it.

She was aware of her mind divided. A part of her transfixed, a part moved solely by curiosity: How would this turn out?

"I want to ask you something. Will you tell me if I overstep?"

She turned to find him gazing at her, intent upon her answer. His mock-decorous manner comical, but tender at the same time. She nodded slowly.

"Why are you here alone?"

She rambled out the story of her tenure at Surplus light. How her husband, Max, secured the position when the previous keeper, who had lost a brother overseas, begged to enlist. How they'd met at a lighthouse station on the St. Lawrence River and married and immediately travelled here, to this tiny island in Malpeque Bay on the sandy north shore of Prince Edward Island, a different landscape than any she'd ever known. How, when they'd found the station in disarray, Max decided they'd be better off to farm. How he was farming now, an hour's drive inland. She did not say: *on a portion of his aunt Lil and uncle Hector's land.* She said he was making money so that they could quit the station for a simpler, more stable life. How this was what Max wanted.

"And your husband's given you the job he signed on to do?"

"I grew up on lights. I am as capable as he is. Maybe more so."

Apparently Peter Cope had no response to this.

She walked on.

In the dune-sheltered cove on the south side of the island he stopped abruptly, drew his braces back and dropped his pants, then felt for the buttons on his shirt.

Underneath his clothes he wore a pair of swimming trunks.

Still.

Sonia had never seen a man disrobe so casually before. Not even Max, in the privacy of their bedroom. Later she wondered if this strange ease with unclothed skin was a function of his medical training or evidence of oddness.

"I'm going for a swim. Will you join me?"

She shook her head. She wanted to swim. But she wasn't in the habit of wearing a swimming costume underneath her clothes.

The second time they met, she was hanging laundry from the clothesline at the station.

He walked up behind her on the path that ran between the dunes, and she didn't see him until he was beside her with a wet shirt in his hands. Her own shirt, from the split-ash basket at her feet. She took it from him and hung it on the line.

"I saw you from the shore," he said. "The lady lightkeeper of Surplus Island."

The naïveté in this remark made him sound like a summer visitor, a dilettante at Island life. How strange this was, since he'd grown up nearby. It made her wonder about the other life he led, at university in Montreal. She'd grown up in Montreal and missed it desperately sometimes: the handsome and historic buildings with their soulful interiors, suffused with mystery; the colour and drama and staccato music of the streets; the art classes she'd been so lucky to fall into. She loved the Island, but she envied him his urban life.

"I thought I'd stroll the beach this lovely morning. Would you be willing to accompany me?"

His smile was like a just lit wick, swallowing all the oxygen around it in a vivid burst of flame. The formal phrasing of his invitation, delivered with a deep, theatrical bow, made her want to laugh.

She knew even as she tied the basket to the clothesline that she shouldn't leave the light. But Max had been back only once in the past month: she felt desperate for conversation with another human being.

He said, "I'll walk—you talk." He said she hadn't told him anything about herself. "Only what your husband's planning for that farm of his."

Your husband. That farm. Something about the lightness of his tone alarmed her slightly, but she didn't stop to wonder why.

He stopped, though. He took hold of her arms and turned her to face him, his expression serious all of a sudden. "Sonia, what is it *you* want?"

What did she want? She turned away, took a breath. This cleared her mind. Still, she didn't know.

He tried again. "Tell me about your life here."

She turned to look at him.

His smile. How his eyes liquefied in the watery light. She considered his simple request: *Tell me about your life.*

What was there to tell? Her life consisted of lightkeeping chores, walks along the beach and rare—very rare—visits from her husband. Surplus Island was uninhabited, so she lived a life of almost perfect solitude.

"You like to walk," he said. "Where do you walk?"

There was nowhere to walk. "Sometimes I cross the causeway to Oyster Cove. When I need meat or milk or eggs I walk across and buy them from a farmer on the shore road."

"George Proffit?"

"You know him?"

"Sure. But what about this place? Tell me about your lighthouse chores."

She wondered if he was off his nut. Who's to say he wasn't?

He smiled. He had a relaxed, sincere face.

"If you like, I'll show you how the lighthouse works. But it's your turn now. Why are you spending the summer in this empty corner of the world?"

His story was the better one. She listened intently. Winters at McGill University, studying medicine. Summers at his parents' home nearby on Malpeque Bay, where he worked part-time as an assistant to the veterinarian, Cy McRae. He liked to cycle, so he toured the area. How he found her, alone on her island—he'd seen the brilliant, flapping laundry on her clothesline. Harold Pyke, the previous keeper, never washed, he said.

She laughed. She said she might have guessed as much from the state she found the station in.

He said, "But Cy McRae is a demon for clean in his veterinary practice." Then he stopped, set a hand on her elbow. "You know Cy?"

She shook her head.

"I'll introduce you."

This seemed unlikely, since she rarely left the light. But she didn't comment.

He talked of Cy a little longer. They walked companionably enough.

There didn't seem to be a natural place to turn around. He said, "So, we'll circumnavigate the island."

They did, and he said it wasn't as long a walk as he imagined it might be. Afterward, as she'd promised, she took him to the light. They circled the woodshed and the house, stuck like barnacles to the four-storey wooden tower. She'd left the tower door open and he went in ahead of her.

"We'll go up to the lantern room," she said, stumbling slightly, made uncertain by his movement through her familiar terrain. "I'll show you how the lamp and reflectors work," she offered. In the sudden dark, she couldn't see him. Mentioning the light was reassuring.

"This way?" His voice near the stairs.

But then he stopped unexpectedly, or he turned, or she misjudged — and they collided. Instinctively, she put her hands up in a gesture of self-defence, and her palms fell flat against his chest.

He felt as resilient as a rubber band.

She brought her hands down, stepped back.

He was tall and slight but strong. He was not as broad as her muscular husband, but his body was finely made in a way that Max's wasn't. She thought, He's only young, probably just a few years older than I am.

He said, "Maybe you should go ahead."

He stepped aside to let her pass, and they made their way up the narrow staircase.

On the landing, she paused to point out the fuel tank and pipes and the pumping mechanism that delivered oil to the lantern room. On the third floor, she showed him her charts and logbook and the supplies she used to maintain the light: chamois, rouge, extra wicks and reflectors. They climbed the final staircase, really a narrow ladder made of boards. In the lantern room she showed him how the lamp was lit and gave him her binoculars to look through. To her what was past the storm panes was no less than the light's dominion, but to him, she knew, it was only view: not complex or threatening, merely picturesque. He was silent for a while as he looked, first with the aid of the binoculars, then without.

"I can see you up here, tending to this light. I can see you climbing up those stairs at night, completely confident of every step."

She nodded. What he said was true. She felt at home on the light.

"I'd like to visit, one night when the lamp is lit. Would that be all right?"

It wouldn't be all right. Of course it wouldn't. But she could not articulate the reason why: her throat had seized up. *The way he was gazing at her.* She nodded assent.

They spent four nights sitting up in the lighthouse, talking through the dark. She loved his company—the stories he told, his calm presence and warm, resonant voice. His ardent curiosity.

Mostly they sat in the lightroom, one floor down from the lantern. During the day that windowless storage room was cool and dark, but at night, when the lamp was lit, a concentrated beam shone from the floor above, illuminating the space between them, the limbs they let fall across that space, the objects they brought into it. Pete entertained himself by reading to Sonia from the instruction booklet that governed her working life.

"*Rules and Instructions for the Guidance of Lightkeepers and of Engineers in Charge of Fog Alarms in the Dominion of Canada,*" he read, and laughed.

"*Rule no. 25. Any scratches in the silvering must be due to dust or careless work, and the keeper will be held accountable for them.*"

"*Rule no. 81. Keepers must conduct themselves with civility to strangers—*" He waggled his eyebrows.

"Are you so casual at school?" she asked, and he just laughed again. They lay with their backs against the floor, their knees in the air, their heads close enough in the uneven light that it seemed possible for them to discern each other's emotion, and intention.

"I think you're pretending," she said. "I think you're more serious than you want me, or anyone, to know." The smell of oil in the air, the bitterness of the rouge she used to polish the reflectors, the dust and the old wood of the structure itself mingled with a clean, piney aroma she now associated just with him.

"I'm not serious," he said, laughing and throwing his arms out, and the motes of dust tumbling in the shaft of light from above seemed to carry that play of fragrances, a careening, seductive scent.

⠿

Near the end of the fourth night, he fell asleep on the lantern-room floor, one arm flung protectively across his eyes.

She drew him lying there.

The slow flare of his arm, its resolute shape emerging from the crumpled sleeve of his thin cotton shirt; the crease in his neck, its depth a match to the spaces between the floorboards; the gentle curve of his jaw at odds with all the straight lines beyond. Drawing is about relationships, her art teacher, Mme Chevalier, had said.

She drew the boundaries around his body and she marvelled at—but could not begin to draw—its intricate movement. She wanted to cup her hands around the tender shapes, to memorialize and console and contain them.

When dawn broke, she extinguished the light and, yearning for sleep herself, woke him by touching his shoulder and his dark, silky hair. "The tide's coming in. You should go."

He seemed to wake, then fell asleep. Struggled, then woke again.

"Don't you have to work today?" she asked.

Throughout these nights she'd thought only of the time they'd shared. Now she realized that he was losing sleep in order to spend his nights with her.

She touched his hair again, and he took her hand and kissed it. "My dear, I'm on my way."

She listened as he stumbled down the stairs. Through the lantern glass, she saw him mount his bicycle and ride down the track toward the causeway. She saw him jump off his bicycle and drag it through the water. The tide had come in so far already that a short stretch of road had disappeared.

He didn't reappear for nine days. Nine fine, quiet days.

These were days of utter innocuousness. A high sun, no wind, moderate heat. From the gallery outside the lantern she watched lobstermen drop their pots—each vessel appearing on the horizon pregnant with a massive, unbalancing dark shape—a mound of stacked pots—then returning

22

to port unburdened. The reeling in of that day, and the sober, steady, rhythmic unspooling of the next: the men hauling their pots back up, emptying or examining them, replacing the bait, releasing them into the depths again. This pattern repeated, repeated, lagged, its sameness enervating. At the base of the tower, waves lapped in a desultory way, incapable without the wind.

Away from the light, she wallowed. She mourned his absence. She walked the beach, plodded through her chores, invented additional chores. From the tower, she watched the shoreline road. Once she saw a farmer, probably George Proffit, his team of horses pulling a trailer with a dark load, manure for a distant field. There was never another soul.

She knew it was a good thing he'd gone. Twice she'd forgotten to listen to "Instructions for Lightkeepers," broadcast in code on the radio.

She loathed this six-times-daily duty. Because she'd never yet heard anything out of the ordinary, it hardly seemed necessary to listen. "Rule Britannia" would play, and then: "Attention lightkeepers. All lightkeepers in East Coast areas. Instruction A—A for Apples—is to be carried out." Since this simply meant "display lights normally," she usually tried to slip in at the last moment so as to avoid as much as possible of the song, whose strident notes inevitably grated against her mood. Of course she would not ever skip "Instructions" by design. One day—you never knew—the government *might* broadcast Instruction B, which meant *extinguish lights*. She had heard tell in a letter from her father of a German submarine in the St. Lawrence River near Cap-aux-Morts—"A Load of Hay," he said they'd called it, on marine radio—and the keeper at North Cape, on the Island's westernmost tip, claimed to have seen a sub cruising in the moonlight.

She was taking linens off the line when he turned up finally, late one afternoon, a swooping dark presence on a clanking bicycle.

Dismounting at a run, he leaned his bicycle against the shed and raced toward her, grinning.

"Sonia! I have a surprise!"

From his pack he removed an empty flour bag full of baby beets—dull purple balls dusted with red earth and white flour—fresh peas and new potatoes. There was a piece of beef, wrapped carefully in the foil from a pound of tea and page after page of newspaper. (This she thought to save for reading.) And there were a dozen hen's eggs packed in sawdust in a biscuit tin.

He laid the gifts on the sand at her feet and she bent toward the bounty.

George Proffit had peas and beans and potatoes in his garden. She'd bought some earlier in the week, and they had been delicious. But somehow they hadn't seemed to shine with promise the way this food of Pete's did.

He smiled when she looked up. "Cy and I did some work for a farmer in Darnley this morning. There was no money, so he loaded us down with food. Cy took his half home. I thought we'd cook this, you and I, and picnic on the beach."

She shook her head and stood.

"Or we can eat in your kitchen—" He nodded toward the station house.

She imagined cooking an elaborate meal for him in her kitchen —something she had rarely found the energy to do for Max. "No...this is your food. Keep it. Take it home to *your mother*."

His face went pale and he bent toward the sand.

Why? Why had she said that?

He began to gather up the food.

I'm sorry, she thought, but did not say.

"I wanted to thank you for showing me the lighthouse and letting me see what it's like up there at night." He wrapped a hand around her ankle. "And...aren't we friends?"

Friends. Could they be friends? She thought of the drawing she'd made while he lay asleep on the lantern-room floor. She imagined tearing that page from her logbook, touching an edge of it to the flame in the lamp and then holding the blazing paper over the gallery rail. The image would collapse into scraps of ash, the wind would take these, and they would vanish before her eyes.

Was friendship what he wanted? All right. She picked up the tin of eggs and led the way toward the kitchen. He carried the bag of food bundled in his arms.

In the kitchen, they laid things on the table, where, somehow, they looked all wrong. "There's really too much food here for two people," she said.

"So, I'll come back tomorrow." He smiled. He reached for her hand.

She had to laugh.

Then there was a rattle in the air, louder than the sound his bicycle had made. He turned toward it.

"Max!" Her heart began to pound.

She looked around — food spread across the kitchen table, his bag slung on a chair, himself.

"You don't need me here," he said, picking up his bag. "I'll leave this for the two of you to share." He indicated all the food. "Oh, and here's your mail. I stopped at the post office yesterday."

He removed a letter from inside his jacket and set it on the table. From the envelope Sonia could see it was nothing special — a standard correspondence from Agent Harry Lank, her tedious, rule-bound boss. It was addressed impersonally, as always: *Keeper, Light Station No. 17, Surplus Is., Malpeque, Prince Edward Is.*

Max's truck sighed and stopped. He'd driven it across the causeway.

She tucked the letter away.

A truck door slammed.

Pete turned to leave.

"Stay," she said. "You can meet Max, and we'll all eat together."

"Not this time."

Then Max walked in, his head hung low, one arm dangling weirdly outside his shirt, the meaty forearm wrapped in a bloodied, torn-up pillowcase. Sonia recognized the tatted edge that bound his wrist, its pattern unique to the linen that had been their wedding gift from his aunt Lil.

"My God, Max!"

He sank into a chair. "I had an accident clearing brush. Lil saw to the arm. I'm all right now."

"My God . . ."

"I'm all right!"

He turned toward the stranger standing in his kitchen. He opened his mouth to say, *Who in hell are you?* But Sonia beat him to it.

"Max, this is Peter Cope from Sea View. One of the oyster-fishing Copes. Peter is a doctor, studying to be a doctor...with Cy McRae..."

Pete stepped forward. "Why don't you let me have a look at that?"

"It's all right. It's tied up now. The drive was rough. I banged it up some on the drive is all."

Sonia crossed her arms. "I bet Lil told you to have that seen to!"

Max stared at Sonia for a moment and set his jaw.

"Didn't she? Let Pete look."

As Sonia watched, one man pulled a chair up to the table and took the other man's hand in his. She blinked and the scene came clear, but still it made no sense: Pete Cope, her new friend, undressing her husband's sliced-up arm.

"This is an awfully neat cut. How did you say this happened?"

"I said already. I was cuttin' brush."

"This cut is from a straight blade, like a folding knife. Saws are serrated. They tear the flesh."

Pete looked at Max. Max held his gaze. Sonia wasn't sure what was happening.

Pete rewrapped the arm. "You need stitches."

"What did you say you were, Cope? A people doctor or a creature doctor?"

Pete stepped away. "Look, I can stitch your arm, but I'll have to cycle home to get supplies. I want you to keep this wrapped. Don't move around. You need to keep the arm immobile or it'll bleed too much." He turned to Sonia, spoke softly. "Give him whisky, if you have any. But just a little. He's trouble enough already."

Max stayed for two full days. He'd parked his truck on the island, snugging it against the station house. He had to wait for low tide to drive back across the causeway. (Spit, Pete had called it: sandbar, tide road, tombolo. He claimed to love the way it vanished and reappeared, like clockwork magic, twice a day. The only way to you, he'd said.)

Surely there were things to do back on the farm, but Max seemed not inclined to leave. "It's too quiet here," he complained. "I don't know how you stand it... But it's good. We need the money... Sonny Laybolt took a hundred dollars off-a me at cards last night. How the hell am I gonna buy seed now?"

His arm bled intermittently. Sonia kept the bandage fresh, changing it when necessary with strips torn from a sun-bleached sheet. She cooked the food that Pete had left, but badly. The meat she burned and the potatoes she under-boiled.

A hundred dollars! How could he have lost *a hundred dollars* at cards? And his arm—was that Sonny Laybolt's doing too? She pictured a knife, steel grey with a chestnut handle. She wondered what threat or act of violence might have provoked its use.

They ate in silence. They walked the sandy shore. They slept like lonesome strangers, afraid to merge, afraid to part.

Finally, Max went home. Alone again, Sonia began to feel combustible, explosive, as though the molecules that composed her body might suddenly fly apart.

What it was: the possibility Pete might return, now that Max's truck was no longer visible beside the tower.

And with Max gone, there was the simple pleasure of solitude, the restoration of her daily rhythm and routines, the ease of oats instead of eggs for breakfast.

She told herself Pete would turn up a few days after Max left, not right away.

After a week alone, she began to feel resentment. Had those days together meant so little? Had he been toying with her? Were they not friends after all?

She could walk across the sandbar at low tide, but she had no transportation on the mainland, no way of reaching him, no option but to wait.

It began to seem he wouldn't ever return, and while it was possible to write a letter, she wasn't about to.

Tidying up one day, she found the letter Pete had brought. Far from being what she'd imagined—a standard communication from the Department of Transport—it was a reprimand. "You're on notice," Agent Lank had written. "Consider this your only warning, Keeper MacAusland."

She'd missed a crucial coded message the day she left the light to walk with Pete. "C for Charlie" had been broadcast, and she was meant to send a written report on hearing it. Now Agent Lank didn't trust her—or rather, Max—to mind the light.

Worse, she realized she could no longer trust herself.

FIVE

January 1965. Prospect, Prince Edward Island.

The memorial service made Stella's disappearance real. For ten days Sonia had been trying to position her daughter's absence as a magic play. Stella's Clever Vanishing Trick, she tried to think of it as, a routine Stella would soon complete with a theatrical flourish. *Ta-da! Here I am!*

But now, as she zipped on a black wool dress, pinned up her hair and slid her feet into pumps, Sonia felt no faith in magic or drama or any other creative force. Stella was gone, and evidently she had made a decision not to return. Having a memorial service imbued this fact with a sickening finality.

It was embarrassing, this proof of her failure as a mother. Her daughter had *run away from home.*

Of course, publicly no one took this view. *Evvie,* they whispered, or *tragic accident.* They were good neighbours. They went to great lengths to make it not her fault.

She entered the church with her two sons and her remaining daughters. Together they walked toward the seats that waited empty for them in the first pew. Dan wore an old suit of his father's. It fit well, and he wore it unselfconsciously, creating an impression of maturity beyond his twenty-one years. Rob was the opposite. His limbs extended too far beyond his dark trousers and white shirt and his skin was unnaturally pale, as though his body had used all its energy in growing and spared none for general health. Even before Stella disappeared, Rob had seemed ill at ease. Turning fifteen, growing so tall in a short space of time, the social and academic challenges of high school—something had unsettled him.

Behind her brothers, Rose was tall and certain, but Frances held her head slung low like a flower felled by frost. As they walked, a hush came loose—the exhalation of three dozen pairs of healthy lungs at once—an obscene sound.

People shuffled in their seats. The wood of a pew creaked lightly as someone arched her back against it, a familiar Sunday morning sound. For a moment this blameless gesture seemed to ripple outward, through one body, into the next. Then, nothing. Evvie walked in and sat down. The church was nearly full, and the silence in it roused in Sonia a feeling of elaborate suffocation—as though a thousand hands wrapped themselves around her throat in quick succession.

Beside her, Frances dropped.

Mum, she heard, or thought she heard. Automatically, she put out her arms and Frances fell into them.

By now Sonia knew something about the experience of collapse, with its curiously inverted stages. First, you felt that captivating sense of reassurance so familiar from childhood, like the fall toward sleep. Then, instead of feeling imbued with calm, you were overcome with panic. Finally, a wave of nausea hit, and you felt an uncanny tug as some essential part of you was drawn away.

Frances looked relieved, as though she'd managed to escape.

But Sonia felt panic. Her voice wouldn't work. She was pinned by her daughter's weight. She could do nothing but look wildly around.

Rob and Dan stood up. Some of the men—men who would have been pallbearers if there had been a casket to carry—came over to help. They carried Frances to the vestibule, where she could wake in privacy, and almost as soon as they set her down, Frances opened her eyes. Sonia watched, a hand on her throat, unsure what to do. Grover Hurry rushed over and began to fan Frances with his large, rough hands, wafting, from the depths of his only suit, odours of rum and egg and the onion-alum pickle he gave away at Christmas. "There you are, my dear," he said. "There you are now." Mae Ladner put a hand behind Frances's back and tilted her body into a half upright position. Sonia moved to kneel beside her. She could see the tiny lines where Mae's lipstick bled into the sweetly fragrant, soft pink powder she'd dusted on her face. "Mary's coming with a cup of tea," Mae said, and Frances nodded.

On the floor beside her daughter, Sonia felt the reassurance that was the beginning of escape. She held her body still in an effort to fend it off. Mae drifted back into the distance next to Grover, who slumped against the door frame, hands stuffed in his pockets.

Sonia watched them closely. She refused to let the uncanny feeling conquer her.

After a moment, Mary Walt floated up. She put a chipped cup full of weak tea cut with milk into Sonia's hands and held them for a moment so she wouldn't let it go.

Mary knew how to manage loss: her husband, Walt, had now been gone a year. "Just drink that slowly, dear," she said. "Take your time."

Later, Sonia sat like a guest in her own living room while Mary Walt and Marina Cray served tea and biscuits and plates of ham and beans and other things the ladies in the community had brought over. Rose herded the ladies, and bossed them. Frances slid from one room to the next to avoid their sympathetic eyes. Sonia watched her, a blank-eyed girl in a black crepe dress searching for a solitary space.

In the hall mirror, the rooms of the house appeared festive, and they were filled with convivial talk. Kate, so adorable at eighteen months, was at the centre of a group of older neighbours who patted her clumsily, like children themselves, in thrall to someone's pet. This is how life is somewhere else, Sonia thought, or how it might have been.

Dan and Rob had vanished. To the barn, maybe, with some of the men?

How lovely it would be to be outdoors. Sonia slipped on her coat. Small groups of people lingered on the porch. She wandered among them. *Stella*, she found herself saying. *Frances. Rose.*

Then she was sitting on a kitchen chair in a corner of the porch, drinking tea with Eddie Mack. "My dear," Eddie said, "it's better for the girls to get on with their lives. It's what they need to do."

What had she said to elicit this? She could not think. Moments of her life kept disappearing even as she lived them.

⠿

Sonia watched Eddie doctor her tea with liquor from his pocket flask. The gesture he used, a casual splash and a neat little turn, was deeply familiar. For years she'd watched him amend her husband Max's tea this way. Things were different now. Gradually, in the seven years since Max died, Eddie had converted Sonia into a replacement for his friend. And Sonia colluded with this. She listened when Eddie told her things. She let him come by whenever he wanted. They sat together. Sometimes they played cards.

He was older, but sometimes he depended on her like a child. *Help me work this out*, he'd say, and the issue might be personal or practical or something to do with the running of his farm. He could have used his own brain, but he didn't bother if hers was available. He was like a cat, saving energy for the tasks he valued most.

But when he wanted to, he could exert enormous power.

Now she wanted to copy that strength. She sat with her wool coat open and her arms across her knees, leaning over her teacup like a man.

"They didn't find her, Ed. How can we get on with things when they haven't found her? We don't know where she is. She could be anywhere. She could've run away."

According to the police, Stella's body was in the river, under ice that varied from two to eighteen inches thick and from smooth to slobby.

They had no proof of this at all.

Stella could have run away. Sonia had worked it out. To get to the village she would have needed a ride. The trip to Charlottetown took an hour more, but people went in all the time. If Stella could get to town, she could disappear. Hardly anyone knew them there.

But why would she do it? This was the part Sonia hadn't been able to understand.

The world they lived in was from a history book, a place apart that neither strife nor progress had reached. Sonia heard news of wars in distant places and her children watched shows on television and listened to the Beatles on the radio, but none of these influences touched them deeply. Sonia had often been startled by change during her own childhood in Montreal. Living with her mother and her grandmother, who kept few secrets, she had been aware from a young age of adult concerns—political matters, domestic disagreement, strained finances. Her children knew a gentler reality. Their daily lives proceeded simply, governed by habits born of poverty but not desperate need. Frances chopped wood for the kitchen stove, Rose helped Sonia grow their food, Dan and Rob ran the farm, and they all worked so hard they fell asleep the minute they hit the bed. They bought clothes from the Eaton's catalogue on those rare occasions they bought new clothes, but mostly they handed them down. They had plenty. They had good lives, lives they were comfortable with.

"My dear, she didn't run away." Eddie had his arms around Sonia now, and he was smoothing back her hair. His voice had grown unnaturally soft, as though he were trying to calm a frightened child.

"We have to find her, Ed."

What could Eddie say? Sonia knew as well as he did that the ice and tides would scour out the river. Either Stella's body would be caught up on the riverbank in spring or it would be carried out to sea.

Unless she had run away.

"My dear," said Eddie, and he kissed the top of Sonia's aching head.

She woke up in the night, remembering the service. She'd dreamed Stella was there, watching from the back of the church, then walking up the aisle and touching all the flowers. Such extravagant flowers, lilies and roses, astonishing in winter. Stella bent to take them in her arms.

It was nearly morning and Sonia's light was on. She'd left it on all night.

At bedtime she had behaved childishly, complaining about the funeral. *Memorial*, Rose had corrected, *not funeral*.

Sonia ignored this. No word could change the terrible finality that pained her so hard that day.

"It isn't right to have a funeral if your child isn't dead," she'd said. "No one knows for sure what happened." She twisted the edges of the sheets around her hands like bandages, turning her fists into stiff white knots.

SIX

Stella ran away.

But Rose said, "Mum, Stella is *drawn* to water. She can't help herself. Remember that seal?"

The week before she disappeared, Stella had been obsessed with a seal cow that came into the yard. The seal was lost, but it seemed miraculous to Stella, a massive sea creature on dry land. She'd crawled up from the river in the night, alternately rolling like a tipped pint of cream and pulling herself forward with her powerful flippers. You could see the track she'd made around the yard, a wide ribbon of packed snow, wavery and lustrous as a slug trail. She looked boneless, her tapered body fattest in the middle, her thick skin smooth and moistly shiny from a distance. Close up, you could see the fear in her big dark eyes.

Seeing that look was what made Sonia think of telephoning out for help. First she called Kip Creamer, the veterinarian in Montague. Then, at his suggestion, she called Clem Sweet, a biology professor at the university. Dr. Sweet said, "Get her in a truck and take her to the shore." That made sense. Rob and Dan herded her to the truck and then lured her up a plywood ramp with a piece of salt cod on a string. Sonia watched her through the rear window of the cab, her liquid look of fear melting to entreaty, then dulling into hopelessness as they drove.

When the seal was in the yard, everyone came outdoors to look. Frances watched it intently, every bit the scientist she yearned to be. Rose crumpled her face in disgust or fear. "Get it away!" Stella, who'd come over from her own house, fixated on the oddness of seeing a water-loving animal on land. She kept laughing over that. "Poor thing, she's out of her element!" Stella would say, and hoist baby Kate high into the air to look down at the seal. It was as though the circus had come around. No one got to work until late, and Stella grew giddy with the idea of creatures switching elements.

Sometimes it seemed Stella was entirely bereft of common sense. Why couldn't she have been more careful? Why didn't she test the ice? Why did she go down to the river in the first place? She was contrary—that was the problem. With Stella, everything had to be upside down and backwards. Sonia thought of smashing the ice, of it coming apart in her hands, of hauling Stella out and Stella wanting to climb in again. She'd been so obstinate as a child.

And the ice itself was perverse. Some of it was lolly, the police had said. Lolly makes a shushing, roaring sound. Sonia knew from childhood. Soft ice, it's called, but in fact it's sharp, not soft at all. You would think it would be cold, but being in it's warm, toasty warm. You can't skate over it like sheet ice or swim in it like water. It's sticky and surprisingly difficult to move through. It builds up on objects that are immersed in it. If it built up on the eyes it would cloud your vision. It's a slobby, slushy, sludgy veil, and it runs much deeper than you would imagine.

The seal cow barked and bared her teeth when they stopped the truck beside the wharf. Rob and Dan let down the gate, and she drove at them so that they backed away, and then she flung herself from the bed of the truck before they had a chance to rig up the plywood ramp. They heard her muscular belly scrape across the snow as she flippered to the ice.

Stella's belly was soft from having given birth to Kate, and looked deflated, like over-risen bread dough. It was the belly of a person who belonged at home, beside the oil stove, with her baby in her arms.

Sonia tried not to picture Stella slipping through the ice, but all she could see was how the jagged edges would have cut into Stella's hands.

If only they'd been there, Rob and Dan could have saved her with some simple object from the truck—a rope or a board or a blanket.

The seal sped up when she reached the ice. She tipped her face toward the sky and bawled, as though to say, I'm home, this icy plane is home. Then, with a crash, she broke right through—and immediately grew graceful, as though her body had turned into water too.

SEVEN

When Sonia woke again, it was to the sound of Frances bickering with Rose. "Shhh," Rose hissed. "You'll wake up Kate!"

Sonia put on her dressing gown. Someone had brought the flowers from the church. The house was filled with them. Daffodils with curved leaves sharp as harrow teeth, blooms still tightly folded inside their dry brown paper wrappers. Lilies bright as saviours. Gaudy mixed bouquets. Sonia watched as Rose flitted from one bunch to another, smelling, touching. For the first time it occurred to her to wonder where these absurdly out-of-season flowers had come from, and why anyone would imagine they'd be worth the expense.

At the stove, Rose unwrapped the paper from a bunch of white narcissi, releasing an explosion of acrid stench. Frances snapped, "Forget it, Rose!"

Didn't Rose see? Flowers weren't going to help.

Against Rose's protests, Sonia gathered the bouquets from their bottles and vases and lugged them dripping out behind the barn to the oil drum Dan burned garbage in.

For a moment she was tempted to touch the cold metal drum with her wet, bare hands. Her fingertips would stick, and she'd rip them away. Then, for a fraction of a second, a searing pain would relieve the anxiety, the dragging emptiness and the aches she could not seem to escape. But the relief wouldn't last.

She could almost see the flowers shrivelling in the biting cold.

Stella had been passionate about the fragrance of flowers. Because of her damaged eyesight she liked to pretend that she could perform feats of extraordinary perception with her other senses. She would listen intently. And she could walk in the door and name the ingredients of a cooking meal. *Pot roast with carrots and celery and summer savoury* she'd announce. *Cod with bread crumbs baked on it, and did someone just make tea?* Sometimes she could say who had been to visit. *Is that Mae's face powder? Was Cece here, sopping bread in milk again?*

Reminded that shutting out one sense intensifies the others, hopeful that in some way she might connect with her absent daughter, Sonia closed her eyes —

But the stink of daffodils and the metallic tang of cold was all she got.

When Sonia came back into the kitchen, her hands and face stiff with cold, Rose was setting out the breakfast things and the stove was spitting hard. Rose had crammed the firebox with birch. Sonia warmed her hands over the stove, then lifted the lid and stirred the fire until it settled.

"Sit down, Mum," Rose said. She dished up eggs, made tea, laid out jam and butter, sliced a loaf of Mary Walt's good bread for toast.

Frances sat too and they focused on their breakfast. "I'm going to clean the house," Rose said. Sonia nodded and buttered and for a moment she felt relief. Yes, she thought. Work is the answer. An animal in harness has no past, only present. Life is easier that way.

The porch door slammed. Rob and Dan, coming in from the barn. Noisily, they kicked off their boots, and in Rose's room, Kate woke up crying. Rose snapped her fingers. "Come on, Frances! We have a lot to do." Sonia watched Rose turn to go to Kate, and her sons strode by, bright cheeks flaming and the bitter scent of frost falling from their clothes.

How she envied them their outdoor lives. She would have traded shovelling manure and milking cows for household chores. She would have bagged and stored grain and graded potatoes. She would have hauled and carried and sweated and built. She would have treasured those tasks for the escape they offered from the house, with its stifling, corrosive and unmovable burden of pain. But she knew the boys didn't really want her in their barn.

And of course there was no escaping the pain, which followed her wherever she chose to go.

Later, the kitchen was warm and the only sound the mumbling of the fire. Kate lay curled on the couch, Rose beside her. Sonia stood at the sink with her hands immersed in oily dishwater, that barking seal slipping away, submerging again and again and again. The image chattered on her mind like a movie jammed in a broken film projector.

"Mum? *Hello!*" Rose snapped her fingers and waved her hands in front of Sonia's face. "Mum. Hey. Where did you go?"

Sonia felt the lurch of panic. What was wrong?

February 1965. Prospect, Prince Edward Island.

When the weather returned to normal, Rose wanted everyone to drag their disrupted lives back to normal too.

Rose said they should establish a routine for Kate. All along, the boys had kept to their daily schedules; the animals required food and care, so Rob and Dan had no choice in this. But Frances and Sonia had allowed themselves to become lost, Rose said. Who is responsible for Kate? she asked Frances, within Sonia's hearing. Who's taking over the chores Mum used to do? She spoke as if her mother wasn't there. So far, Rose and Frances hadn't worked these questions out. They simply stumbled in a haphazard manner from one moment to the next, allowing chaos to build up like snow around the house.

It was not possible to let things slide. Heat depended on splitting kindling and getting in wood. Meals required homemade bread and soup or beans or salt beef brought up from a barrel in the wellhouse, then thawed, rinsed off, drained and cooked. Someone had to gather eggs, start oatmeal porridge simmering on the stove, set the bread. Someone had to soak and wash the clothes and linens and all Kate's things. These had to be put through the mangle, as it was so accurately called, and hung out on the line and then brought in to defrost and be ironed dry.

In addition to all this, Frances was missing school, and Rose had abandoned her correspondence course in secretarial.

Weeks of disorder had built up in the house before Rose spoke. Now she pointed out clothes and toys strewn around, Kate crying all the time, the boys complaining there was no tea, no food. Rob wanted clean thermal shirts and socks. They'd run out of butter, flour, salt. The floors were dirty, the towels musty, the porch awash in mud.

Recovery seemed impossible to Sonia, but Rose was more pragmatic. She made a list, assigning tasks and issuing orders her mother and sister weren't always up to following.

EIGHT

We've grown apart from one another, Sonia thought, and our lives are so different from how they were before.

Even at night the boys were in the barn, never in the house. Frances became silent, and Rose cultivated a jangled, forced jollity that everyone but Kate ran from.

Most days, after cleaning up the breakfast things, Rose would lie on the kitchen couch and cuddle Kate. She'd sing a little ditty and twirl her finger on Kate's small, fat palm.

Until they'd worked out some more permanent arrangement with Evvie, Sonia, Rose and Frances were supposed to share in looking after Kate. This was what Frances and Rose had decided. But the way it turned out, Rose managed all the daily baby care—diapers and feedings and crying jags—and she played with Kate too, or pretended to.

Even as they lolled on the couch, Rose kept her arm tensed between Kate's tiny, mobile body and the edge. Kate didn't notice that Rose was obsessively on guard. Her fat little fingers stuck out at all angles like starfish limbs and she laughed with her mouth opened wide.

Sometimes it seemed wrong to Sonia that Kate spent more time with Rose than anyone else, but mostly she felt relief. It was so long since she'd cared for a small child that she felt uncertain what to do—she could not be solely responsible. And it was apparent this arrangement was good for Rose. Caring for Kate filled some need she had, or salved some guilt.

March 1965. Prospect, Prince Edward Island.

While Rose looked after Kate, Sonia used the phone to call the RCMP. What had they learned since Stella ran away? She called the train station, the taxi company in the city, the few friends Stella had in high school and hadn't mentioned since, the city police, the hospitals.

Without these tasks, she had no reason to get up.

Yet sometimes she didn't get up.

Sometimes she forgot her role and wandered like a ghost, not changing from her nightgown, not eating more than toast and tea, hardly speaking, even when addressed directly. Rose and Frances brought her meals on a tray. Eddie Mack came by, her neighbour Marina Cray, a few other ladies. Sonia didn't get up for any of them. "She needs her rest," she heard Marina say. "Just give her time."

Loudly, Rose complained, "But that's what we've been doing."

Some days she was absent—she couldn't help it. She was *somewhere else*, just as Rose had said.

NINE

Time passed. Sonia couldn't say how much.

Her daughters milled around uncertainly, or made repetitive suggestions about getting on with things. They annoyed one another — she noticed this.

She noticed sound — too high, too low, too loud. Or no sound. Nothing, nothing, nothing, for hours on end. She noticed pain in her limbs, her chest. Her heart ached. Why did she have such intense *physical* pain?

She noticed the surfaces of things. Their flatness and lack of depth, the dullness of their colours.

She noticed the hardness of her bed, the dryness of toast, the tastelessness of tea.

She noticed quiet, quiet, quiet, like a raging noise. And the inescapability of the central question: *Why?*

"You have to get up, Mum," Rose said. "You have to get outside."

Was there some way in which this terrible grief was helpful?

Sonia leaned on the hope that it was healing, necessary, the way a scab is necessary to protect new tissue growing underneath.

Were they growing stronger? Did their hearts only appear to be wrecked beyond repair?

Sonia could not imagine ever feeling calm again. Her heart beat too fast. All the time she felt anxious and overwhelmed.

Rose screamed in the woodshed—not the house—so Kate wouldn't be alarmed. *Goddamn. Goddamn. Goddamn you all to hell!*

Sonia heard. Dan and Rob heard, though they pretended not to. Frances must have heard, from her room at the back of the house.

And what did the boys do, to express their pain?

They were hardly around, they barely spoke, so Sonia could only imagine.

What she remembers of those hellish weeks: Rose became absorbed in looking after Kate. Frances returned to school and poured herself into her studies. Rob and Dan wired the barn. Was this their way of moving on? Out there with their rolls of black, cloth-covered line, each with a pocket full of staples and a hammer in his hand. The deliberate way they'd have to work: selecting each staple by its rounded—not its double-pointed—end; carefully positioning it around the wire; hammering the staple without denting the wire, without piercing its fabric skin or copper core.

Less productively, Sonia huddled in her room—desperate, sleepless, lost to everyone. She felt as though she too had gone away.

She tried to imagine Stella coming home. What would bring her back?

But there was never any news, and Sonia could not imagine a way out of her dark, solitary cave.

Sometimes she felt tormented by a feeling of responsibility for Stella's disappearance.

Had she paid enough attention to Stella?

In her memory, she turns her back on her daughter, annoyed (*annoyed!*) by the troubles in her life, made impatient by her constant need for help: Stella's washer won't start, her head aches, her bread won't rise, a cupboard door keeps getting jammed, the flour bin has fallen apart. Small things bother Stella too much, tiny problems she could solve herself. *Mum?* she says, her voice pathetically low and mild, her expression pleading, tentative. *Mum?*

You are grown up, Sonia wants to remind her, *married.*

She'd wanted to deny her child. Again and again she'd turned away, ignored her pleas, pretended not to hear.

She'd come to believe Stella needed to learn how to help herself. It was the wrong approach. But in the chaos of the moment, she could not see far enough ahead.

All through those weeks, Sonia kept her bedroom door closed to contain the torment, to quiet the scrabbling in her mind. She was like a squirrel in a box trap — climbing the walls, smashing the lamps — or she was a nightie-clad wraith in a terrible race, chasing memory, fleeing guilt.

October 1939. Pointe d'Espoir, Quebec.

A sunless day — balmy, still, the world enclosed in colourless vapour as familiar and moderate as breath.

Sonia was picking cranberries in the clearing, marvelling at the extent of their chromatic range (vermilion, orange, yellow, celery, cream), and everywhere glistening beads of fallen fog (subtle, watery tints, berylline through glaucous grey), when suddenly out of the silence a motorboat drew up and cut its engine at the slip. After a time she saw her father's hand lantern go bobbing down the cliffside path. She gathered her bowl of berries and headed back toward the house. Daniel would expect a meal to offer whomever he brought up from the river.

She'd lived with her father at his lighthouse station in Pointe d'Espoir, Quebec, since completing school in early spring. After fifteen years with her mother and sisters at her grandparents' home in Montreal, only visiting her father on holidays, she asked for the chance to try out as assistant lighthouse keeper. Daniel promised he would teach her everything a keeper ought to know. Only after she moved in did she discover he had been humouring her with this promise. He did not reveal to the Department of Transport that she was living at the station. "DOT won't pay for an assistant keeper at Pointe d'Espoir," he said when she pressed him to explain. "It's such a simple light to run."

Though not simple enough for Sonia, apparently.

At first she didn't care. She had her dyes and a supply of wool.

But then Max arrived, and everything changed.

The first time Sonia saw Max, she was taken with his sandy hair and brows, frosted sugar-white in places from sun. His pale blue eyes bored right into her. For a moment she was frightened of his gaze. Then she decided he was merely anxious, and not much older than she was — nineteen, maybe twenty. She looked more closely. His mouth was broad, and his smile as lively as a strand of kelp dancing on an August sea. He wore a hand-knit scarf and toque, an oiled slicker like her father's, and underneath an expertly knitted, un-dyed sweater of a plain design, a worn blue flannel shirt. His clothing spoke of thrift and maternal care. Sonia asked who knitted for him. His mother made his things, he said. Her name was Nova Byrne MacAusland. *Nova*, Sonia thought, studying the sweater, *I would like to meet you.*

Daniel introduced Max carelessly to Sonia as a member of the crew of the lightvessel *Brilliant*, the floating beacon moored permanently in dangerous shallows opposite Cap-aux-Morts. Then he outlined a plan. He would take the motorboat downriver to repair a broken lamp on *Brilliant*; Max would remain behind to mind Daniel's light.

   In later years Sonia's memory of the fury she felt then mellowed somewhat, but she never did forget. A fiery feeling like a blend of flame and tar, thick and sticky, burning hot, had filled her lungs. She saw black. *She* was assistant keeper. *She* was!

   But there was no point in trying to discuss a thing with Daniel. There never had been. Even as a child she knew better than to ask her father twice for something. *Maybe* just hardened into *No*. Daniel's decisions were his own, and they were always final.

She busied herself with domestic chores, stoking the wood stove and making chowder from cans of milk and clams. There was relief in familiar work, in slamming pots and sticks of wood around — and in testing the limits of Daniel's temper. She could be as bloody-minded as her father, he would see.

She tried to listen as Max explained to Daniel the problem with the optic on the lightship. "Spray of fuel," "line" and "spring" were the only words she heard. Every other sound was drowned out by the roar of anger and disappointment in her ears. Why would her father never trust her to do work she'd proved herself amply capable of? In wartime, women took on many more complex jobs than this one Sonia held informally. Soon, women the world over would assume significant responsibilities. Sonia knew this for a fact because she read the paper from Montreal, whenever her father or the supply truck driver remembered to bring it with him.

She burned the biscuits, but neither Max nor Daniel appeared to notice. While they ate, she swept the floor around them, banging their shins with the broom. Then she went upstairs to pack her father's bag. "Only two days on the water," he said happily when he came up. "All I really need is my slicker and a couple of pairs of dry wool socks!" He rubbed her back as she folded socks, and her anger began to melt away. Daniel adored an adventure; she could not begrudge him this rare chance to escape his station chores. She packed his Thermos, three apples from the cellar and the bar of chocolate she'd been saving from her mother's latest care package. Her father would be fine, and she'd sort out Max MacAusland somehow.

When Daniel had gone, Max did something in the engine room while in the kitchen Sonia filled an old jam kettle with boiling water and powdered dye to soak a skein of wool. She stirred the mass with a driftwood stick, lifting it from the dye bath every thirty seconds to see what colour she'd achieved. She knew wool looked three shades darker wet than it would dry. She aimed for something close to navy, hoping to achieve a blue with both depth and light. When the dye had taken, she added vinegar as a mordant, then rinsed the wool in clear fresh water, rinsed, and rinsed again. She rolled it in an old piece of flannel to draw the water out. Slowly, carefully, she spread its heavy strands along a broomstick that hung from the rafters of the whistle house and left it there to dry.

Outside, the wind was up. It was colder now. What had her father taken on, going downriver in such changeable weather?

⁙

For supper she plucked and stewed the hen Daniel had killed that morning. She cooked cranberries with honey, boiled turnip and potatoes and opened a jar of pickles from the pantry.

"Do you always eat this well?" Max said when he was served.

Was that an accusation of some kind? "This is how we eat when I cook a hen."

"On the ship," he said, smiling as he ate his chicken, "we only have a hot plate, so it's cans of stuff or nothing."

Sonia poured the tea.

"You're lucky here, you know," he said. "On the ship — well, here you have — "

She sighed. She looked out at the water.

Since leaving school, Max said, he'd been living aboard *Brilliant*. The primitive, crowded conditions (five other men worked *Brilliant*) and the decrepitude of the vessel with its coal-burning generator and its temperamental gas-fuelled lamps made life on board an especially monstrous kind of hell. Max wanted to get some experience on a station light, then find a station of his own.

He hoped, he admitted, for a recommendation from an older keeper, like Daniel Greer...

Of course you do, she thought.

She knew her father would never recommend her to DOT if he recommended this ambitious young man.

What Max wanted from lightkeeping was not what Sonia wanted. The solitude and the importance of the work appealed to her. No one *needed* pictures — not in the way they needed water, air or food — but if that lamp did not stay lit, fishermen would die.

Max only wanted a job. Almost any job would have sufficed. But lightkeeping was all he knew.

She closed her eyes and he began to enumerate the things he'd said he loved about the station (woods, house, food). She went to the oven for the biscuits, dumped them in their basket and sat down again.

"Would you like some butter?" In spite of the tea, her mouth felt dry as paper.

"It's a lovely meal," he said. "A very lovely meal."

They ate in silence after that.

She left the table before her plate was clean, to get another stick of wood to brighten up the fire. The woodbox in the porch was empty, so she went out to the woodpile on the lee side of the house. By the time she made it back into the kitchen, Max had vanished into the tower again.

She spent the evening working near her bedroom window, bathed in intermittent light—coloured wool illuminated every twenty seconds by the turning of the lamp's occulting lens.

The abstract picture she was making drew from skies she'd watched out the windows of the lighthouse tower, and from horizon lines she'd studied in all kinds of light. She'd traced lines on paper to record the play of shapes she liked, she'd meticulously prepared the dyes, she'd spun the wool herself, and now she threaded lengths of saturated colour onto a canvas frame she'd built. She knotted the wool in places, loosened it in others. She smoothed it to emphasize its sheen, or she encouraged its halo to flare out. She added one colour—another, another.

In this way, hours passed.

Sonia woke as usual at six. The morning was cold. She dressed and went straight downstairs to build up the fire in the kitchen stove and put water on to boil. Max was asleep on the kitchen couch, fully dressed, covered with his coat. He woke when she dropped the lifter on the stove. "Funny how you miss the pitch and roll," he said, rubbing a hand across his eyes. "Feels like I barely got to sleep."

She began to prepare a pot of tea, a plate of toast and boiled eggs. "Porridge?" she said.

"Yes, ma'am."

She filled a bowl with oats from the pot on the back of the stove, added brown sugar and fresh cream.

"I could get used to this," he said, grinning as he spooned his porridge up.

After breakfast, she went outside to do her chores. She started up the tower stairs. Then, halfway, she turned around, compelled by a vision of the jewel-like skein of cerulean lambswool hanging in the whistle house. What did it matter if she didn't do her chores? Her father had put him in charge.

A ragged gust wrenched the door of the whistle house from her hand. She had to lean against it to push it closed. She looked around, collecting evidence the wind was up: whitecaps on the river, flattened weeds in the meadow, the big trees near the bank waving freely, as though trying to escape their roots.

She wondered, Is the wind this bad in Cap-aux-Morts?

Sonia worried about her father whenever he was away. Every trip downriver, it seemed to her, would be his last. Daniel Greer was a skilful mechanic and electrician, regularly called upon to do repairs at other stations. But on the water he was a nightmare—clumsy in the boat, terrible at navigation and prone to losing oars (or, if in a motorboat, forgetting to gas up). As soon as he had said he was required at Cap-aux-Morts, she'd felt sick. He would not come back. Sometimes she knew important things this way. She hoped they wouldn't happen, but she hoped against a kind of certain knowledge, only so the inevitable wouldn't disappoint as much. Already she missed her father's whistle and his sandpapery singing voice. As she pumped up the air compressor, she counted to distract her mind. Then she oiled and polished the diaphone with a soft old chamois, collected the skein of sky blue wool and closed the whistle house, walked out to the little vented weather box in the clearing and read the wind and temperature gauges bolted to an iron post inside.

Max was passed out on the couch again when she came back into the kitchen. Had he not seen to the light after all? She turned around and ran up the tower stairs.

In the lantern room, she opened up the keeper's log and made a note.

October 22. Visitor to station—Max MacAusland, off Lightvessel No. 2. Sky slightly overcast, storm cloud moving in from N. Wind N-NE. 38 degrees. Primed foghorn compressor, oiled piston on resonator, polished lens and—

Here she paused and looked around. The storm panes were rimed with salt spray. *—washed storm panes,* she wrote. *Head keeper still away.*

Taking up a linen cloth, she polished every prism of the lens. She fetched a bucket of water from the wellhouse to wash the heavy windowpanes and counted out the tower steps on her way back up. There were eighteen, a bearable number. Nearly every day her father said a little laughing prayer of thanks for the small stature of their tower, which rested on a cliff two hundred and eighty feet above the sea. Hauling gear up from the water was arduous work, but getting supplies to the station was not. Most came by truck from Montreal to neighbour Clément Dionne's farm. M. Dionne helped Daniel and Sonia, loading forty-five-gallon drums of fuel and boxes of supplies onto the trailer he hauled wood in, then using his team of Clydesdales, Babette and Belle, to tow the trailer down the eleven-mile logging road that ended near their isolated station. For this trouble, and a barrel of beef, Daniel paid Dionne forty dollars a year. Sometimes M. Dionne came by with bottles of fresh cream and blocks of salted butter. He had a sideshow look: enormous shoulder muscles and a funny handlebar moustache. But he was kind as well as strong. If anything happened to Daniel, he would help.

Back downstairs, she collected the skein of wool she'd left in the porch, snuck past the sleeping man on her kitchen couch and climbed another eighteen steps, up to her attic workroom. Here, on a level with the lighthouse lamp, were all the colours she'd copied so carefully from life.

"Your fingers are blue!" Max had said when she passed his plate to him. "It's not poison? This isn't from the light?"

She shivered. From her mother she'd heard stories of the keepers' wives on isolated stations who'd lost their minds — not from the isolation, but from the brain poison, mercury, which the husbands carried in their blood and passed into the bodies of their yielding wives.

But the optic at Pointe d'Espoir did not revolve in a mercury bath.

"What is this blue?" He touched her fingertips.

"Just colour."

Later, she would wonder what prevented her from answering his question properly. Was it instinct? Or the voice of Mme Chevalier echoing in the art room? *Don't let anyone take this away from you*, she used to say. *People will try. They'll say other things matter more. But, girls, this is not true! Art nourishes the soul. Without it, we cannot be complete.*

Mme Chevalier had been her own person, like no one Sonia had ever met.

By supper, the wind had shifted again. She studied the sky and checked the gauges in the weather box. Every hour she climbed the tower stairs to look out over the river and make note of any changes in the log.

1 p.m. Wind direction N-NE. Fresh breeze. Gusts to 50 knots
2 p.m. Light rain. Water choppy.
3 p.m. Wind N. 40 knots, gusts to 60.
4 p.m. No change.
5 p.m. Wind 40 knots, N-NE. Gusts to 80. Brief hail. Water very rough. Lamp at St-Ange-sur-Mer in sight—visibility reduced. 33 degrees, temperature falling.

Whenever the ecclesiastical light at St-Ange-sur-Mer disappeared from view, Daniel started up the horn. She would have to do that soon.

Reheating meat from the bird she'd stewed the day before, she paused to wonder where Max had gone. Surely he wasn't upstairs in their private family quarters, and she herself had been in and out of the lighthouse all day. That left the whistle house. But why would he be in the whistle house?

Then she realized she'd forgotten to start the horn. She pulled on her boots and jacket in a rush.

She found Max sitting on the concrete floor of the whistle house, surrounded by compressor engine parts. "I just flipped the switch to turn it on," he said. "Nothing happened."

"It's fussy after it's been oiled, but nothing's broken—at least, nothing was broken." Sonia pulled her jacket closed against the cold, and studied the parts laid out in lines across the floor. "Look, if you can get it back together inside twenty minutes, I won't have to send a radio message out. Just come and get me when it's fixed. I'll start it this time!"

She turned and left. Transforming leftover chicken into dinner suddenly seemed an unimportant chore.

·:::·

The foghorn blasted as she bent toward the stove. She felt its prolonged moan as a pressure in her chest. This close, you didn't merely hear the warning: it became a part of you.

Max appeared a few minutes after the foghorn blew, grease-covered and grinning hard.

"You can wash up here," she said. "Supper's ready." She poured warm kettle water over his hands, and he scrubbed with the yellow soap her mother regularly sent down from Montreal.

"Thank you," he said. He sat on the couch. Then, right away, he jumped up and rummaged in his bag. "Would you like to share?" In his grease-stained hands he held a bottle of dark wine. *Vin de table, France,* the label read, in ornate script. No one in her family drank alcohol, so wine was an enticing mystery. And getting scarce, she'd heard, since the war in Europe had begun.

She had made a hash of potatoes fried with onions, gravy and chicken. Also a salad of Brussels sprouts dressed with vinegar and bacon. Later they could have cheese and apples from the cellar. While she set out plates, he opened the wine and poured it into teacups.

They talked and ate as they drank, but for Sonia it was the revelation of the bright-tasting wine that would stand out in her memory. That, and the devastation he enacted on her romantic picture of the lightship.

She'd seen the floating beacon glimmer on the water many times, on her way to town. She never thought *white for danger*, as a mariner would. She loved the way it shone, luminescence spreading out in concentric circles from the ship. It was brighter than the Christmas lights in Montreal.

"It isn't pretty on board," he said. "The ship's a thousand years old, and the crew is a bunch of hooligans."

She tipped her cup back. Only to be conversational, she asked their names.

"Huh." He drew a breath. "Mathieu's the oldest. Everyone calls him Goose. He's worked on lightships for twenty years. He says he has a family in Montreal, but he never seems to visit them. On leave, he always heads straight for Rivière-du-Loup. Whatever he's got going on there... Well, Goose is quite a character..." He filled her cup. "Gilles is our fireman. He comes from Chicoutimi. You wouldn't know he's a Quebecker, his English is so good. Goose says Gilles was a Department of Transport bureaucrat who got caught dipping into the petty cash... René is six foot six, with straight black hair. It sticks out all over his head like a chimney brush. He's from up near Chibougamau and speaks an incomprehensible *joual*, so we don't talk much. Étienne works the engine room. He comes from Chibougamau also. I call him Mosquito because he *whines*."

Sonia laughed.

"Maggot is a crazy anglo Montrealer. He used to pilot barges down the river, but one night he got into a brawl. He lost the fight and can't see straight anymore. He shouldn't be on a lightship, either, with that handicap, but he memorized the eye chart for his test... so..."

It was her turn to speak, but she could not think of what to say. Was this catalogue of criminality Max's life?

Of course it was. *Of course* these were the kind of men who worked on lightships. And Max was one of them. For a moment her brain throbbed like a hammered thumb. She was *alone* with this man.

How had he come to be working on that ship? And if it was so awful, why did he stay?

But she couldn't articulate her questions. Her tongue was wool. Instead of a response, she decided, she'd simply smile.

He filled her cup.

Alone in her room, Sonia sipped the last of the delicious wine. She felt a pleasant whirling feeling. She looked out at the water. She could see whitecaps on the river where the lantern beam played across the waves. Soon it would be time for bed. She yawned. Lay down. Max MacAusland would see to the light...

The first thing Sonia knew when she woke up was that something had gone very wrong. She rubbed her eyes and listened. It was unusually quiet. The light inside her room was blue. Slowly it dawned on her that this was because the windows were iced over.

She stumbled into overalls, a flannel shirt and her warmest double-knit wool sweater.

In the kitchen, Max's couch was empty, the fire almost out. She threw a handful of kindling and a birch stick on the failing fire, pulled on her jacket, boots and mitts.

She found Max in the lantern room, writing in the log. "That was a bad one, eh?" he said.

He shouldn't be writing in my log, she thought, enraged.

Then she read his entry.

Gale-force winds overnight. Hurricane? Temp. 26 degrees at 8 a.m. Foghorn on all night. Scraped panes at 3 a.m., 4 a.m., 5 a.m. and 7 a.m. Several station buildings damaged. Peapod boat smashed on slip. Windborne ice scraped paint off tower.

She looked at Max. His eyes were dull, his hair was lank. "Were you up all night?"

"Yes, ma'am. That's my job."

"Which buildings were damaged?"

"That rickety little one out back? I guess it's gone."

"The henhouse? Oh my God!"

"Do you mean to say you slept through all of that?"

"What do you mean you *guess* the henhouse is gone?"

"I mean, I never really noticed it was a henhouse. It's definitely gone."

She put the logbook on the shelf and went down the tower stairs. If the henhouse was gone, how had the lightship fared? Why was Max not worried about her father and the lightship crew? She wrenched open the tower door, slammed it closed. She walked around and behind the house, tracking snow as she went. The chicken coop was gone.

Instinctively, helplessly, she began to run. The mossy trail to the weather box no longer felt like a pillow underfoot. The ground was frozen in places. She picked up a small branch that had fallen across the path. The loss of the henhouse—not even a feather left—prompted a vision of all the eiderdown she'd gathered with her father on L'Île des Oeufs that spring. Three flour bags full: a fat handful out of every sea duck nest. Daniel had taken two dozen duck eggs, a dozen for them and a dozen for Clément Dionne. The bags of down had fetched fifteen dollars each.

Near the weather box, she slid on a patch of ice, righted herself, and saw again the snowy, empty space where the henhouse used to be. They had to radio out, she realized. They could send a message to the station at Cap-aux-Morts, across the river from *Brilliant*. She turned and strode back along the trail, toward the tower. How had she slept through such a storm? Her head ached. Her father was gone.

She couldn't make the radio work. Her voice went out—at least, she thought it did—but no one spoke back. All she heard was interference. Perhaps the battery was dead? She unhooked it and connected the spare. This changed nothing.

Max walked in to find her slumped in front of the radio, tugging at her hair. "That isn't going to work today," he said. "The VHF antenna's fallen down."

Sonia stood. "Can we fix it?"

"Yes. But not without some wire rope."

She threw her arms into the air. "So we'll rig up something temporary."

"I'll look at it. Why don't you get some breakfast?" He held out the small fir branch she had carried from the woods, wrapped, she saw now, with a length of the bright yarn she seemed always to have in her pocket.

"Is this yours?"

The smell of fir oil represented comfort and stability to Sonia. At Christmas her mother and sisters would come to the station from the home in Montreal that they shared with Grandma Murray. Daniel would chop a fir tree, Mairi and the girls would decorate it, and for a few days there would be laughter and conversation in the house. None of this would have been possible in Brighid Murray's house. Nor would it ever be possible to sustain past the three or four carefree days of Christmas. Mairi almost couldn't stand to stay that long. Even to Sonia, who didn't want to see it, her mother's antipathy toward the light station, and its single-minded keeper, was all too obvious.

She filled the porridge pot and set it on the stove. She picked up her mother's wooden spoon and heard her father say, *If you're going to live life, expect loss.* She dropped the spoon into the pot, slipped on her boots and ran back out to the engine room.

He turned around fast, surprised.

"Aren't you desperate to know that the lightship survived the storm?" she demanded. "Aren't you worried about your friends on board? *I* am worried about my father!" Her voice was high and pleading. It seemed to reverberate in her skull: a scary, foreign sound.

"Sonia..." He sighed and set down the bent antenna and the pliers he'd been using. "I've been on board that lightship in worse blow-downs than this. The ship is anchored in four places. It would have bounced around on the water all night and made the crew feel sick, but I'm certain that's the worst that happened. Don't worry. We'll send a message out when I get this set of tin sticks fixed."

She sank against the concrete wall. "Are you absolutely sure?"

"I promise you."

He fiddled with the radio antenna all morning long. Finally he got a message out to Malcolm Jeffrey, the keeper at Cap-aux-Morts, who said he would relay a message to Daniel Greer on *Brilliant.* Now they simply had to wait for a response.

Over supper, he plied her with questions about her life at school in Montreal and about her sisters. She allowed herself not to worry.

She closed her eyes and listened to his almost familiar voice, with its soothing, faintly Gaelic lilt, only slightly more pronounced than her father's. All the lighthouse keepers in Quebec were Scottish, or of Scottish descent. She allowed this frivolous coincidence to reassure her.

Now she felt at rest somehow, released from the pressure of a burden she hadn't realized she carried. This was just like when they'd drunk the wine. She believed it was an abdication of responsibility to relax when she had not yet heard from her father. But it felt good to relinquish this anxiety.

Daniel was okay: Max had *promised* her.

⁝

Max carried his plate to the sink and stopped to watch her as she cut a slice of ginger cake. She smiled. She couldn't help it: he was leaning over her and grinning. She raised an eyebrow, and composed her mouth into a questioning crescent, but he said nothing. She smiled some more, like an idiot. She *was* an idiot. An abdicating idiot. She didn't care. She looked at him. She looked away. When she looked back, his expression had changed. So confident a moment earlier, now it revealed a stormy interior battle between eagerness and doubt. "Have some ginger cake," she said, stepping decisively outside the radiant sphere of energy their bodies suddenly seemed to generate.

When she came down into the kitchen at nine o'clock to make a cup of tea, she found him slumped on the couch with an old newspaper in his hand. He wasn't reading. He looked fretful and concerned.

Why did I believe him, she wondered, just because he used the word *promise*?

But then he looked up, and smiled, and her fear dissolved again. She said, "Would you like some tea?" She wanted his company.

"Will you stay to drink it with me?"

"Of course I will."

"Then I want tea."

They sat together on the narrow, backless couch long past the time the tea grew cold. He described the pod of whales he'd seen from the tower gallery, awe enlivening his voice. "We rarely see whales as far downriver as *Brilliant*."

She described the beached blue whale she'd seen the previous summer, its belly ridged like a bicycle tire. She had been amazed that such a majestic animal could look so homely on close inspection. He asked about her absent mother, and she explained that Mairi Greer preferred to live in town. He said that he would prefer to live in town himself. "In Montreal," he clarified, "not Rivière-du-Loup..." They leaned back on the couch and made up names for the characteristic of *Brilliant*'s light, which produced a sequence of one flash followed by ten seconds of darkness, four flashes, darkness, three flashes, and finally darkness again.

In town, anglophones called it the *I Love You* light, matching the numbers of the flash characteristic, 1-4-3, to the letters in the words—and playing off the name of nearby Cap-aux-Morts, which could sound like Cap-Amour to a careless anglo ear.

He said the crew on board the ship thought *I Love You* sickening, and preferred a saltier name. She said, "What name?"

He smiled and crossed his eyes. She laughed, and closed her own.

The soothing rhythm of his words, the captivating giddy-headedness she felt—it was delicious, this blind surrender. She shook away her mother's voice, shrill inside her head: *What you see—or do not wish to see—constitutes a choice.*

When she finally slept that night, she felt she'd tumbled overboard. Bliss: her mind submerged—the world an ancient, lightless underwater cave.

All of *Brilliant*'s crew came back with Daniel in the morning. "Yes, she sank," he said. "But not before I fixed her!" He whistled, he sang, he unearthed a bottle of fiery liquid from somewhere for the men. "My darling girl!" he said, hugging her. He'd had his adventure. He noticed nothing new.

TEN

March 1965. Prospect, Prince Edward Island.

As the days lengthened, Sonia yearned for the pattern of her life to become more normal.

She began to understand that except for the pain she felt, the anxiety of not knowing — except for the crying spells and the black days and the frustration to which she privately gave vent (pulling her hair and screaming silently, the dry air scouring her throat; hammering her fists into her thighs until they throbbed so hard she was certain she'd bruised the bone) — except for wondering what she, Sonia, could — *should* — have done for her vanished daughter — she was fine, really.

They all were. The boys were too busy, Rose was overly controlling and Frances was worryingly quiet. But this was to be expected, wasn't it? She told herself they managed.

Then Evvie came by.

Rose answered the door. Frances was ironing, and Sonia was rocking in the chair by the stove, rocking and trying to puzzle out an answer to the questions that plagued her. *Where had Stella gone? Why?*

Evvie stumbled in, and both girls turned pleading looks on Sonia, as if she would know what to do.

He'd been drinking. You could smell it, and you could see the glint of manic energy in his eyes.

"Sonia," he said, and nodded. "I come to pick up Kate."

For a moment no one spoke.

"*Sonia*," Evvie said again, as though she were an idiot.

Frances lifted the heavy iron by its spiral handle and set it on the stove to heat. The ironing board was between her and him.

"Just a minute," Rose said, and blocked his way.

That morning, Rose had insisted they were going to have to talk to Evvie, to get Kate's things from him. They needed Kate's high chair and crib, she said. What she meant was that she wanted to settle, once and forever, where Kate would live. But Sonia could not imagine having such a conversation with Evvie. Just wait, she'd said. But Rose didn't want to wait. She stood glaring at Sonia, clutching Kate in her arms like a point she'd won. Rose had been ferocious then, but for all that earlier bravado she cowered now, her head bent, her shoulder curved around her heart.

"*Sonia*." Evvie stepped forward again. He was nose to nose with Rose now.

"I'll look in on her," Sonia said. She wasn't going to argue with Evvie. But she wasn't going to give Kate over to him, drunk like that, either. Maybe if she left the room he would back down.

Sonia stood to leave.

Evvie swayed beside the table.

Frances gripped the handle of the iron as though she was prepared to use it on him.

Sonia walked down the hall. Kate was asleep in Rose's bed. I'll just wait, she thought. I'll just give him a minute.

Rose appeared. "Mum, will you talk to him?"

Sonia walked back to the kitchen and looked at Evvie, now sitting in his barn coat and grubby boots, hunched over his knees on the far side of the couch beside the door.

Evvie stood. "I come to take my daughter home. Off your hands."

Sonia nodded.

"*No!*" Rose screamed.

Evvie made a gesture like a shrug and turned to leave.

They watched the door slam shut. After a moment the lights of Evvie's truck swung around the kitchen.

Rose tugged the mop across the dirty puddle his boots had left on the floor beside the kitchen couch and Sonia reversed her journey down the hall.

Rose followed her. "Mum, Evvie isn't capable of taking care of Kate."

"No, dear. But you can see he doesn't want to."

Evvie was driven, like a hungry animal. There was something he wanted, but it wasn't Kate. For the life of her, Sonia could not imagine what it might be.

She'd seen Evvie lose his temper twice. Once over a trivial disagreement with Rose. The reason hadn't even registered at the time. Rose had voiced some opinion and Evvie exploded. All she could remember after was the sudden ferocity of his rage and the miraculous way he'd calmed when Stella spoke to him.

The second time was after Stella stayed overnight with Kate. Sonia remembered every word because the moment had seemed, at first, like a turning point. Stella had finished with her tea and was dressing Kate to go home. Evvie had been wild, she agreed, but it was a new day, and now he'd be better. Frances was not convinced. "Just gather up Kate's things and come back," she said. Stella insisted she could handle Evvie, that he was gentle most of the time, it was only when he drank. She'd hoisted Kate in her arms. "He has his good points," she said. "He isn't that different from any of the other men around."

Sonia was reluctant to get involved. Pushing Stella into things never worked. But Frances didn't hesitate. "Wake up, Stella," she said. "He's a brute!"

That was when Evvie walked in. "A brute, eh?" At first he seemed wryly amused, even proud of this assessment. He winked at Sonia. Then rapidly, and without warning, his face changed its cast. Stella set Kate down and pinned Evvie's arms at his sides, whispered to him in a soothing voice. The urgency she must have felt was hidden and, incredibly, again Evvie calmed.

A few times Sonia had mimicked Stella's tactic. Evvie liked being spoken to softly. He'd relinquish his anger if you flattered and agreed with him. Sorry, Evvie, she'd said. You're right.

But things were different now, with Stella gone.

Evvie's visit lit a fire under Sonia. Stella was the only one who could control him. They needed her back. Sonia didn't think this out. She just applied herself to the job she now saw she ought not to have abandoned, because no one else was going to do it. She sat at the table and picked up the telephone. *Hello, this is Sonia MacAusland of Prospect. Can you help me?*

The answers were always the same, and the rhythm of the dialing quickly became anodyne. But at least she was doing something. By the time Cece and Mae Ladner came over late that same day, she felt charged with energy, but baffled as to why.

Cece and Mae were Stella's nearest neighbours. They'd always been good to her. Since Stella disappeared, Sonia had seen a lot of them.

Now she rested in their presence while Rose poured tea, and Mae inquired gently, How are you, Rose? How are you, Frances, dear? How is little Kate?

She listened to her daughters answer Mae's questions with one part of her brain. With another part she watched Cece tip his teacup so a milky waterfall spilled onto his saucer. He tapped his cup on the edge of his saucer to release the drips, then rested the cup on his knee and brought the saucer to his mouth. "How are the boys?" Mae asked, and Cece supped his tea, slurping loudly from the saucer and sighing deeply.

When his tea was gone, Cece said, "I dropped some culverts off to Evvie for the lane to that new field he cleared, and he asked if I'd bring some things to you." With his halting, old man's hands, Cece described Kate's crib and high chair, and Sonia saw that Mae had brought in two brown paper bags filled with baby things. One was stamped *Roger's Hardware*. Pink wool and crocheted lace peeped out the top.

Cece stood and wiped his hands across his pants and flushed apologetically. "Them other things is in the truck."

Rose held the door so Cece and Frances could carry in the high chair and the disassembled crib.

In this way it was settled. But why had Evvie agreed so readily?

While Rose and Frances began to put the crib together, Sonia sat down by the phone. She opened the phone book at the page headed with the letter C. In Rose's room, she heard Frances say, "I think he *pushed* her through a hole in the ice..."

Rose said, "Uh, huh." She wasn't listening to Frances, or she didn't agree. Rose and Frances were born opposites.

Sonia put her finger on the page. *Cantwell, Donald & Betty. Bristol.* She heard what sounded like a bolt tumble to the floor. "Hey, Frances—" Rose snapped. "Hold up your end."

Then Sonia saw Kate toddling down the hall, and she heard Rose raise her voice again. "Why are you so determined to blame Evvie for Stella's disappearance?"

Cantwell, Donald & Betty.

Frances changed her tack. "Okay, maybe he lured her onto the ice, and he let her walk where it was soft."

Rose came into the hall and snatched Kate up in her arms.

Cantwell, Donald & Betty.

The scene Frances described seduced Sonia slowly. Evvie on the ice, calling out to Stella. Evvie angry. Evvie showing Stella the unsafe route across the ice. He wouldn't even have had to push...

But, no. Stella had run away.

Rose said, "No." Rose didn't want things to be that way either. "*No*," she said, and there was the sound of more hardware falling to the floor. "I don't believe it. He's a mean drunk, but he didn't *lure* Stella. Stella fell. Frances, you've completely lost your sense." Another bang. "*Forget it*, Frances."

Sonia could understand Frances's desperation. She felt desperate herself. But Frances was wrong. Stella had run away.

"Wah!" Kate said.

"*Come on, Frances,*" Rose begged, her voice steadier now, calculated to soothe Frances, to not alarm Kate. "We don't know what happened. You have no proof. *It was an accident.* Let's just forget."

"For God's sake! Stella could hardly see. Even if he didn't push her, even if all he did was fail to lead her off the ice, isn't it still his fault?"

Rose did not respond. She came out of the room with Kate, leaving Frances to finish assembling the crib.

Sonia turned back to the phone book. She put her finger down. *Cantwell, Donald & Betty.* She turned the crank on the phone and Mary

Walt came on the line. "Switchboard," Mary said, and Sonia pictured her in the little room beside the village post office. Sonia could see her sitting on a hardwood kitchen chair, alone in the closet-like room with a mug of tea beside her and a book in her hand. Sonia too had a mug of tea at hand. She and Mary were several miles apart, but in a way, Sonia thought, Mary kept her company.

Except in the last little while Mary had begun to speak impatiently. Reminded of this, Sonia became businesslike. "Bristol. Put me through," she said, and read out Donald and Betty Cantwell's telephone number.

"No, dear," Betty Cantwell said, less than a minute later. "I'm sorry."

A few days later, the RCMP came by to give a "preliminary report." It was old Harry MacLeod and a skinny young fellow from up east who was training with him. Sonia emerged from her room—but only just.

She thought Harry looked slack and sad, all trembly belly and grey skin. His eyes had that opaque cast you sometimes see in people who are profoundly bored. He wasn't bored, though. He was intent: still as oil, focused, waiting. He let the boy introduce himself.

Sonia shook her head in response. "You're so young," she said sadly, as though it were his lost life they'd come together to lament.

Harry and the boy took off their caps and bowed their heads. Then the boy straightened his back. "Mrs. MacAusland?" he said. He nodded at Sonia, though she had said nothing and had not changed her demeanour. He looked imploringly at her, quaking a little. He seemed to be waiting for her to deliver him from his obligation.

After a long moment, she nodded back at him.

"Yes," he said.

Sonia waited. Yes, *what?*

Then, without warning, he spit out his message: "I'm sorry she must of went through the ice," and he reached into the case he carried and pulled out Stella's white wool hat with the bobble on it, the one Rose knit for her the same as Kate's.

Harry MacLeod said, "We found this on the ice, Sonia. It looks like she went through. Her tracks led down there, and her husband says he saw her. We talked to him. I'm sorry. The case is closed. There's nothing more we can do."

Sonia looked to Harry and the boy for more, but apparently this was all they were prepared to say. No real explanation. Just, *Stella drowned. Nothing more we can do.*

She clenched her jaw and exhaled loudly. What incompetents they were! They didn't care. They hadn't really looked. They'd wasted all this time.

That hat wasn't proof of anything. Stella could have lost it any time. Sonia hadn't seen her wear it in ages.

Stella hadn't drowned. She'd run away.

Sonia felt her heart speed up. No one understood how impossible it was that Stella could have drowned. That would mean she was gone. She could not be gone. In what kind of world was that possible?

Sonia reached for the door frame. Was she going to pass out? In front of her, Harry waited. Her vision cleared a little and she shook her head at him. He had a job to do.

She shook her head again, and Harry gripped the boy's arm and locked eyes with her. "Sonia, people do it all the time," he said. "Go through, I mean. You'd be amazed."

She said nothing. She cut her eyes at Harry. "My daughter ran away. You were supposed to look for her. She's a missing person. Did you call the hospitals, the train station, the ferry captains, police in Halifax and Montreal and Toronto? Did you call anyone?"

After a moment, Harry let the boy go and put his hat back on. "We are very sorry for your loss," he said, his voice gentle but firm.

"*You didn't even try!*" She shook her head in disgust. Harry was the one who should be sorry.

The minute they'd gone, Rose got the mop from the porch and scrubbed the dirty boot tracks they'd left behind.

Later, Sonia could hear Rose and Frances bickering in Rose's room.

Frances was louder than usual. "Give me a break, Rose!" she said.

"Mum never cried. Not the day Stella vanished. Not since," Rose said. "Don't you think that's a little weird?"

Rose was right, Sonia thought. She felt baffled and lost, flayed, in physical pain — but were these feelings grief?

"It hasn't hit her yet," Frances said.

"Uh, huh." Rose had trouble understanding other people's points of view. Wisely, Frances didn't say another word.

It hasn't hit her yet. What did that mean?

ELEVEN

The thing was that Sonia could understand why Stella would want to get away. She herself had wanted to run away, in the first years of her marriage. But where could she have gone? (She'd yearned for Surplus Island as soon as she left. But someone else had been installed as keeper there.)

Stella's situation was different. Stella had gone away before. Sonia lifted the handset of the phone, wound the crank around. "Operator?" she heard, and recognized Annie Donnelly, from the village.

"Union Station, Toronto," she said. "Could you put me through?"

She remembered the morning Stella came back from Toronto—nineteen years old and all grown up, after less than a year away.

No one had been expecting Stella, so her return was a shock. Her new appearance, too. She'd cut her hair and it was set in an unnaturally buoyant permanent wave. She walked in the door and struck a pose to show off this hair and the new car coat and shiny boots she wore. For a moment Sonia didn't recognize her own daughter. Then Stella took off her coat and boots and sat down at the table, and finally Sonia could see her in the way this jittery Toronto woman touched the tips of her fingers to her brow. Her one bright eye danced around the room, its useless mate at rest.

"Frances!" Stella said. "Look at you. All grown up!" Stella embraced her sister, a new gesture, entirely at odds with the physically restrained girl everyone remembered. "I have books in my bag for you," she said, turning away. "And, Rose, I bought the cutest blouse for you!"

Sonia set down cups and saucers and Stella said, "Mummy, I have something for you too." She lifted her suitcase onto the kitchen couch and, with a flourish, released both metal clasps. Sonia wondered where her reserved, quiet daughter had gone, and would she ever understand this new person Stella had become?

Stella rifled through the good suitcase she'd borrowed ten months earlier, when she left the Island to look for work. Most of the bag's contents were clothes, and the items she removed were nothing like the things she'd taken up there. Sonia recognized styles from the catalogue, skirts and blouses the old Stella would never have worn. Clothes too formal for Island life, or too prissy. Other things as well — a slip and nightie Eaton's didn't carry and a pair of fine leather gloves the colour of Moirs chocolate drops.

"Mummy, these are for you." Stella held out the gloves, and Sonia felt her face harden. She had nowhere to wear such fancy gloves. And Stella had spent so much money!

"These are lovely, Stella. But you shouldn't be so extravagant."

"Mummy, try them on."

Sonia slid one hand into a glove. Physically, Stella was her duplicate. The handsome glove fit perfectly.

"They're beautiful, dear. Thank you."

For Rose, Stella had a blouse made of creamy nylon with pink polka dots. It was tailored and stylishly short and it glimmered like the inside of a mussel shell.

Rose ran a finger along the row of transparent buttons. "Thank you, Stella." No one else would have a blouse like it, she said.

Last, Stella pulled out two field guides, books Frances had asked her for.

"Oh, Stella!" Frances said, line drawings of birds and animals and fine Latin text leaping to life at her touch.

Stella smiled, and her face crumpled in a way that seemed familiar, finally. This was a relief, and it allowed Sonia the respite to wonder why she had come home.

Rose said, "I'm just going to check on the hens. I'll be right back," so Sonia went down the hall to look in on Kate. Of course Kate was asleep — Rose wouldn't have stepped out otherwise. The pieces of Kate's crib leaned against one wall, and Kate herself lay curled in the bed that, as a child, Rose had shared with Frances. As Sonia watched, she sighed and turned against the heavy blanket Rose had rolled into a bolster to prevent her falling out of bed. She flung an arm out, and suddenly it was clear to Sonia why Rose was not as close to Frances as Stella had been. The narrow bed was barely large enough for one spread-eagled child, let alone two sets of warring knees and elbows.

As the eldest girl, Stella had her own room, so she never fought with anyone.

Stella was home from Toronto for more than a week before anyone learned about Evvie. Evvie was also from the Island, but Stella had met him in Toronto.

Was that why she accepted him? Had the city of Toronto bestowed its magic on Evvie, and made him seem to shine with unearned promise?

Kate stirred in her sleep and Sonia watched her eyes fly open and fall shut again.

When she went to Toronto, Stella had seemed captivated by its possibilities. In her letters she'd described so much that was new: electric heat, coloured television, streetcars, elevators, going out, a million strangers, better clothes, a job she rode the streetcar to. But back at home the confidence she'd earned quickly vanished.

Sonia was sorry Stella let the interesting urban life she'd begun to establish simply slip away. People said Toronto was hot, noisy, busy, fast. But Stella had seemed to flourish there. She'd made friends; she mentioned them in her letters. On the Island she became meek and quiet and worn out again, neglecting her appearance, hiding in the house, and giving in to whatever Evvie asked.

She'd been injured in a haying accident when she was thirteen and lost the vision in one eye. Even with her glasses on, she spilled food on herself and bumped into things. More than once she poured tea directly onto the tablecloth *beside* the cup she'd set in place.

She said, When you lose one sense, the others compensate.

But Sonia could see no evidence of compensation. Compromise, maybe.

Maybe compromise was the reason Stella had settled so easily for

69

Evvie, who, with his taut, neatly muscled limbs and narrow mouth, looked ungovernable: a potent form of trouble.

Evvie was a piece of work, and he made no effort to conceal the fact. Stella must have felt he was all she deserved.

TWELVE

By the end of the week, Sonia had reached the letter L. There were nineteen pages of names in their exchange. She was halfway through. She was about to ask for *Lyall, Albert* when Dan came into the kitchen. He held a sheaf of papers in his hand.

This is about Stella, Sonia thought, and set the telephone down.

But it was not.

"Mum. Can you help me?" Dan spread his papers on the table and Sonia recognized the forms for his Farm Credit application. She'd helped him fill them out already.

"I thought these were done." She watched Dan frown and fidget with the pen in his hand.

"I want Evvie off the application, Mum," he said.

On their own they did not qualify for an expansion grant. This was why Dan had asked Evvie to make a joint application. They could do this because they were family. It would give them more manpower and more equipment to work the additional land Dan wanted to buy. In theory, anyway, so long as Evvie did his part of the work. Six months ago Dan had explained, "We need the extra land, Mum, or we'll never get ahead." Now he wanted to erase Evvie and put Cece Ladner on the application instead. But Cece was old, and he could barely manage the work of his own small farm.

Sonia said, "Cece isn't family."

"Isn't he? Distantly? A second cousin or something?"

Sonia shook her head.

"We could just say."

"Hmmm." Farm Credit sent inspectors around, and Sonia hated the idea of asking Cece to lie.

"Mum. There isn't any other way."

Sonia looked at the form. What did the fine print say? She'd been staring at the phone book for so long her vision was blurred. She rubbed her eyes.

Dan said, "It's okay, Mum. I'll ask Frances. She's good at math." He patted the kitchen cot. "Maybe you should lie down for a while."

When she woke from her nap, Dan was gone. She found him in the barn, leaning against the horses' stall, Frances with him, tapping a pencil against her teeth. Dan hated anything to do with math, but Frances loved it. She was in her glory. They had the pages of paperwork spread out on a plank of wood.

Frances gestured at a page. "Okay," she said, "just put another zero there."

"But I don't have—"

"Are you with me, Danny Boy? Just write the number. You don't have any choice, unless you want to farm with Evvie."

Dan hesitated.

"You could leave his name on, and just tell him how things are going to be."

One of Sonia's hands was tingling where she'd slept on it. She shook it out.

"Hi, Mum," Frances said and grinned.

Dan made a mark on the paper. "Like hell I will," he said.

And then something in him sprang away. Some filter, or his sense of restraint. "Evvie pushed Stella," he said. "Or if he didn't push her in, he might as well have."

Frances stopped smiling.

Dan narrowed his eyes. "*You* didn't hear him talk about that day." He imitated Evvie: "*It was bright enough out, and flat-arsed calm. Only an idiot wouldn't a seen that hole in the ice.*"

Then he was silent for a minute, waiting.

Sonia didn't know what to say—couldn't think—and Frances just stared at her brother.

"You know how Evvie is," Dan said. "I think he pushed her to the point where she was willing to walk through the ice."

They were all silent then.

Frances was still dressed for school in her black vinyl zip-up boots and duffle coat. She looked incongruous next to Dan in his flannel shirt and the wool-lined canvas vest he wore for work, beads of sweat gathered at his temples. Sonia couldn't wrap her mind around the accusation Dan was making. She couldn't understand it in the context of that familiar, homely place, with its animal smells, its gentle sounds. Frances had already said something similar. But coming from Dan, this assertion sounded more serious. Dan was her most moderate child.

Around them, cattle lowed.

She looked at her placid, loyal son who never criticized a soul, and all she could see was fury. Suddenly he reminded her of Evvie, who was often angry in this same explosive way.

"Oh, Dan," she said. She thought, *Please don't lose it too.*

Dan looked hard at her. "I swear to God. That's what he said." He threw a bale of hay toward Doll and Hellie, then kicked the bale open so the mares could eat, his muscles tensed and popping, face alight with rage.

"He was always cutting her down. Don't you remember?" he demanded.

Again, he described the night he'd spent at the river, standing vigil near the place Stella's tracks had disappeared and taking turns with Evvie to walk the ice and call her name. They'd searched the woods on snowshoes, skied up and down the river, calling, shouting themselves hoarse.

When it seemed that Stella wasn't anywhere, they'd lit that fire on the bank. Rose had brought them Thermoses of tea. But Evvie had scorned the tea for rye.

Evvie had been drunk when he called Stella an idiot. What came to Dan now, though, was not the harshness of that word but rather Evvie's clear specificity.

That hole in the ice, Evvie had said. As though he knew the hole was there, and precisely where it was.

That hole in the ice. Sonia repeated the phrase to herself. She focused on the words so closely they began to lose their meaning. She thought, Dan could be right about Evvie, but why would Stella let him do that to her?

Beside her, Frances went slack, her body slumped, her eyes glazed.

Sonia could picture Stella on the ice, and Evvie beside her, goading or pushing her, reaching out with a fist or a shoving, flat hand. Stella too frozen with fear to run.

But things didn't happen that way, did they? Not really.

The idea was ludicrous. That anyone could be so evil.

She thought, We all want answers badly and we're all just trying to bully though.

"No, Dan," she said. She left her children and went inside and opened the phone book and found the letter L.

THIRTEEN

"Take a break from the phone," Mary Walt said. "Rest for a few hours, and then I'll put another call through."

Away from the phone, Sonia didn't know what to do. She wandered the house. Frances was at school, and Rose was out somewhere with Kate. She washed the few dishes on the counter. She took out the broom. She put it back. Finally she opened her bottom bureau drawer and took out the photo album.

Nowhere in the album were there pictures of the years before the children. There were several formal portraits: Sonia's parents being married in Montreal, Max's mother at a spinning wheel and Max's father beside a little boat. Aunt Lil as a pale young woman, gussied up and gleaming.

But of Max and Sonia together, or of Sonia in her adult life before the children, there was nothing.

Most of the pictures had come from Lil. Sonia had taken only a few. In the best of these — the clearest, truest image — Stella stood between Dan and Max, holding baby Rose. Rob and Frances hadn't yet been born, and their now decrepit truck, in front of which they'd lined up, was then almost new.

Sonia held the photo up to the light to study Stella, skinny and severe and proud, wearing a checked cotton dress and braids, and holding her baby sister in her arms. Beside her, Dan looked wild and grubby, like any little boy. Before Sonia clicked the shutter, Max — in his overalls, with his dirty blond, sticking-up hair and hesitant, lopsided smile — had laid an arm across his daughter's shoulder, and Rose, whom Kate so resembled, had squirmed and reached out for the camera Sonia held.

Want dat! she'd said. Sonia could clearly remember. *Want dat!* had been Rose's favourite phrase for years.

Stella had never wanted things. Stella at six had been insubstantial, a wraithlike assemblage of three component parts: pale skin, a stripy shirt and stringy hair.

At least, this was what Sonia remembered.

But now Sonia could see that the girl in this photograph didn't look like the daughter she remembered. Holding Rose, she looked as strong as a new fence post. And calm too, as though she could easily set Rose down and walk away, whenever the squirming and the wanting became too much.

If only there were a picture of Stella as a baby, with her father holding her — or of silent Max alone, as Dan liked to be alone — or of the ice on the ocean off Surplus Island, piled up onshore the way the ice rafted onto the riverbank at the end of winter.

Sonia imagined photos that would explain the absence she felt, an emptiness her life with Max had not solved. His departure either.

Max's heart had given out when he was thirty-seven. After that, she didn't *think*. She was overwhelmed just trying to maintain the farm he'd run. The children, too. Rose and Dan had worked like dogs at first, Rose helping in the house and Dan taking over most of his father's daily chores. Rose had been twelve and Dan fourteen. They'd given up what remained of their childhood in order to work the farm — in order to survive.

Eddie Mack had asked, at the wake for Max, did they need help, and Dan said confidently, *We don't.* Sonia loved her son unreasonably in that moment. But the work had not been easy after Max was gone. It changed them all.

Rose helped run the household, and she became obsessed with order and with rules of every kind. Frances and Rob, too young to do as much as their older siblings, became for a time wild and spoiled things, not liable to think of other people's needs. Stella, almost sixteen when her father died, was hardest hit, escape all she ever seemed to think of. *When I go to Toronto*, she would say, as though merely uttering this incantation could change her life. Sonia watched them all for signs of loss. She tried to make up on Sundays for the hours she spent out in the barn and fields through the week. But she felt despairing, so much of the time, and she was sure her moods affected them.

Memories of Max come to her in unguarded moments, and as she saw him bend to pull on his rubber boots or shrug into his work clothes—lifting shoulders over-muscled from carrying bales of hay and bags of oats, pushing machinery and pulling animals—she felt regret. She'd hardly known him. Oh, she knew his gestures, and she knew what he had made of the moments of his life. But that was all, and in the end it hadn't been enough to bridge the distance between them.

How much had changed? And how much was still the same? Without a picture, it was impossible to know.

Something had happened to Stella as a teenager. After the accident, when for so long she wasn't able to see very much at all, Stella had retreated. She became less able, stopped trying to do things on her own, needed to be looked after instead of looking after others. Sonia's opinion was that before she lost an eye Stella did too much looking-after, as Rose did now. Competence could be a form of weakness. How Sonia wished her daughter had been able to find a balance between doing things for others and living for herself. But she never did. There had been that period of revelling in her loss, when she lay in bed, her bandaged face dark and puffy, recuperating from the accident that took half her eyesight and—though it needn't have—her confidence. Sonia tried to get Stella moving, tried not to indulge her. But Stella wanted indulgence—and she got it from Rose, then still a child, and eager to be helpful.

For weeks Rose waited on her sister. Then, after, there was that acquiescence Sonia couldn't bear, that sense Stella seemed to have that she was a less important person.

Thinking about her daughter's self-denial could still exasperate Sonia.

Max had been compassionate with Stella in the first few days, generous with the comfort and encouragement she craved. But just as in the period after her birth, only a short time passed before he reverted to his usual inattentive way.

Maybe they'd all been inattentive. No wonder she left.

FOURTEEN

Sonia slept and woke, slept and woke, dreams and memories standing in for human contact. Someone brought her food. Tea, she drank cold.

Everything was cold.

She remembered how cold she'd been, going out to Surplus light with Max that first winter.

February 1941. Surplus Island, Malpeque Bay, Prince Edward Island.

They were still new to the Island then, renting an apartment in Charlottetown for the winter months, and with just one summer of solo lightkeeping experience behind them.

He'd taken her out by horse and sleigh, and they surfed the roads like waves, skimming turns banked high after a winter of bad storms. It had been a cold, astonishingly bright day. Every surface—fields and sky—shocked white.

Her goal had been to catalogue and report any damage to the lighthouse from onshore winds, or from a storm surge that had destroyed wharves up and down the north shore. But the trip had worked out differently than she'd expected. Instead of examining damaged equipment and noting parts to order for repair—there was no need since the station had hardly been touched—she'd witnessed damage she couldn't fix, or even fairly mourn.

That day there had been fishing boats on the water—far out, where the ice pans were breaking up. Sonia had studied them through the telescope in the light tower. It was her first winter on the Island, so she had never seen the seal hunt. The quantity of blood on the ice came as a gruesome surprise, as had the soundless violence of the blows the fishermen dealt the ice. Sonia couldn't see the white seal pups she knew were lying wherever the sealers struck. But she understood that what she saw was fishermen smashing skulls and skinning carcasses with knives.

Red bloomed on white as far as the eye could see, and for the first time Sonia understood how separate the fishery was from her role in watching over it. She'd felt a distance then, both from the light it was her duty to maintain eight months a year and from the fishermen for whom she performed the role of guardian.

Max hadn't understood. When he saw the hunt was on, he looked away, as he always looked away from events he could not endure. This was the first winter of their life together, during which, for no reason Sonia could fathom, they'd grown apart.

She was mystified by her marriage, which turned out to be so different from her expectations. Max did not say *I love you*, as she understood husbands were supposed to. He barely looked at her. His silence could be scalding. His rages, too. After a time she felt as though in some essential way she'd disappeared.

All that night, she dreamed of violence. In her mind she didn't blame the fishermen, whose survival depended on the harvest of seal pelts. Life required death; she understood that much about the hunt.

No, it wasn't the hunt. Something else about that journey troubled her.

It was that moment Max looked away. Her realization that he saw what he wanted to see, and did not trouble himself to wonder about the hidden depths of life — or about the people around him. He didn't see her, and he wasn't interested in trying to understand.

July 1941. Surplus Island, Malpeque Bay, Prince Edward Island.

Max returned one rainy Saturday toting sacks of summer vegetables — carrots, peas, Swiss chard, green and yellow beans, new potatoes — a bundle of recent newspapers, a pint of cream and a pail of raspberries from Lil's garden. Because the rain had made the causeway soft, he'd parked his truck on the mainland and walked across the swollen sand. Sonia was napping when he crept in. She woke to see him standing over her in the limpid gleam of that wet afternoon, eyes alight, freckles standing out against his tan, hair slicked back—shades darker, dripping rain from its curling ends. She hauled herself upright and tried to focus. His arm had healed, though it was apparent now that there would be a scar. He sat down carefully on the edge of the bed. Haying would resume as soon as the rain stopped and the fields dried out. "One day!" he said. That was all he'd spare. Sonia marvelled at how tightly wound he seemed, as though anxious to get *past* this one day off and back to work. He stroked her hand. She closed her eyes and thought: I remember you.

Her first few days with Max had been heady, joyful days. She was seventeen and careless. She had been sure she was the thing that he was smitten with. It was only after her father had helped him to secure this position—lightkeeper of Surplus Station—that she began to wonder if he'd confused her with the means to get away from a job he hated. His manner changed. He grew distant. He rarely spoke. And even before he took up his late uncle's farm, leaving Surplus Station in her care, she understood that the bond she'd imagined between them had broken somehow. If it had ever been there.

It was hard to believe they'd known each other eighteen months. They'd been apart more than half of that.

For a short time, they'd been happy. Gratitude can look like love, easily enough. She was convinced by little things: his ability to repair any broken thing; the few stories he told; the way he studied her, amazed. But living together demands more than mutual illusions.

In the chaotic days before their move from Quebec to Prince Edward Island, she made several errors. Ceding decisions to him was one. Leaving her dyes and equipment and supply of wools behind was another. Without a creative outlet she soon lost track of who she was. Daniel had warned: You won't have time for those pictures with Max to fuss over and cook for. Even in that moment she knew her father's advice was horribly misguided. But something about the state of being wed and moving with a man to a foreign place had stripped her of her status as a sentient being. Your *hobby*, Daniel said, takes too much time. And Max, who had seemed at first to understand how much colour and line meant to her, had not disagreed.

How foolish she had been. She left everything—brushes and paints and dyes, even her first small scissors and wooden knitting needles, treasured since childhood—behind. To Max and Daniel, this was evidence of womanly commitment. By giving up the many hours she spent dyeing wool and making pictures, she'd freed herself to focus on Max's lighthouse work, and on Max himself.

She bitterly regretted those losses now. It had been a year and a half since she'd created anything of significance with her hands. Occasionally, making entries in the station logbook, she'd find her pencil moving of its own accord, sketching an image of the horizon line or a group of lowering clouds, all she could see from the station tower. She always stopped herself, rubbed the illustration out.

What point was there in drawing what she could not reproduce in colour?

Even now that Max was living elsewhere, she had no intention of trying to retrieve her things. Surely her father would send whatever she asked for in the mail, but she did not ask. Pride kept her silent. She felt resentment roil in her as Max drew his hand across her thigh, as he kissed her neck toward the back, where her hairline met her collar. *Pete*, she thought, and closed her eyes. Her body loosened its hold on rage. "Sonia," Max said softly. *Pete*, she thought. His familiar hands were everywhere. She leaned; she pulled him back against the bed. *Pete*.

"Sonia?"

She squeezed her eyes tight. Vivid puce and orange shards struck like lightning on the scrim inside her brain. She pushed against his shoulders, and he broke away.

The rain had stopped and the sun was out. They were on the sandy lane off the shore road, loading the truck with eelgrass for Lil's garden, when Pete appeared. He'd seen the vehicle, he said. He'd come down to check on Max's arm.

Max pulled back his sleeve to display the scar. "You done good work, Doc."

"Good, good. Excellent. You look after yourself, now." He turned and headed back inland without specifically acknowledging Sonia.

After Max had gone, the weather changed again. Thunderheads began to mass against the white clouds to the west. The sky grew dark. Sonia inhaled the astringent tang of approaching rain and felt the prickle of hair lifting off her bare arms as she walked. Piercing expressions of agony—the cries of seagulls—and the strafing attacks of terns drew her attention so that she almost didn't see the small red fox that crossed her path, trotting fast in a rough zigzag from tide line to dune. When she did see him, she stopped. He held his head high, his jaw stretched wide to hold his prize, a limp, buff-coloured bird, its head suspended like a plumb bob from its broken neck. He looked at once victorious, brave and cruel. *He,* she thought. But it could just as easily have been a female fox. Probably it was, in fact: a vixen with a pair of kits to feed.

Still, she regretted the death of the dear, harmless bird, as pale as sand. It had been a piping plover, the skittish shorebird with the mournful cry. Ghost bird, people called it, for its faint colouring and its habit of invisibility.

It wasn't invisible now. She marvelled that a creature so adept at disappearing could look so obvious and plain in death.

As the rain began, she turned and strode toward the station. It was time to get to work, to light the lantern for the night and make a list of the tasks she'd left aside all summer. It turned out her father was right: she was a lousy lighthouse keeper. No better, really, than Harold Pyke, her predecessor, who'd left dead flies to rot on all the windowsills. Some of the things she hadn't done: paint the tower inside and out, repair the motor in the lifeboat (which moaned and coughed and complained of death), create an inventory of station equipment and compile a list of necessary supplies, send an order off to DOT. This last was very late—the supply boat was due to pass the station in six weeks' time.

She kicked at the dampening sand as she walked, dislodging clots of kelp and eelgrass from the plane surface of the beach. Recently it seemed her days all blurred together. How many miles had she walked on this bloody island where there was nothing distracting or enlivening to do?

Now she determined to submerge herself in work. Work was as good a cure as any for the mess she'd made of things. Pete would go back to Montreal in a few weeks, perhaps never to return, and soon, Max said, they'd give up the lighthouse posting to concentrate on farming. Sonia had tried to argue with this, but Max was like her father—he'd decided, and that was that.

Because Sonia dreaded the idea of moving to Max's landlocked little farm, she'd made a decision of her own: she'd declare herself to DOT and ask them to keep her on. With the number of men heading off to Europe now, it was just possible they'd have no option but to say yes. *Dear Sirs*, she'd write, *Please permit me to explain—*

No. She couldn't sound that weak.

Sir: I am writing to inform you of the situation at Light Station No. 17, Surplus Island—

Could she say that Max had left? No. He could be charged for having left the light. She'd have to get around that part somehow.

She shivered in the sudden breeze and unhooked the door of the lighthouse tower. The wind was really picking up. Maybe she should close the lantern windows just in case.

After the storm, Sonia examined Surplus Island and found it changed.

Several sandbars had disappeared. Three massive rocks she'd never seen lay exposed in a deepened channel on the island's western edge. She stared at these, astounded.

The world had shifted all around.

She saw objects in the distance and began to walk toward them. Solid black shapes eerily backlit by the sun. Be positive, she told herself, praying none were bodies. Be prepared to witness mystery, not loss.

Loss was always a possibility, but so far she'd been spared. No missing boats or fishermen. No beached whales. Instead, she'd felt relieved and amazed at the objects she found thrown up on the beach. When the sea was rough, sugar kelp and jellyfish littered the foreshore—also crab shells, dead lobsters, shells of mussels, limpets, starfish—sometimes a stingray—sometimes manmade objects. Several times she'd found glass spheres the size of rutabagas tied with twine made of supple, grassy stuff; often there was driftwood and pieces of knotted line; once there had been a hand lantern, its globe miraculously intact; once a biscuit tin with a picture of King George VI on it; once a good canvas bucket. Today—she could see the black shapes clearly now—there were lobster pots unmoored by the storm.

As she walked, she pulled at the pots scattered amongst the wrack along the shore. She tied three together in a train and dragged them to the station, and then went out again and again, the heavy traps rasping the sand with deafening force, until at last she had seventeen lobster pots stacked neatly against the woodshed. She sat on her stone front step. She could hear the wind and the waves again. What bliss the quiet was! Even in near silence there was so much to hear. The sough of the wind in the marram grass. The laughing of a gull. A tractor coughing on the shore road.

The stranger walked halfway around the island before he saw the wall of pots Sonia had salvaged, now drying in the sun. Poor man! she thought, noticing his weary gait.

"I knew they washed up somewhere," he said, resting a proprietary hand on a damaged trap. He lifted the hand and held it out to her. "Grenfell Hillyard."

"Sonia." She offered him a glass of cold tea.

He ignored the offer, shook his head sadly. "It was good of you folks to drag them pots back here for me," he said. Against his deeply lined, sun-darkened skin, his pale blue eyes were riveting. The irises, struck with sun, seemed faceted like gems. How lovely, Sonia thought—the brilliant contrast of white and beryl, the various dull reds and browns of his cracked, dry lips. His mouth opened. He was smiling, laughing at himself, changing his mind. "Thank you, dear. I'd love that drink," he said.

She left him on the step while she went to get the jar of tea she'd sunk into the surf to cool.

She poured them each a glass and cut two slices from a lemon she'd been saving in the cellar.

"Oh, will you look at that!" he said. "My God, you're good!" He took a long drink. "You know, I thought I'd have to drag those pots the length of the island myself, and here you folks have gone and done it for me!" He glanced around. She could see that he was about to ask for Max. She wondered what she'd say.

But he did not ask. Instead, he drained his glass in a single draft, exhaled vocally like a child, then reached for her drink, still untouched in her hand. "My land," he said, "that's good tea."

They sat together on the rip-rap barrier that breasted the waves in front of the lighthouse tower's concrete base. He was in no hurry. He wanted to wait until the tide was high enough to float his pots across the causeway. He said he came out after every storm to look for lost traps cast onshore. He sighed and sipped from his second glass of tea. He caught her eye and said, "Your husband's into town for the day, now, is he?" And she nodded, looking away, reluctant to lie even by omission to this soft-spoken, gentle man.

"I've been fishing off here since 1917," he said.

She did the math — twenty-four years on the water — but she couldn't begin to guess his age. His face was weathered, but his hair was not completely grey. He could be anywhere from forty-five to sixty.

"Back then," he said, "the fish were so thick this place deserved its name. *Surplus* Island." He spoke the word longingly, the way you would say a lover's name.

All this time she'd believed the island was surplus goods — used up and no longer wanted — that this was why it was uninhabited and how it had earned its name. Unconsciously she'd transferred this slur against the island and the light to herself, its keeper.

Grenfell Hillyard was gazing out to sea. "You could never get rich off fish, of course, but it was good fishing here, twenty, twenty-five years ago. Too many blinks now," he said. And then, seeing Sonia's look of incomprehension, he added, "The little ones, too small to keep."

Blink. The word suggested those small fish that swam flashing through the nearshore shallows. Illusory creatures. She tried to imagine the good days: men upending bushel baskets full of fish onto their boat decks, silvery scales becoming coins of light as they fell. It wasn't difficult to picture fishing boats weighed down with bulging nets, seals gorging themselves under the ice, hordes of mergansers, cormorants and herons (beaked demons of the nearshore) stabbing the shallow water — and the fish vanishing like passenger pigeons.

But of course all this was impossible. The ocean was full of fish. "The boats are so far out on the water now," she said. "I can see them from the tower. But even with my binoculars they're tiny specks."

"Yes." He smiled gently. Perhaps like Sonia he knew how surprisingly little you could see from atop a lighthouse tower.

"What happened to the fish inshore?"

Grenfell Hillyard shrugged. "It was mostly lobsters we got here. Like all creatures, lobsters move around. They decide for themselves where they want to live. And shorelines change." He talked about wave action, storm history and the configuration of the dunes. "I remember when those dunes were twice that high and there was a hundred feet of land in front of this lighthouse tower. That's why there's no point in building a break like this." He got up from the rip-rap barrier and set down his glass. "You might as well spit on a fire in a barn full of straw."

Island stone wore away. Sandy beaches moved. After an especially fierce storm the shoreline might not look familiar anymore. But the human mind would adapt.

Grenfell Hillyard began to walk away.

"You cannot hold a thing like water back," he said. "It will cut the earth right out from under you."

FIFTEEN

March 1965. Prospect, Prince Edward Island.

Sonia called train stations all over the Maritimes, RCMP detachments in cities and small towns, operators in the city of Toronto. She called the ferries and the hospitals, both Protestant and Catholic.

Everyone said, *I'm sorry, dear. I don't think so.* No. In some part of her mind Sonia understood these answers weren't going to change. But she couldn't imagine what else she might do.

The frustration she felt was a physical torment. Her heart was knotted, yet it raced. Her lungs felt compressed, as though her body had been tightly bound. She longed for release, or escape.

But from what? From the need to search for Stella? But who would do it if she didn't?

Late one night when she put down the phone, she heard Rose's voice say, *Mum, you have to get outside*, and she slipped away from the house.

Snow, deep on the ground, necessitated snowshoes, so she laced on Dan's, taking them down from where he kept them, on a spike hammered into the back wall of the porch. The night air felt good to Sonia, cool and sharp inside her lungs. She breathed deeply, and the sudden pain invigorated her. She stepped briskly away from the house and yard, her lungs full of air so cold it seemed a gaseous form of frost. After so long inside, the idea of this vast, quiet dark was giddy-making.

Near the woods, she turned her flashlight on. The moon was faint, and clouds hovered all around it. As she strode, sinking slightly in the slumpy snow, her yellow flashlight beam bobbed ahead, illuminating tree trunks shaggy with old man's beard and great spread mounds of ground yew iced like cake. In the wintry dark, her own familiar woods seemed alien, the shriek and gasp of tree limbs as they moved, an eerie chorus. But Sonia had nothing to be afraid of. What could be worse than the losses she'd already suffered? She was like a superhero from one of Rob's comic books: so freakishly damaged that she was immune to ordinary pain.

She strode half blind through the dark woods, smashing small, buried shrubs and young trees with Dan's big snowshoes. The snow was dense, sticky stuff. She sank into it, and it clung to the snowshoes. Walking through it required muscle, but she felt glad to use her body vigorously again. She'd spent too many days inside, idle days in bed or in her wicker chair. What she wanted now, desperately, was *action*.

A twig snapped beneath her foot and part of it flew up into her face. Startled, she stopped and looked around.

How had this happened? Without meaning to, she'd stomped her way to the river. She was only a few hundred yards from the place where Stella had supposedly disappeared, and she felt alarm at the sight of the frozen river. When had she last been here? In her imagination the ice was clear and solid. Not in reality. Even in the dark, Sonia could see that the river had begun to change. Slabs of ice had rafted onshore, and open water was clearly visible in the centre of the river, where the current ran deepest. On the opposite bank, less than a hundred feet away, snow and ice had melted enough to reveal a stand of broken cattails and bent-over rushes, remnants of the vanished year.

It's almost spring, Sonia thought. I've slept the winter away.

She made her way along the riverbank. Her flashlight had gone out, but some clouds had drifted away from the moon, so there was enough light to see by. Where the jagged ice floes piled on the bank made snowshoeing difficult, she walked on the frozen river. The edge still held, in most places.

Once, she stopped to adjust the straps around her boots and heard a breath of sound. Another time, she stopped to listen: a fox or a rabbit was travelling through the woods nearby.

Then, without warning, Dan's dog, Buddy, appeared beside her on the ice. He danced on and around the snowshoes. How had he got loose? Without realizing it, Sonia herself must have let the old dog out of the house.

"Go home, boy! Go on!"

But Buddy stayed until snow began to fall in fat, bright flakes, and Sonia turned back, heading along the river toward her farm. By the time she reached the house, the wind had come up and the heavily falling snow swirled everywhere in a disorienting tempest.

She paused to rest by the paper birches that bordered the farm, and Buddy raced ahead, inflamed by the unearthly screams of an ermine hunting near the road. Silly old pup, she thought. Weasels slink around, they hide in crevices. They squeeze themselves into places dogs just can't fit.

She slowed her steps as she approached the house. She wanted to stay outside where the air was fresh and there was only the snow and the cold to think about.

It was Rose who noticed the dog was missing. Rose, because Kate wanted to play horsey with him.

"He'll turn up," Dan said. "He's probably chasing rabbits in the woods."

But Buddy didn't turn up. And it snowed so heavily overnight and all the next day that there were no tracks to follow when, finally, an insistent desire to look for Buddy kept Dan from his work.

Sonia watched him put on his boots. She stood with her shoulders hunched, her arms across her chest. *No*, she thought. *Not this too*. The feeling was urgent, but she kept quiet because Kate was beside her.

Please, not anything else.

SIXTEEN

There was no break in the weather. The snow that started the night Buddy disappeared continued to fall. Plows were out every day, creating cuttings that built up along the roads almost to the height of the telephone lines. By the time a week had passed, everyone had given up on Buddy. Rose and Rob and Dan turned away from each other, toward the work they used to hide their suffering. Frances focused on studying for exams at school.

The old dog was a trooper, but out in the cold without food and water for so long, he must certainly have perished.

Sonia retreated to her room again. For a few days she was visited regularly by Rob—the youngest and the most affected by Buddy's disappearance. Buddy had been Max's dog, then Dan's, but it was Rob he followed everywhere, and Rob's bed he slept on every night.

"Mum," Rob said whenever he came into Sonia's room, "can I get you anything?" He didn't ask for comfort or consolation of any kind. But Sonia understood that this newly solicitous behaviour was Rob's way of reaching out.

"I don't need anything, dear," she'd say. "Sit with me awhile, if you like."

Rob would sit on the end of Sonia's bed, near her wicker chair. They would be silent together in the murky room. Then Rob would leave, closing the door softly after him.

One shadowy late afternoon, Rob's face took on a childish cast, and Sonia was reminded of his distress over the stuffed bear he'd lost. She'd felt terrible, sure that she herself had misplaced the bear, mixing it up with the laundry, perhaps. She had promised to help look for the bear, or make a new one, whatever it took. "It can't be a *new one!*" Rob had wailed. "It can only be him!" He'd burst into tears, and Max had laid his hand down hard on the table. "Be a man!" he said. "Sonia, you baby him!"

Why had she not defended Rob? Protected him better?

Thinking of this, she began to weep. Rob patted her shoulder awkwardly for only a moment before escaping. After that, he stayed away.

Sonia understood she'd failed him. But what could she have done? The loss of Buddy was almost nothing to her. She refused to think of the dog, and she never admitted she'd likely been the one who let him out.

SEVENTEEN

April 1965. Prospect, Prince Edward Island.

The day the snow stopped falling and began to melt instead, Dan shovelled out the lane. Sonia watched him from the kitchen as she filled the sink. He dug as though possessed, as though he might find gold rather than shale under all that snow, as though he had no other work to do. He dug in order to tame his fury. Ever since he'd spoken about Evvie on the ice, he'd been enraged. It was wrong that Evvie was free while they mourned Stella. And what about Kate? he said. It was wrong, too, that Sonia remained tormented by the notion Stella had run away.

Sonia felt touched by Dan's concern for her. But his thinking was muddled. *How many times had she explained?* She wasn't tormented by the idea Stella ran away; she was impatient for Stella to return.

Dan shovelled, and snow piled up beside him. As Sonia watched, her feeling of incompetence grew. She'd failed at helping Dan.

Meanwhile, Rose announced she was going into town. *With Ray*, she said, and sighed dramatically.

This was Sonia's fault too.

Ray Vermeer had come into their lives the previous fall. Frances found his wallet when she was fishing with Mart Decoursey and Lyman Cray. The wallet had been underwater. Lyman slipped on it when he got out to haul the boat. You could see it clear as anything, Frances said, a neat rectangle among rounded slabs of sandstone, completely out of place in the silt on the river bottom.

Raymond Francis Vermeer, the licence read. The leather wallet couldn't have been in the water long: it was only slightly swollen and the dollar bills it contained were good as new. Besides the licence there was no other identification, only two water-ghosted photographs, whose subjects — a woman in a fifties updo and a stylish new car — remained, despite their blurred and scrofulous images, insistent.

Right in front of Mart and Frances, Lyman pocketed the money. Frances took the wallet and the licence home. Two hours later she picked up the phone and asked the operator for Vermeer, in Charlottetown.

It was that easy. The operator rang a number and Ray came on the line. He arranged to collect the wallet the following Saturday. He was grateful for her thoughtfulness. Prim as a schoolteacher, Frances said later, not a bit like his real self.

Ray claimed he was a teacher, but he was nothing of the kind. Dressed for fishing when he stopped by the house that Saturday, he'd hit it off with Dan, who was up from the barn for morning tea when Ray's late-model Chevy pulled in the lane. Ray slurped the tea Sonia poured, clattered his cup, swept biscuit crumbs to the floor.

Several days later, Ray telephoned to ask Dan and Frances to go fishing. Frances said no. After a week or so, he called again. On and off, he called all winter, dropping Dan's name from the invitations. *No*, she would say, and hang up. But Ray was persistent. Duck hunting? Grouse hunting? Ice fishing? A movie? A walk? A skate?

When Frances stopped answering the telephone, Ray replaced her with Rose. How lucky for him their voices were so much the same, he said. As if Frances and Rose were interchangeable.

One day Sonia answered, then slammed the phone down.

Rose immediately picked up the phone and called Ray.

I said, *Is your daughter there?* Ray explained, and she hung up on me.

My sister is gone, Rose said. You'd better not call again. Then she hung up on him. "I'm sorry, Mum," she said, explaining this.

But Ray was not the kind to quit. Somehow, over the course of several weeks, he wormed his way into Rose's life.

And now Rose was entranced by Ray. While Sonia washed dishes, out the window Dan dug into the packed snow. At the kitchen table, Kate tried to peel the paper wrappers off her crayons. But Rose simply sat, lazy and thinking of nothing but this man Sonia didn't trust. *Ray*, she sighed.

And from beside her came the parrot sigh of Kate, so focused on her crayons she would not look up or speak. Sonia felt choked—her heart shredded by the sight of that pile of worm-shaped paper labels and the gleam on Kate's tiny, perfect face, her lips pursed in concentration.

Stella had once looked just the same.

"Mum," Rose said then, "do you know Ray's going to take me dancing at the Rollaway Club?"

Sonia turned and saw the hope in Rose's eyes.

He'd talked to her about a job at the telephone company in town, Rose said. Of course, she couldn't take a job like that and still look after Kate, but wasn't it sweet he had ideas for her? He was so thoughtful, she said.

Sonia wanted to remind Rose that she knew very little about Ray. They'd been talking on the telephone every two or three days for several weeks, but they hadn't met in person and he'd asked so many questions, she'd had no time to ask her own. She said, "Ask him where he comes from, and who his people are. Who was that woman in his wallet photo? What does he do for a living, and why won't he say?"

But Rose was focused on his looks. She'd refused to allow Frances to describe him. "You don't like him. You'll spoil it." She had an idea he was tall, probably Dan's height—with straight dark hair and a healthy, ruddy complexion. She felt he was wiry: muscular but slim. She decided this based on the way he spoke. There was always a lot of energy in his voice, she said, and he never wasted any time.

Sonia wished she could set her daughter straight: Broad, not tall. Wavy hair, greased black. Fanatical about his own interests. Impatient. Loud.

But Rose would not hear a word against Ray. She preferred her imagined version of him to what anyone else might say. She preferred his *mystery*. Soon there'd be an end to that. Ray had promised to pick her up on Friday and take her into town for the evening. Rose had asked

Frances and Sonia to watch Kate so she could go. Of course they agreed, but thinking about this planned evening made Sonia feel guilty and negligent somehow.

Once, much earlier, Ray had asked Frances to describe Rose. *Does she look like her sister?* And Frances—distracted by his slick manner, forgetting somehow that he'd only met Dan and herself—had wondered, *Which sister?*

Mum! she'd wailed, telling this story. *There's only Rose now.* And Sonia understood a little better what Frances felt she had lost.

"*Help!*" Kate said, startling Sonia and almost falling as she climbed backwards off her chair, bits of crayon paper scattering like confetti. She tugged at Rose's skirt, then climbed into her lap. "*Draw!*" she commanded, and for a few minutes, until Kate became engrossed again, Rose distracted her with sketches of candy-coloured cows eating lilac grass under an ingratiating, smiley face sun.

And then Dan was in the porch, leaning across the threshold. "*Hey!*" he croaked, as if he'd lost his voice. "*Help!*" Then he was gone.

Sonia let the dishcloth slide into the sink, slipped on her boots and jacket and followed him.

Near the mailbox he kept hearing something. "*Listen,*" he pleaded. "Where is it coming from?"

She listened. Maybe she heard a moan. She wasn't sure. But Dan needed her to be sure. And she needed to help him. She'd already failed Rob and Rose.

"Please, Mum," he said.

Maybe all of this had been too hard on Dan.

He bore his doubt and pain in silence. His role as eldest male was to protect everyone else, to run the farm and to bear up. That's how he seemed to see it. It's what he'd been doing since his father died. For years he'd gone to school all day then worked through the afternoon and evenings, as Rob did now. He'd worked in the fields every summer and all through harvesting and planting seasons without the benefit of whatever was going on in school. Somehow he'd graduated. But looking at him now, Sonia thought she could see the wear on his face.

"Do you hear it, Mum?"

She couldn't hear anything. But Dan needed her to help him, so she guessed. "Dig there," she said, pointing to the near edge of the ditch where the snow had been packed all winter by the snowplow into a giant mound. This will keep him busy, she reasoned, and he'll work the tension out of his body.

As Dan put his back into the heavy snow, she thought of Wile E. Coyote, foolish and ever hopeful, gamely wielding an ACME digging tool against insuperable odds.

But when she listened again, there was definitely a moan, or a whimper.

She took a turn with the shovel, then swallowed her racing breath while Dan dug.

Finally, after what seemed like hours, Dan revealed a blue hole in the snow, a small cold cave with something alive inside it. *Rrrr*. Dan threw the shovel down.

Before he could even bend toward the hole, a weak growl and a moan resolved into a picture of Buddy in the culvert underneath the lane. And then the look on Dan's face: an impenetrable expression comprising reverence and hope and desperation.

She hadn't seen Dan's heart exposed this way since childhood.

"Don't worry, boy," Dan said. He fell onto his stomach in the snow and, reaching down, tugged Buddy's stiff and emaciated body back into the light.

Dan carried Buddy into the house and they examined him more carefully. It was difficult to recognize the dog at first, his body was so wasted, his coat so dull and matted. His eyes were closed. He was unbelievably cold. His nose felt chapped. Was he alive? Dan detected a moist wisp of breath, or imagined that he did. "Lay him here," Rose said, opening the oven door, taking charge. "Get a blanket from the closet in the hall and lay it on him."

Kate left her crayons for this new excitement. "Dog?" she said. She reached with her small pink hand toward a paw that seemed entirely made up of bone and sinew.

Buddy growled weakly.

"*No!*" Rose said. Then, more gently, "Dog is sick."

Kate flung herself across the room and hid her face in the pillow on the couch.

Sonia could see she was hurt, but in the chaos of that moment the dog seemed more important. She felt ashamed of this decision later. It was the same kind of emotional triage by which she'd so failed Stella. All Kate needed was a bit of attention, and to be included. *One of us could have gone to her*, Sonia thought. *I could have.*

Dan came back with a grey wool blanket and Rose said, "All right. I'm going to make some baby formula. That's what we'll feed him until he gets his strength back."

Dan patted Buddy, and Rose punched two holes in a can of milk.

"How about that, Rose?" he said. "How about that, eh? It's a miracle."

Soon the odour of dog was rising in the warm kitchen and it seemed to Sonia that everyone would smell it, and that when they did they would look at Buddy and think of Stella.

It was a miracle the dog survived, but it had been so much longer since Stella disappeared. Two miracles was too much to hope for.

EIGHTEEN

August 1941. Surplus Island, Malpeque Bay, Prince Edward Island.

Now Sonia devoted her days to the chores she'd let slide all summer: scraping, painting, scrubbing, greasing, washing, oiling, mending, beating, airing. She scoured the tower and the house. She canned jam and vegetables, put up pickles. She tried to fix the lifeboat, failed, spent the better part of an hour sending a message to Malpeque Harbour to hire Grenfell Hillyard, who got it working in an afternoon. She oiled a crateful of extra parts supplied by DOT (some duplicates, some meant for machinery no longer in evidence at Surplus Station). She brought the lighthouse up to inspection standard, and then she stayed awake each night, twitchy with doubt and indecision. She could have slept. Her only nightly obligations were to light the lamp at dusk and extinguish it at dawn and to listen to "Instructions for Lightkeepers." She had managed this since she'd arrived, carrying an alarm clock to her bedside and listening in the dark at 11:30 p.m. and 3:30 a.m. for the by-now-familiar message: "Instruction A—A for Apples—is to be carried out." She'd become accustomed to getting the rest she needed in four-hour increments.

But now she could not seem to rest.

After weeks of staying up all night, sleep deprived and unhinged by solitude, she began to believe she craved the dark. Several times she became dizzy in the sun, and daylight itself began to assume a hallucinogenic quality.

Every morning before she doused the light, she paused to observe the progress of dawn. The spectacle was compelling, yet she couldn't fathom why. There was really nothing to it—just that shimmering with a glare beneath it, and then the brilliant, full-on glare itself.

When Pete returned at last, she was asleep in bed at noon. She woke to the unfamiliar sounds of cooking in her kitchen, someone banging the kettle around and opening a cupboard door. She came down and found him with a jar of her raspberry jam in one hand, a teaspoon in the other. He'd made toast and tea and fried an egg for each of them. Turning her gaze from the stove, she caught a glimpse of unfamiliar colour. He'd set the table. The pot of silver spoons was in the middle of the table, next to a water glass with vivid fuchsia beach pea blossoms in it. There were napkins, cups and saucers, knives and forks on either side of the plates. He beamed beside the table he'd set for her.

His feet were bare, and he'd tracked sand across her newly waxed and polished floor. A spill of crystals glinted on the dull, dark wood. The sand was lustrous—in contrast to the floorboards she'd lavished with attention, which remained (she now saw) utterly, stubbornly dull.

She wondered why he'd come. She wondered if she cared. When would she learn to take control of this backwards life she lived? Damn it, why had she bothered to wax and polish that wrecked old floor?

Gripping the jam and the spoon together in one hand, he pulled out a chair and held it for her.

Obediently, she sat.

Without speaking, he dished up the eggs and toast and poured the tea. She thought of Max, meals she'd given him. This awkward silence seemed similar.

Pete cooked eggs so they were crispy at the edges, soft and yielding in the centre. His toast was the bright brown of caramel all over, and he'd sliced it neatly into fingers.

He took two small bowls from the cupboard and set one at each place and sat down at the table with her. He twisted the screw band off the jam jar and lifted away its bubbled green glass cap. He used his butter knife to ease out the disc of wax with which she'd sealed the jam. This he set on the edge of his plate. He stirred the jam and spooned a little into each of their dishes. He licked his spoon and set it down and looked at her.

But suddenly she was too woozy to eat. "Excuse me," she said, and got up carefully and went out the door.

Was it the smell of the eggs? That he'd opened her new jam?

By the time she'd walked a few paces in the breeze, she was fine. It was just the surprise of seeing him, the fact that she was not yet fully awake, that her kitchen was stuffy from having been closed up overnight. It had been unbearably hot and muggy for days. It was eighty-three on the thermostat, the air as still as soup.

She climbed over the breakwater and bent toward the surf. She splashed salt water in her hands and ran her wet palms up and down both arms. That felt better. She wet her hands again and touched them to her face. She could go back inside now. She'd be fine.

She came inside with white sand clinging to her own bare feet. So much for the floors. But what could you expect, really, living in such a place? All the work she'd done was — how had Grenfell Hillyard put it? — like spitting into the face of a raging fire.

He stroked her wet arms and took away the greasy egg. He gave her a clean plate. As she spooned ruby jam on toast, he covered her sandy feet with his own.

It was too difficult to eat.

He began to explain himself, and she lifted her cup of lukewarm tea and drank to his words (lies and excuses).

Cy had kept him busy. There was a disease in the calves on three neighbouring farms. His mother had been ill, so it hadn't seemed right to sneak away.

Then the feeble truth: his mother had noticed his absence the night he'd slept on the floor of the lighthouse. Someone had seen him crossing the causeway with his bicycle and told her and she'd guessed where he was. She hadn't been pleased.

Unless Pete's mother was very different from other Island women, it would be impossible to count the number of people to whom she'd told *a version* of Pete's story. This explained the reception Sonia had received at the Proffit farm a few weeks earlier when she'd gone across intending to negotiate a price for firewood.

She'd found Marg Proffit in her flower garden. Marg had glossy straight black hair that she wore pinned in a bun at the back of her head. She was a handsome woman, but that afternoon she had looked dull as a mouse among the glories of her garden. Sonia drank in its colours: tall, deepwater blue larkspur, impossibly dark orange lilies, phlox both red and white; the sweet, almost artificial pink of musk mallow and the clear pale lemon of a tiny day lily. If there had been a way to burn the colours onto her retinas, she would have done it. But she couldn't even paint a picture. She had no watercolours or dyes; she had given up all that.

She turned away.

A proper married woman would have a home and a garden of her own to tend, she thought. She would wear a look of peace, like Marg.

"Sonia? Is something wrong, my dear?"

A proper married woman would express concern for others.

With a small pair of scissors she took from her pocket, Marg began to cut her flowers.

Sonia followed her as she assembled a bouquet and bound the stems together with a piece of string from her pocket. "For you," Marg said with a gentle smile. This was pity, Sonia realized. But she found she didn't mind — the flowers were so lovely.

Marg ducked through her open porch door and emerged a moment later with a damp rag in her hand. This she wrapped around the cut ends of the bouquet. "I set eggs and cream aside for you in the cellar," she said. "Now why don't you choose what you'd like from the cold room in the storage barn? Georgie's out there, he'll give you a hand."

Sonia made her way slowly along the path that led from Marg's garden to the barn. The path was made of flat pieces of Island stone set neatly level with the earth, but weeds thrived between each stone just as they did throughout Marg's lush jungle of a garden. Everything about the Proffit farm was like this: rampant, carefree and disordered. In the garden there were tangles of hedge bindweed; amongst the grass, a rusting collection of broken equipment, mounds of wood slabs; hillocks made of tumbled birch logs (the very wood she hoped to buy for winter) were hedged all around with thistle; on the paths, roving wild gangs of fowl; and everywhere — in spite of the Proffits' apparent inattention — an overabundance of ripe fruits and vegetables and tall green growth. How Sonia admired George and

Marg's capacity to grow what they needed. How full and serene their life here seemed. And how different it was from her own, which was ruled by the clock, the light and the stringent regulations of the DOT.

In the barn, George was standing with his hands stuffed in his pockets, rocking on his heels and speaking softly with another man. Sonia had noticed a truck in the yard and assumed it belonged to another customer for produce or a neighbouring farmer. But this man did not look like he was buying vegetables. He certainly wasn't asking for advice on balky cows. If anything, he was giving it. Sonia could see from their stances and the way they glanced her way that these two men were friends and social equals, respectful of each other, and familiar enough to trade intimacies. This was the kind of relationship her father had had with their neighbour Clément Dionne. They were almost as close as women. M. Dionne knew more about the failure of her parents' marriage than she did, just as Daniel no doubt knew about whatever troubles M. Dionne had confided. She hoped one day to have a friend like that. There had been girls at school she'd liked enough to share her time with, but no one she'd considered close enough to confide deeply in. Briefly she'd felt close to Max's mother, who knit so beautifully. But Nova MacAusland grew ill with croup before Max and Sonia married, and she died a short while later. Max had moved away; Pete kept disappearing. Was she deficient in some aspect of character essential to friendship?

George said something to the other man and clapped him on the back. They laughed quietly together for a moment while they studied the dirt on their boots. Then simultaneously they looked at Sonia. "Come over, dear," George said, waving vigorously. "I'll help you find something to eat."

George stored his vegetables in covered crates and large jute bags in a cool, dark corner of the barn. It was just a corner with a partial wall, but he referred to the space as his "cold room," and he liked to take out the vegetables himself and present them one by one to Sonia. She always allowed a generous length of time for buying vegetables. There was a ritual to these meetings, which began and ended with a handshake.

She held her hand out now, but instead of taking it, George put his arm around the other man and said, "Sonia, you know Cy McRae."

A chill ran down her spine. She *did* know that name. But *how?*

Then it came to her. Cy McRae was Pete's employer.

He wasn't anything like she'd expected. Pete had described a gentle, soft-spoken man and she'd imagined a placid grandfatherly figure, small and stout perhaps, with wavy, greying hair. The real Cy McRae was tall, sharp-featured, wiry, vibrantly alert.

"We haven't met," she said. She offered her hand. His grip was firm and he looked into her eyes in a steady, interested way.

George did not say, Cy, this is Sonia MacAusland. This failure of courtesy told her that George had already spoken her name to Cy. It said plainly that *she* was the object of interest here. She felt cornered, thought: *run*.

Cy said, "So you keep the light?"

"Yes."

"Must be quiet, living out there."

"It's quiet. I like it."

"So, you're all alone out there? You manage all the equipment, the foghorn, the light in the tower?"

"It's not so difficult, really."

"And you're on your own out there," repeated George, who knew damn well she was, and why.

She said nothing.

"Where is your husband, anyway?"

She hated him! She would never come to his farm again! She'd buy food and firewood somewhere else!

"I mean, he shouldn't have left you, dear. And for what? To farm. It's a job for fools." Here he laughed, gestured all around. "There's better ways to earn your bread." His chuckle turned into a grimace of self-deprecation, and for a long moment Cy bestowed on George what must have been meant as a sympathetic smile.

"Too dry this year, too many sick cattle around," George added, and Cy nodded his head in agreement.

Then they both turned back to Sonia, and Cy spoke: "Do you mind being on your own there, dear?"

"No." She'd answered this question already.

"Things were probably better years ago, when more people lived down on the shore," he offered.

"Yup," said George.

"You know, years ago there was a big community living on the sandhills up in Freeland," Cy said, all history teacher and grandiosity. "At least a hundred people moved out to those shanties and cabins every summer, and the lighthouse keeper was the centre of all that. I had to go up a few times, to look after the horses that worked the moss."

"I had a cousin, Claretta, that ran a lobster cannery up there," George said, stepping closer to Cy. "It was quite a place...Cy! Remember Ace Walfield?"

"One time I helped a woman up there give birth," Cy said. "There was no doctor anywhere around..."

"Every evening there would be a time," George said.

"...the laughing and crying! And those flimsy shacks, with the wind whistling through them, and sand sifting between the boards..."

The two men were in separate worlds of memory now.

"I can hear Danny Adams put the bow to the fiddle," George said, and began to sing: *"My mummy told me if I was goodie, that she would buy me a rubber dolly. / My auntie told her I kissed a soldier, now she won't buy me a rubber dolly. / Ohhh..."*

"*Hmmmm*," Cy chimed in, and George took a mouth organ from the breast pocket of his overalls and began to play.

The sound George made was rich and deep and vibrant, but Cy had a sharp, wavery voice, too high for the song.

George sang, his voice low and mock solemn, and with his mouth organ he made the sound of clapping hands.

Cy slapped his knee. "Lay the leather to the hardwood!" Again they laughed.

Then George turned back to Sonia and assumed a solemn expression. "Ah, you missed them times, dear." In the sudden quiet he looked sincerely sorry, but Cy waved a hand through the humid air.

"It wasn't anything. You can't go around regretting what you haven't known."

While George sorted through his vegetables, Cy rattled on about what he'd seen and the wisdom experience had imparted. Sonia listened grudgingly. Pete had described Cy as a talker, but he hadn't mentioned this didactic streak. The worst thing was that he brought out the native bossiness in George.

"Take some of these beets," George said. "They're a decent size now. You'll not be sorry." She hated cooking beets once they'd grown past the tender baby stage, but George was determined to force them on her. "I'll tell you what, take all these. That'll do you for a while."

"George," said Cy, "she'll not eat those beets in a month of Sundays." He turned to her. "Because you're by yourself now, dear, aren't you?"

Why were they so stuck on this question?

"Maybe you have visitors sometimes," George said. "A person wants to have their cellar stocked just in case." He peered around Cy to look at her, a sly look on his face, the bag of beets dangling open from his hand.

Both men waited, but she did not respond.

"You know," said Cy, "it's natural to need the company of other folks. A solitary life can be lonesome. A person can go a little loony, start making bad decisions. Take that Harold Pyke, whose post you took over at the lighthouse."

"He used to visit me," George said.

"Yes, and he kept company with Mary Gormley after old Hew died. Then Mary died herself. After that he broke down, I guess."

"But nobody blamed him. A person needs companionship."

What were they saying? They thought she was crazy from living alone?

"Let me help you with those things, dear." Cy lifted two jute sacks half full of produce. With the sacks in his hands, he began to walk out of the barn. She followed him.

At the door of the barn, he turned around. "I guess the difference is, Mary wasn't married anymore."

Beside her, George began to nod.

"Pete talks about you," Cy said quietly. Gently, he touched her hand, and she looked down and saw that she'd crushed the stems of Marg's bouquet. "Pete's a good man," he continued. "But he's leaving in a week or two, and I'd hate to see you two young people hurt."

So this was the point they wanted to make.

She felt shamed by the baldness of Cy's statement. He held out the sacks of vegetables and she took them from him. How presumptuous he was! What did he know of her relationship with Max? Was Cy the reason Pete had not been back to see her in so long? Had he spoken to Pete in this same insinuating way? Perhaps he had been even more blunt with Pete: *Love is blind, but the neighbours aren't. Har, har.*

She felt her eyes well as she walked away with the bags slung over her shoulder, beets like rocks slamming into the soft part of her back. She did not stop in at the house for the eggs and cream Marg had said she'd set aside.

In her dream that night, she was a part of the crowd at the sandhills. She belonged there, among the shanties like tents with crevices everywhere that let in the air and the sand, among the folding tables, camp beds, portable stoves, and the galvanized tubs used to wash people, clothes, linens and dishes. There was condensed milk in cans, not fresh. Possessions hung from nails in the studs of the walls and life was lived in open view of all. It was a life apart but dense with other people. Close like an ant colony: collaborative, but fractious too. Because that's how it is when people are together. Passion overtakes reason and they do things to harm one another. They love and they lash out. On rainy days there would be games of cribbage and forty-fives. On mild evenings there would be a co-operative supper in the cookhouse followed by a dance. And then after the dance there would always be a fight.

But she would have the sense to leave before the dance got rough. And she would walk along the shore where the waves lapped softly on the sand. And Pete would be waiting for her, taking her hand, strolling with her in the moonlight through the gentle surf.

Then Pete would say her name, and she would wake.

"Sonia?"

He touched her hands, which she held wrapped around her cooling tea.

"You don't have to eat that toast if you're not hungry. I only made it as a way to keep busy until you got up. I came to see you — not to cook."

She shook her head. "It's delicious."

He wrapped his big hands around her small ones. This felt suffocating. She pulled her own away.

"I'm sorry not to have come back before now. My classes start next week. I have to leave tomorrow."

So what was the point of coming back? She wondered if he ever thought before he spoke.

"Let's spend the day together. Let's have a nice time. Friendship should be about the time you spend, not something else."

Not what people say, he meant.

They walked down to the shore in the manner of summer visitors, holding hands, dressed in bathing clothes and lugging a blanket and hats and Pete's pack, which they'd filled with food. She was determined to enjoy his company this one last day. She tried not to think, He's leaving, but rather, *He's here now.*

This was what she had been hungry for, she realized. In his absence, all the hues of her life had been greyed out.

First they swam, the water so sharply cold it stung. Then they raced up and down the beach to calm the chill that burned their skin. They sank onto their blanket on the sand and let the weak, late summer sun do its best to dry and warm them in their clammy suits. They ate the bread and cheese he'd brought, and he talked about the classes he would attend when he returned to Montreal. He would begin to train in surgery this year, he said, and learn to find his way around the hospital. She listened, nodding, asking questions, but not volunteering any of her own plans for the fall. Finally he fell silent, and she simply gazed at him. There was nothing she could say about her own plans that would meet with his approval. She knew that now. "You can't stay here," he'd said when she'd suggested spending the winter at the station. It wasn't safe, he argued, and of course he was right. In November the station would be boarded up for the winter, and the road would be closed when the snow came.

He said he didn't like the idea of her going to the farm to live with Max. But she and Max were married and that was the thing she had to do, he implied.

Of course, this was true. Whenever she'd talked of this subject, though, attempting to argue a way out of the cage she'd built, Pete became tense. "I could go back to Montreal too," she'd offered once, and he'd held his breath, said, "*Oh!*" — and then immediately retreated. "But... I don't want to be responsible..."

Whenever she tried to parse the meaning of this, she came up against a wall of doubt.

Pete would be her friend, but he would not be responsible.

Whatever that meant.

So she said nothing. Instead, she turned gently away, and for a time they drowsed in the sun, which was warmer now, but distant — not like the bright, strong sun they'd enjoyed those spring and early summer days when nothing had come between them and Pete had seemed to Sonia to become a part of her.

She woke because the wind was up, blowing sand around, the sand scraping her exposed skin. Beside her Pete lay asleep. She touched his shoulder and he woke. "It's late." If he was going to leave on the train in the morning, he would have to cross the causeway before the tide came in.

They went back to the station house, and he followed her upstairs for towels — somehow they had forgotten them earlier — and when she turned with the towels in her arms, he caught hold of her by the shoulders and kissed her.

They had never kissed. It had been easy to deny themselves this — she was married, wasn't she?

It had been easy for Sonia because simultaneously she thought, married — and saw Max's bloodied arm.

But now Pete's mouth on hers was like a powerful form of light, erasing everything — Max, respectability, rules.

"Sonia — " He took the towels from her and squeezed her arms and seemed to be turning some thought over in his mind.

But then he discarded whatever it was he was about to say and simply bent to unbutton the shirt she'd put on over her swimsuit. She allowed this, as she allowed him to pull the straps of her heavy black suit down over her arms and the suit itself down past her hips and to the floor. She stepped out of it. From her feet when she lifted them a smattering of sand drifted down onto the pale painted floor. She turned her face to his. Taking hold of her hands, he stepped away, to look at all of her.

And in an instant she saw his face collapse in shock and then contort in anger — or disappointment, or some mixture of the two — and she remembered what it was she had been trying so hard to shut out of her mind.

"When?" he demanded. "How far along are you, Sonia?"

Through the thick double layers of her swimming suit you could not see the swelling in her belly for what it was, she supposed. But Pete was a doctor and knew the meaning of the shape like a large pear where normally only the formless, level plane of belly ought to be.

"Have you seen a doctor, or a midwife? Why are you still working? My God, Sonia, you shouldn't be here *alone*. All those stairs. What if you fell? It's so *unsafe*."

This was his professional voice. She had lost him now, she realized. And it was her own fault. She picked up a towel to use as a covering and sat down on her bed.

"It was the end of April," she said. "Max followed me here, and I tried to make him go back to the farm, but we fought and...I was confused... This was *long* before I met you..."

She could hear the incoherence in her voice, which came through the bones of her head sounding distant and cold, like the voice of the waves at the onset of winter when they were thick with the intention of ice.

"Never mind..." he said.

He was crying, or she was. He sat down behind her on the bed and wrapped his arms around her and around the towel and held her fiercely and pressed his mouth into the back of her neck. "Promise me you'll leave the station. At least for the winter. You should be in a warmer, sheltered place."

Did she actually speak? In her mind she nodded her head in agreement with this request. But in reality? Afterward, she could never remember.

NINETEEN

April 1965. Prospect, Prince Edward Island.

"Mum, since you're up..."

Sonia turned to Rose and saw in her daughter's eyes the doubt she'd been seeing there so often recently. What happened to the constant child she'd been? Sensible Rose, who let propriety and order rule her life, was willing to give up on a person because she *fell apart a little bit*? Rose's problem was that she expected life to stay the *same* from one moment to the next. Well, there was no same anymore.

Sonia returned her attention to Buddy, who needed something. Needed help.

But Rose didn't go away.

"Mum?" Rose bent down with Kate, crowding Sonia and the dog. What did she want?

"Mama?" Kate tugged at Rose's sleeve. Kate had been doing this so much lately, asking for her mother, or asking for the kind of reassurance mothers give but which Sonia was fairly certain Stella hadn't been able to offer.

"Darling girl," said Rose, and stood up with Kate in her arms, forgetting Sonia.

Sonia poured warm diluted milk into a pie pan and attempted to feed it to Buddy by the stove. She felt unmoored, torn between relief and redundancy. What was her role, if Rose was going to be the mother of the family?

She cooed over Buddy and petted him. But the dog took none of the liquid from the pan.

She filled a baby bottle with milk, set the nipple into place and screwed the cap on. Then she set the bottle in a pan of water on the stove and sat in the rocker to wait. Beside her, Buddy strained to breathe.

She tested a drop of milk against her wrist. Perfect—warm as blood. She shook the bottle to release a drop and nudged the nipple against Buddy's chapped pink and charcoal lips.

But Buddy didn't take the nipple. He didn't move, didn't blink.

She shook the bottle and pushed it into place again. Nothing. Was there no way to get some liquid into him?

TWENTY

A day made so little difference, and so much.

Buddy languished by the stove, seemingly unable to eat. Frances was up, desperately trying to nurse him into life. Rose was clinging helplessly to Kate.

Outside, the world had turned sharply green.

Rain had melted so much snow overnight that grass was visible in front of the house. Blackbirds stalked the yard, puffed up with pride over their glossy, iridescent heads and the rudder-shaped tails they dragged behind them like wedding trains, their cockiness all at odds with their high, strangled voices (like a clothesline being pulled) and the witless way they looked at you with their one bright staring eye. Sonia loved their enthusiasm. Squeak, they said, and she focused all her attention out the window at them, tried to block out Rose, who would not stop fantasizing about her date with Ray Vermeer. We'll do this, we'll do that, she kept saying, and Ray will be perfect. It seemed that she'd forgotten Stella. Since Frances got up and took over with Buddy, Rose had forgotten him too.

Ray, Ray, Ray, she said, and she was like those feathered drinking birds you set on the edge of a glass: up and down, up and down they bob their blown glass heads.

There was never silence anymore; Rose filled it up. Sonia yearned for silence.

But then she was sorry for what she'd wished when Rose went suddenly quiet, staring out the kitchen window, and Evvie's truck pulled in the lane.

Evvie, Rose breathed, and she scuttled back to her room.

Evvie came in loaded down with a box of Stella's dresses. "Someone may as well get the use of these," he said, and set the big box on the kitchen couch. The bottom was muddy from having been in the back of his truck. "Mmmm," he said, sniffing the air. "Smells like boiled dinner."

Frances screwed up her face and rolled her eyes. "Of course, you're welcome to stay for dinner," she had to say, then caught her breath.

"Nah," said Evvie. "Ate already." He walked across the kitchen in his boots and bent down to pet Buddy, who opened his eyes and lifted his chin. Then Evvie turned back to Sonia. "You should give the dog some of that broth."

In the hall, Kate called *Mama! Mama!* She tore into the kitchen dragging a sock with a block inside it. She ran straight at Evvie — then pulled up short. *Mama,* she said softly, sadly. She nudged Evvie's knee, then whipped around and ran out of the room again.

Evvie nodded at Sonia, turned toward Buddy again. "Put that meat juice on a rag and squeeze it in his mouth. He's not looking great."

Then he stood and turned and went out the door.

"Oh—" Rose said, lifting one of the dresses from the box and holding it up in front of her body. "Look."

Rose held the dress, a shiny champagne shirtwaist Sonia had never seen before, and Frances fell—

Later, Rose marvelled that she fell "like a stone" to the floor. Her voice was rich with awe, as though fainting were an accomplishment of some kind. What Frances was good at.

TWENTY-ONE

As Frances lay on the floor and Rose knelt beside her, it seemed to Sonia that Stella spoke—

. . . always a whirlwind of noise. At the dinner table, all trying to talk at once. . . how it is—was—most of the time. . . there're so many of us, and each one trying to sort out something different.
I missed that noise, when I moved away with Evvie.

She knew it wasn't Stella's voice she heard, but rather some version of her own. She was desperate, she realized, to know that her daughter had been happy, even briefly.

This must be why older people spoke so reverently of *peace*. Mary Walt invoked the word at Stella's memorial, and Cece and Mae chimed in, "Someday, dear, you will see she's in a good place now." Sonia had imagined they meant something churchy by their canned assurances. Not simply, *Stella is free of all that troubled her.*

Rose patted Frances's hand as she came to, and suddenly Sonia understood how many of her mothering tasks she'd handed off to her girls.

She hadn't known Stella as well as she should have, and now she was letting go of Rose and Frances too. As children they'd been so needy and she'd been so very busy.

But wasn't this how it had to be? They were all going to leave. They were leaving from the moment they were born, each one of her unique and incomprehensible children.

"When you come right down to it," Rose liked to say, "it is impossible to know another person."

Now Rose was distracted by the clothes in the box, so many of which she'd never seen before. Frances rested on the kitchen cot, and Sonia sat beside her. Frances patted her hand as though she were the one who had fallen.

Later, Cece and Mae arrived, and Dan, still baffled and amazed, told the story of his discovery of Buddy.

"Well, somehow he got out on us. He got himself into a culvert and he must have fell asleep. Then it snowed. The plow came by. Buddy got buried under all that snow. I only found him by accident when I was digging out the lane."

Dan said nothing about the look in Buddy's eyes, the way the light had fallen on him, the uncanny colour of the walls in his snow cave. Maybe Dan hadn't noticed any of those things, but Sonia believed he had.

Cece and Mae listened quietly to Dan. When he was through, Mae said, "It's something he was able to last that long, without food or water."

"I guess he wasn't thirsty. He was licking snow."

Cece nodded and that was the end of the conversation, but it seemed for a moment that Cece and Mae were waiting for Dan to say something more.

The first time Sonia heard him tell this story, Dan was in the milk room with Rob. Dan washing out the separator and Rob drying its parts with one of the towels kept specifically for that purpose. She'd come in to get cream for dinner. She waited while Dan spoke. Rob's hands, with their bony, blue-veined look, made her think of Buddy in the culvert, then of Stella, lost in Toronto or somewhere else. And Dan's voice, so fraught and full of wonder, seemed to contain every nuance of the conflicting emotions she felt. "I dunno," she said into the silence after Dan stopped speaking, as though in answer to some question he or Rob had asked. Both boys looked at her. They'd forgotten—or had never noticed—she was there.

It seemed to her then that Dan's bafflement confirmed what Rose asserted all along: there is no way to understand the events of life, not any more than you can fathom the mind of another person.

TWENTY-TWO

After Evvie left, Rose dipped up a ladleful of liquid from the boiled dinner and bathed a clean dishcloth in the meaty broth. She put a pie plate under Buddy's chin and squeezed the liquid from the dishcloth over his dry, lolling tongue. His withered body vibrated as though from a shock. He moved his jaws. Rose squeezed some more broth, and Buddy raised his head and blinked at Rose. "Oh, Buddy," she said. "You're alive again!"

She dampened the cloth and squeezed more broth. Sonia could hear him swallow. It seemed to cause him pain. Rose squeezed the cloth and Sonia stared at the point where they connected, Rose and Buddy, willing him to live. Buddy made a rasping noise, and Rose went very still. "Don't worry, Mum," she said. "The liquid will lubricate his throat."

Later, Sonia lay on the cot, breathing in the musty odour from the box of dresses. She could smell the dresses, their history, yet all she could see was Evvie with the box.

It was Stella's face she yearned for.

When the girls were little, they liked to play a game called Dress Up and Pretend, and the roles Stella favoured were traditional ones, informed by what she knew. Dress up and pretend to be a mother, dress up and pretend to be a bride. Rose used to dress up and pretend to go out dancing, what she most wanted to do. Frances liked to dress a different way each time, and she never performed the same roles as her sisters. Dress up and pretend to be a lawyer. Dress up and pretend to be a vet, dispensing stern advice to farmers and fawning sympathy toward the cats from the barn. Dress up and pretend to be a science teacher, like lucky Dan's good science teacher, Una Hearne.

As a child, Sonia's favourite thing was to dress up and pretend to be his own self, Inspector Sherlock Holmes. It wasn't the idea of detecting she liked; it was the hat, a hand-me-down from her Montreal neighbour's English husband, who had always been a smartly dressed gentleman. In that hat Sonia felt grown and powerful and full of knowledge, nothing like her real self.

The first time Stella brought Evvie home, Sonia watched him closely. Stella was keyed up, as though his presence at the table were an honour of some kind. Sonia wanted to say: Evvie's not the Queen of England! Of course, she would never be so rude.

Evvie dominated that first supper and the hours after. He made himself at home — sitting down without being invited to do so, stretching out his legs, gazing frankly all around. Dan and Sonia asked questions — not many — and he answered them: Age twenty-one, same as Stella. Parents George and Loleta, a Trainor from Pisquid. Home a mixed farm in Martinvale with a dozen head of cattle, a flock of chickens and a half a dozen hogs.

Dan and Rose behaved as though they liked him. But for no reason she could name, Sonia thought: He's a brazen, cocky bastard. She didn't like the way he held his shoulders back, or the way he looked her in the eye and blinked unsmilingly at Stella.

What did Stella see in him?

Sonia believed Rob and Dan would say "brazen and cocky" too. But later she learned she was wrong about this. Mysteriously, Dan liked him. Rob did not.

During dinner, Evvie talked when he was spoken to and otherwise just ate. He ate ravenously, but no one commented. After dinner, when Stella served the rhubarb pie she'd made, with tea for the family and coffee for Evvie, he claimed Sonia's rocker by the stove and went on about the old Hickman farm he planned to buy, down the road. *So Stella can be near her family.* Making this remark, he grinned unctuously around the room and Sonia began to really worry. Something was wrong with the way

Evvie went about things. At the time — even now — she couldn't name the thing that set her teeth on edge. But it was there.

Other dinners followed. Evvie always dominated the room, as though because he was the eldest male he should assume the place of patriarch. But that place still belonged to Max. Even Dan never tried to take it over.

Was it only this that bothered her: that Evvie wanted to take control? Or was there something else?

After Stella and Evvie married and set up their own house, Stella was always home alone whenever anyone dropped by. Evvie disappeared for long stretches and no one knew where he went. He never seemed to be around when Stella needed help with Kate. Rose said once she'd seen Evvie slam a door and yell at Stella, and Frances said, *Aha!* But Rose said nothing more, had seen nothing more, as far as Sonia knew.

TWENTY-THREE

The weather on the day of Rose's date with Ray was beautifully mild. But the evening of that day a fog rolled in, enclosing Prospect valley and all the roads out of it in a cool, thick mist that snuck inside the house and settled like dew. (That strange fog was a sign, Rose said later. Mum, why did you let me go out in it?)

Frances had burned something horrible in the oven, a science project of some kind. The smell was so bad that Rose had to help Frances get the storm panes off so they could open the kitchen windows to clear the air.

After that, Rose complained she felt smothered and chilly. Her rayon blouse clung unattractively to her arms and her wool skirt smelled of sheep. "Wear your coat," Sonia suggested. But Rose was tired of her winter coat (which was wool in any case and would smell no better damp than the skirt). Rose mentioned Stella's gabardine Toronto car coat. "Remember how she looked in it? Like Audrey Hepburn in *Breakfast at Tiffany's*."

They'd gone through the box of clothes soon after Evvie brought it over. For Sonia it was a relief to handle them, but she could not bear to listen as Frances and Rose debated what to do. "Stella will want these," she said, "when she comes home." But Rose made a job of it, selecting things to save for Kate and things to give away.

In the end, Rose said, it wasn't a difficult task because the clothes had lost their lustre. They were only fabric after all. Unfolded slightly crumpled from the box, none of Stella's things looked the way they had looked on Stella—unremarkable Stella, who had been transformed by the quality articles she'd brought back from Toronto.

The car coat hadn't been in the box. Maybe Stella gave it away in one of her impulsive fits of generosity, Rose said. Maybe we all imagined it.

No, Sonia thought. She took it with her.

Ray appeared as promised on the spot of six. He stood grinning on the step in a shiny leather jacket, the porch light gleaming off his grease-combed hair. He looked like Johnny Cash: brash and handsome, but oddly vulnerable too. Sonia explained to him that Rose would be out right away. She said it was really better not to come in. "Frances cooked something nasty in the oven."

"Burnt mouse, it smells like," Ray suggested. He stepped across the threshold.

Rose, who'd opted to change her skirt and blouse, was nearly ready. "Just wait right there," Sonia said.

Ray smiled. "All right," he said. He swung off his coat and stepped inside, passing quickly through the empty kitchen into the living room, plopping down beside Rob and Buddy in front of the television.

Sonia racked her brain: what more could she have done?

Ray talked at quiet Rob. *Coloured television!* he exclaimed. He'd seen a set in Charlottetown. Rob wouldn't believe the difference colour made. *You have to get one! Save your pennies for it!*

Poor Rob. He didn't have a dollar to call his own, and even if he had, he would never waste it on a frivolity like television.

Rose said Ray had lectured her like this too.

Lately he'd been on about Switchboard. He wanted Rose to move to town, and Switchboard was a way. A relative of his—he'd said her name: Chevette Gallant—was giving up her switchboard job, which Ray had gotten for her. The telephone company would need a replacement and he could easily put in a word with Blondie McLean, his friend who managed all the girls, that is, the operators.

You'll love it! Ray said continually.

After one of Ray's long phone calls, Rose had sought out Sonia for advice. "Mum," she said, "I don't know what to do!" The house was quiet and Rose's panic bloomed in the silence.

She worried he would eventually wear her down. Already she almost didn't care, she said. She just wished to hear no more about the friend with the job. This was the awful part, the greasy friend and the job interview, which Rose dreaded.

Sonia nodded, and Rose went on talking as though unable to stop. The work itself she believed she'd like. She'd seen the switchboard in the village, and could imagine the one in Charlottetown as the same, only larger. The switchboard in the village with its hundreds of plugs and tangled mass of crossing wires that always wanted sorting out was utterly compelling to Rose. But it would be better to get on at the switchboard in town. Ray had told her about the coming change to dial telephones and how soon only jobs for the operators in Charlottetown would remain.

But first there was the interview to get through, then the move to town, and before all that, figuring out what to do about Kate. Because Frances was going to university in the fall. If Rose left too, Sonia would have to look after Kate all alone.

Rose looked at Sonia, and Sonia bit her lip.

When Rose mentioned this difficulty to Ray, she said, he brushed it off. He could find Rose a little car to get to work in, he said, as though transportation were her main concern.

You can pay on the instalment plan, he'd said, and winked.

Rose demonstrated this manoeuvre, squinting one eye as though in pain, and Sonia laughed. She didn't understand how Rose could make fun of Ray and date him at the same time. Perhaps this question played across her face. "Don't worry, Mum. It's just for now," Rose said.

Sonia thought about telling Rose she was making a mistake. Nothing is ever *just for now*. Our impulses have consequences.

But of course Rose would not want to be told what to do.

Sonia thought about the times one of her girls had gotten into trouble—or just barely missed out on getting into trouble—because of just this kind of impulsive choice.

Frances sometimes got around with Marina Cray's son Lyman, who knew every type of badness a person could get up to. He knew what went on in the back room of Joe Gormely's corner store, how to get to the poison mushroom field behind Norm and Elva Corrigan's place, where to find the bootlegger on the Sandy Cape Road and when people met to play cards for money at Virgil Rooney's house. Frances had once been stranded with him out in Peakes after dark and forced to walk through miles of marshy, half-frozen fields until she came to a house with a telephone. A lot of Lyman's ideas revealed their badness from the start, but it always seemed as if Frances would have a moment of weakness and go along with them anyway.

Someone almost died after a fight up east and Lyman had been there. Marina had said, "He wouldn't hurt another person. He's just young, drawn to wherever the action is."

But Sonia believed Lyman's talent for trouble was contagious, and she didn't want her daughters to catch it. What if Ray was the same?

The problem was that Frances and Rose could both be too accommodating.

And of course for Rose there was more at stake than whatever trouble Ray might get her into. There was also Kate.

Rose complained that Kate cried Mama, Mama all day long but was calmed if Rob or Frances or anyone picked her up. Of course she was. Rose was not Kate's mama any more than Buddy the dog or the cows in the barn, whose velvet noses she so loved to be held up to pet.

But Sonia was not Kate's mother either. And Sonia was no good at being a mother, as Stella's disappearance clearly demonstrated.

She was afraid of looking after Kate on her own.

"What are you worried about, Mum?" Rose said when Sonia voiced this concern. "You looked after all of us."

This was precisely what made Sonia anxious.

Some mother, Max had said, so many times. She could hear him still. And why? Because she'd wanted to protect her children? Because she dared put their needs before his? The first years with Stella were hard, but when Dan was born something crucial had clicked into place. And then it became easier to know what they needed after Max was gone. Before, life had been governed by his continual hurry and his need to be the centre of attention.

"Thanks for listening, Mum," Rose said, and Sonia nodded, not certain how she had helped but reassured by the calm on her daughter's face.

Rose wanted Sonia to listen again after her date with Ray. Sonia paid attention: this detailed reporting was so out of character for Rose.

Sonia was worried about Rose. Has he confused you? she wondered. Are you who you were before?

It seemed to Sonia that Rose had left her self behind and migrated into this extroverted personality that fit her as badly as someone else's tailored suit.

But maybe this unfamiliar person *was* Rose. Or an aspect of Rose that Sonia didn't know. Again she wondered if she knew her own children at all.

"Mum?" Rose said.

Sonia turned her attention to her daughter again. I can immerse myself, she thought, so that when Rose tells her story I have a chance of understanding.

In the car Ray turned frequently to grin at her, Rose said, and she marvelled at the way the sun seemed to rise out of the earth as they drove toward higher ground. Often when it was foggy in Prospect valley, it was perfectly nice elsewhere. That day, golden light reflected off the windows of homes and barns, sifted through trees and hedgerows and glittered at the edges of the road where the weeds were wet. Even weeds can be beautiful if you look at them in the right light, don't you think, Mum? Rose said.

The date would not start until they got to town, Rose believed. She hoped to be taken out to dance at the Rollaway Club downtown.

But the date was on a Friday—and dances at the Rollaway were held on Saturdays. Don't worry, Sonia had said the week before, when Rose broached this problem. You'll have fun.

But Rose did not exactly have fun.

Ray parked outside a smoke shop on Elm Avenue, a shop Rose had never noticed on her few previous trips to town. Leaving her on the sidewalk, Ray ran into this shop to buy a pack of cigarettes. As she stood waiting, watching fond-looking couples and pairs of businessmen in suits stroll past, Rose realized this was not an auspicious beginning to the evening. She would have liked for Ray to sweep her into a restaurant on his arm, gently pushing her ahead of him the way men did in films when walking into public places with their gals.

Ray is no movie star, Sonia thought, when Rose told this part.

After the cigarettes, he took her by the arm and guided her around the streets of town. "*Town*," Sonia said, and thought of Montreal. How small her life had become.

For a few minutes, Rose said, it was interesting to stroll around with Ray. She enjoyed peering in the window of Adela's Millinery with its ranks of tiny cardboard boxes filled with silk flowers, satin ribbons and tiny, brightly coloured papier mâché birds. She'd never seen the shop before, and she would have loved to go in and discuss the design for a hat with Adela—if Adela was the delicate older lady bowing her head behind the counter. Instead, Ray led her to the Town and Country, where they ate a plain meal of ham steak with canned green peas and soggy chips. Rose had tea and Ray had beer with his.

Afterward, there was a visit to what Ray called his club, where men sat astride battered stools at a long counter and were offered clear and amber beverages in chunky tumblers. Ray consumed several of these while Rose waited. All the while he talked about Switchboard, and the apartment she might get if she lived in town, and how they would go out like this on weekend nights.

Sonia could picture this scene easily. She imagined that Ray touched Rose's knee as he spoke, and tried to put an arm around her waist, and that Rose shrugged these gestures off.

After, Rose said, Ray drove her by the Island Telephone Company, a boxy brick building whose third and highest floor was brightly lit against the dark. That's where the long-distance operators work, he explained.

Then they detoured to the other side of town, and he showed her where he lived, gesturing down a narrow street. But there was nothing she could see. Ray's street did not have lights.

On the long drive home, Rose gazed out onto the grey, moonlit fields while Ray talked about his car, a lacklustre Chrysler Imperial that he insisted was "only borrowed from a friend." His own vehicle was a new Ford Mustang coupe, he said, "Candy Red in colour."

But it was "presently in the shop."

This was simple boasting, so far as Sonia could see.

But Ray was not all bad, Rose insisted. He had positive qualities. He was enthusiastic. He thought about Rose's future. That must count for something.

"Maybe," Sonia said.

The drive back home had frightened Rose. The car was big and cold, and there was black ice on the road. Rose wished for summer: Ray drove *too fast*. Near Scotchfort he jammed on the brakes to keep from hitting an animal on the road. In the pale glow of the headlight beams, Rose saw it dash into the ditch, eyes all aflame: a small black fox with a pure white tail.

Ray whispered, Silver fox.

Thilver, the word came out. Ray was drunk.

A few miles farther on, the car swerved off the pavement. Ray hauled it back. But by now all Rose could think was: I never want to do this drive again.

Perhaps she did want to live in town.

Maybe I want to be one of those women who stay up at night answering long-distance calls from across the Island and around the world, she said.

Connected, Sonia thought, but alone in a wire-and-button world.

Yes, Rose said, eventually she wanted to earn money of her own, to rent her own apartment, to buy stylish clothes and shoes and a made-to-order hat from Adela's, if she wished. She wanted to avoid this driving back and forth, except to visit home and family and Kate. When Sonia was ready to look after Kate, Rose qualified. "When you're ready, Mum. Okay?"

Sonia nodded. But how could she think about Rose leaving? About looking after Kate alone? And soon Frances would leave too—

Rose was still talking. Pay attention, Sonia thought. She hasn't left yet.

Ray had his good qualities, Rose said. She could rhyme them off. He was handsome. You could say he was handsome. He was strong, with dark, wavy hair and a squared-off jaw that made him seem simultaneously dangerous and reliable. He could carry on a conversation with anyone. He was never worried or afraid, so far as anyone could see. He was persistent. He tried to do nice things for Rose. Someday, for sure, he would take her dancing at the Rollaway Club.

She said she'd liked how they had walked from street to street, looking into shops, sitting down for drinks at various establishments. They had taken in the town. How theatrical it had all been, she said later—the look of the shops, the people out and about, the liveliness. She had never been in town on a Friday night. There was something freeing about walking around in town when other people were out, also walking. It felt like she was part of an event.

Talking it all out, she said she had felt buoyed by possibility. Sonia could imagine this feeling too.

Rose said, "Maybe that was what Toronto was like for Stella."

Is like, Sonia thought. Maybe that's what Toronto *is* like for Stella.

Rose went to bed then, and Sonia stepped outside.

The night had grown black and the stars pressing down from within that darkness seemed to her uncomfortably numerous, and at the same time too faint to be of any use.

TWENTY-FOUR

October 1941. Prospect, Prince Edward Island.

Sonia dreamed of the sandhills all that fall. She dreamed of people around her, busy with work and friendship and dancing in the evenings. She dreamed of women friends bending their heads intimately toward her own, sharing stories and advice. On the sandhills in the evenings the light was yellow and orange, so warm it erased even the chill from the onshore wind. It was impossible to see beyond this light given out by camp stoves and lanterns and bonfires. But in that circle of light was all she needed. Pete was there, tending to whatever required his attention. Max's cut arm. A boy in a sling. Someone's baby. She would look at him, or speak, and he would turn, smiling, toward her.

The dreams became a habit. She could return to that world by imagining the feeling of sand against her skin, or the sound of waves. She began to crave sleep like a drug.

But she woke from the dreams feeling unrefreshed, more tired than if she hadn't slept at all. In the mornings, up before Max, when out the window there was barely enough light to see, she could hear crows calling overhead as they flew from their roosts in the woods to their feeding grounds on the fields. This was how she knew, every morning, that something had gone badly wrong. On Surplus Island, in her sandy bed, she'd woken to the keening of gulls and the high, competing calls of terns—their vibrant, confident voices. Now she felt soft cotton sheets above and beneath her and the restrictive weight of three wool blankets, and she tore herself from the pull of sleep only with great reluctance.

The strangest thing had been losing touch with people she'd begun to know—Marg and George Proffit, Grenfell Hillyard and the fishermen who sometimes put in at Surplus Island to gather or repair their traps. All these people knew her as a person with an important job to do. At the farm, she was only Max's wife, stuck at home. She knew no one, and no one knew who she was or what she could do.

She missed the daily rituals she'd established: lighting the lamp at dusk and extinguishing it at dawn, pulling closed the canvas drapes that shielded the powerful lens from sunlight, polishing the reflector until it shone. She missed the expanse of sea and sky, the lines of sight she'd had, the way subtle ocean colours changed from hour to hour and with the weather. She missed her independence.

The letter she sent to DOT had failed completely. So far as she was able, she'd followed regulations: Use the special, lined memo paper. Write on one side only. Address only one topic per letter.

It was her topic that proved troubling. No, they wouldn't have a woman lighthouse keeper. If Max didn't want the post, fine. There were men who could take over from him. Plenty of men wanted to help their country but weren't able, for one reason or another, to go overseas.

She felt sorry about this response. But in the end, she realized, it wouldn't have mattered what DOT had said. In two months, a baby would be born.

If the baby was a boy, she'd call him Daniel, for her father.

She had no girl's name. She wanted a girl, but how awful to bring another girl into this world. Girls had so little choice in life. They could dream and hope, but what they did was up to men—fathers or bosses or husbands.

Sometimes in her dreams of the sandhills Pete would appear with a child. Her child. They would be holding hands, walking through the surf, and when they saw Sonia, the child would break away from Pete and run to her. Nothing was like life. Not the serenity of the scene. Not the relaxed look of certainty on Pete's face. Not the fact that Pete cared for this child, which in the dream was his as well as hers, but which in reality of course belonged to Max.

She loved the dream. The little girl had champagne-coloured curls and a warm, understanding smile. She forgave Sonia for whatever mistakes she had made. Slipping out of bed to build up the fire and put water on for tea, Sonia marvelled at the way her life had changed. This farm, cold, empty, landlocked, was becoming more familiar with every passing day. Whenever she made a set of curtains, or a meal, or dressed the bed, she performed an act of commitment to the place, and by extension to her husband, Max. This was how familiarity worked: it bred commitment against a person's will. Soon she would no longer dream of life away. Pete and the sandhills would become for her what they had always really been: a figment of imagination, nothing more.

Sonia gave birth at the end of a fall so long and mild that bales of straw left out on the fields grew tender green caps of seedling oats.

She experienced a dreamless night of physical discomfort, then woke to a clear realization of pain. The cramps were dull at first. She believed she could endure them. She let Max get up to make the tea, saying nothing. She would wait as long as she could, keep this to herself. Throughout the morning Max kept coming into the house from the barn, certain something was happening in spite of her many denials. She refused to drive to the hospital in town. It's not time, she said.

By noon, there was no way to carry on alone. She was sick in a basin, the pain so unrelenting now there was no evading it. Max went for Lil, who had been a midwife to other women in the community, and when Lil came into the house, Sonia felt a sudden lightening of the weight she carried in her mind. She would get through this agony with Lil's hand on her back, Lil's whispered words and the damp cloth Lil smoothed across her face.

A gentle breeze across the sandhills became a constant wind, whirled up into a ferocious storm, threw sand and crashing salt-sharp waves on everything, destroyed buildings, wharves and boats, chased inhabitants away.

Still, when the storm abated, the naked dunes would be fine and strong. They were a glory in and of themselves.

At first the baby cried reluctantly.

Sonia was amazed. She felt torn up emotionally—how was this infant so able to restrain herself?

The tiny creature looked around, gazing into her mother's eyes, and Lil's, as though there were worlds available to her inside each of them.

She was so fiercely alive and yet so fragile.

Sonia felt profoundly incapable of looking after her.

You'll be fine, Lil said.

But Lil meant physically. Your body will survive, she meant.

At Lil's suggestion, they named her for the sky when she was born. It had been a clear, cold night. The first really cold evening of that winter. Stars hung thickly overhead, their light exploding as though through holes in a heavy blanket.

It's weighted, Sonia thought, bearing down on us, the piercing white points of it boring into me.

In the morning, every surface was covered in a fine skiff of dry snow and still one star shone in the high, pale sky.

"*Stella*," Lil said.

To Sonia that one star seemed a sign that the winter would go on forever.

Her despair came on quickly. That first look in Stella's slate-blue eyes had been a slap. You're not fit, it had said, and nothing Lil or Max or anyone could say would change that clean, sharp truth. She plodded through the tasks required of her, but she didn't actually want to touch or hold *that baby Lil had named*, as she thought of Stella then. Something was in the way, some blockage or barrier between Sonia and the pale, strange infant she was supposed to love. There was nothing Sonia could do to change this. But she fed the baby and kept it clean and put it down to sleep. And Max came in to check on them—came in early from his work to hold the baby in the rocker, if she was awake, or to tidy up the house and try to jolly Sonia out of what must have seemed a deep, unfathomable sorrow.

Max's tenderness with the child seemed to Sonia as improbable as her own apathy, those first days. In the baby's presence his face flared like a lantern touched with flame. She could almost hear the breathy rush of fuel and the sudden, unsubtle gasp of ignition. Max was captivated and Sonia felt mystified by this—and plagued with guilt. What was wrong with her that suddenly seemed right with him?

Lil began to come by more often in the weeks after Stella's birth. At first she kept her visits short, taking time only to gather dirty laundry to take back to her own house or to put dishes of food in the icebox, and to sit with Stella in the rocker by the stove so Sonia could have her "rest." Apart from feeding Stella, Sonia did nothing all day but rest, yet it seemed that she was always tired.

One morning Lil found Stella bawling in her crib, her bedding and clothes a sodden mess—and Sonia crumpled like a rag, screaming silently, eyes wild, hands pressed against her ears.

Lil saw to Stella first, soothing her with sugar water dripped from her little finger. While she changed Stella's clothes and diaper, Sonia came up and reached for her.

"*I am not so far gone I can entirely forget to feed my baby!*"

Lil made the tea that morning, oatmeal and eggs to nourish Sonia and a lunch for Max. Then, for months afterward, Lil came back each morning, and gradually Sonia overcame some of her hopelessness—or sorrow, or grief—whatever it was that had stood between herself and motherhood. Lil was not the one to judge.

Sonia overheard Lil on the telephone one day: *It's quite an adjustment for her. She's never had to be responsible for anything before.*

She was surprised by the simplicity of this practical assessment. Lil had not expressed anger, or hurt, or (as Sonia's own mother had recently written) *disappointment*. She had spoken in a soft, forgiving voice.

How comforting this was. Because of course Sonia *had* been charged with responsibility before. She'd been the keeper of Surplus Island Light Station. She'd been a negligent and inattentive keeper, much of the time. A failure at lighthouse keeping. But she'd done it.

Lil didn't care. Lightkeeping was not the same as motherhood. Learning to be a mother takes time, she said. And you need support.

In this way Sonia came to understand that Lil intended to stay by her side, and this meant that she, Sonia, was not alone.

TWENTY-FIVE

July 1943. Cavendish, Prince Edward Island.

Sonia followed a path through marram-covered dunes to a beach so crowded she barely recognized it.

Beside her, a flame-haired woman in a ruby swimsuit swept her arms over a small, attentive group — *Waddya say, kids? Let's get wet! Last one in* — then she ran like a child, sand flying, hair flying, towing five young men behind her on an invisible string.

All around, people were living it up, paired off in couples or massed in knots of giggling girls. No one was alone, and no one else had a child clinging to her hand, so far as Sonia could see. What did other parents do — leave their children home?

The sand was bleached white, glittering, and the crowd a whirl of movement and colour. Cobalt jars of Nivea lay wherever they'd been tossed onto red-and-white-striped, ash grey blankets.

Sweating, open bottles lay everywhere. The sugary gold of ginger ale and the lovely underwater green of 7UP. Stubby brown beers half buried in the dry blond sand.

People lounged among the dunes, their clothing bundled into makeshift pillows, teasing, laughing at each other's jokes, smoking cigarettes, enthralled by secrets or gossip they shared.

Small flocks of sandpipers swept over the crowd like a breeze of air, setting down in the flotsam and falling up into the sky again, their fluid movements governed by wind or whim or, perhaps, no force at all.

This beach seemed dull to Sonia, compared to the shore of Surplus Island. It had been tamed by habitation, like Sonia herself, bound, now, to a family she barely understood. Every day Max spoke to her about the baby and the farm. (His pride, disappointments, anxieties. *She's smart like me, not you. There's no money in a farm. Grain better sell this year!*) So few of his words reached her. Stella was eighteen months old. Sonia pretended affection in the hope that she would eventually learn to love the child.

She worried Stella would grow up maimed by inattention. She worried she wouldn't love the second baby she now knew she carried. But she hoped things would be different this time around.

Stella spied a jellyfish and tried to pick it up. "No, no!" Sonia cried. The creature was a delicate pale puce all through, like grape juice watered down. "Mummy! Pretty!" Stella said, reaching for it, and Sonia realized with a sudden hit of pleasure that her daughter possessed a love of colour like her own.

Something softened in Sonia then. But she pushed the feeling back.

On the high tide line, small shells and bits of driftwood from broken lobster pots swam among waves of dry seaweed. Stella played amongst these, selecting shells and setting them in little piles, while beside her Sonia watched the sea.

The empty sea. Boring and still, from a civilian perspective. She didn't know this particular stretch of shore or the fishermen whose boats were visible on the horizon, so the view was as inaccessible as a foreign word whose meaning she could not decode.

She consulted her watch.

Max had promised to collect them at three o'clock, but that meant an hour more to wait. She was tired of lying around doing nothing, and now the sky was starting to cloud over.

"Shall we play at the edge, sweetie, or go in the water?"

"No!" Stella stacked shells determinedly, building a tiny tower.

Sonia stood. If she walked away, Stella would follow her. She couldn't stand to sit still a moment longer.

"*Mama!*" Stella flung a shell from her hand and grabbed for Sonia.

"Let's just take a little walk."

"O-tay!"

What a relief: Stella was having a compliant day.

Sonia turned to face away from the crowds. They'd walk up the shore and perhaps by the time they walked back down Max would have arrived to take them home.

But before she'd taken a step, Stella bent to grab the shell she'd tossed away, hauling down on her mother's arm, then relaxing her hold as she straightened up.

"Let's go now," Sonia said.

"No!" Stella dug her heels into the sand.

Sonia hesitated, torn between following her plan and giving in to Stella, who looked ready to have a spectacular tantrum. Gently, Stella tugged her daughter's arm again, and just as she did, a firm adult hand pressed Sonia's opposite shoulder.

Max, she thought. For an instant she felt torn two ways at once.

"Hello."

Sonia loosened her grip on Stella's hand and turned around, confused. *She knew that voice.*

"*Sonia*," Pete whispered.

She blinked, narrowed her eyes. Was this real?

"I saw you from over there." He pointed back toward the crowd of people, clotted up now in a single mass.

Something about him had changed.

"And who are you?" He touched the top of Stella's head and Stella turned her face up and gazed curiously into his eyes.

"I thought you weren't ever coming back." She spoke so quickly it came out sounding like an accusation.

"I never said that."

"No?"

She thought defensively, *I remember every word you ever said to me.*

This wasn't true, of course. She had no idea what he'd said the last time they'd been together. She could remember distinctly how she'd felt, but not — she realized now — the actual words he'd spoken. She had been too panicked to think.

"Sonia," he whispered, "she's a beautiful little girl. She looks just like you."

Max found them in the water, splashing with Stella. The sun had gone behind a bank of clouds, but the air was still quite warm. "Doctor Pete!" Max smiled as he approached, and the two men shook hands.

"Not 'Doctor' anymore, actually," Pete said. "I gave that up."

"*No!*" Max glanced at the scar on his arm. Sonia could see what he was thinking. You didn't just give up a skill once you'd mastered it.

"Anyway," said Pete. He started to walk away. "I left my clothes back there." He pointed toward the crowd up the beach.

"Good to see you, Doc. Uh, *Pete*."

Sonia dove into the water. Now that Max was here, she could leave Stella for a moment. As fast as she was able, she swam out past the sandbar.

Pete had kept saying her name, as though he couldn't quite believe his luck. Yet he was the one who'd left. He left everything, it seemed. He said he'd given up medicine after something went wrong in a delivery room.

"It was an emergency Caesarean," he'd said. "I kept dwelling on the person behind the green drapes instead of what I was supposed to do. In surgery, a doctor can't be distracted like that. Part of the function of drapes is to keep the surgeon from seeing the person whose body he has to cut into. The mind resists harming another human being."

The mind resists harming another human being. (Was that true of everyone?)

He'd had to leave the operating theatre. He quit that day. He said he didn't know what he was going to do instead. He was working as a clerk in a bookstore for the year. In another month he might go back to school, he wasn't sure.

He asked many questions, but she answered only one or two. She couldn't confide in him about her difficulty being a mother to Stella—he thought Stella was adorable. She couldn't discuss Max. What else was there? Finally they'd gone with Stella into the water. Pete held Stella's hand and jumped over little waves, clowning for her.

For months after, she would summon up this encounter, rearranging it, changing her responses, or his.

The image of Pete holding Stella in his arms impressed on her mind like a brand.

TWENTY-SIX

May 1965. Prospect, Prince Edward Island.

Rose professed ambivalence, but she was still swayed by Ray. She let him take her into town to be interviewed, and she accepted the switchboard job when it was offered.

"Congratulations," Sonia said, but now she was worried. As Rose's life changed, so would her own.

She watched Rose strip off nylons and her good skirt and put on what she called her "comfies," wool work socks and worn jeans. "This is what we need, Mum," Rose said. "It's what I need, and it's what you need too. Kate is so sweet. She likes you. You'll have fun."

It's what you need.

Sonia remembered Max saying something like that to her, one desperate day in Stella's first year. Lil had not been by and dishes were piling up, laundry, clutter. Sonia's hair wasn't washed, her head hurt, her breasts ached. Stella was crying.

"You need to keep up," he'd said. "You. Not me. This is your job."

After the first week, he'd lost interest in Stella. She was a job now. Sonia's, not his.

Later, when Max became more insistent, and Sonia began to feel she needed to leave, he spoke as though he'd changed his mind about Stella. "You go!" he'd said. "You're not taking the baby. You're a terrible mother anyway!"

He'd barred the way to Stella's room, and Sonia knew by the look in his eyes that he meant to hurt her if she took another step toward him.

She couldn't leave Stella. So she stayed.

She couldn't have left anyway. She was pregnant again.

After that, for a long time, she was afraid to need them, these children he could take from her.

He was warm one day, cruel the next. And if he did the least little thing to comfort her, Sonia would forgive him weeks of brutality. Forgive and forget.

The things she forgot.

His raging; doors slammed, his fists put through them; objects thrown, broken, thrown *at her*. Was it her fault?

You made me do it!

She had repaired the damage, swept up the glass, erased the memories. Only the kids did not forget. "Why don't they like me?" he'd asked once. "My own children!"

She hadn't dared to answer.

Other people seemed to like him. Neighbours, farmers, other men. Had they noticed his hardness? Perhaps they had not.

TWENTY-SEVEN

Rose got drives with Harry McLellan, into town and home again. Harry McLellan worked for the government, so he said she didn't need to help him pay for gas. Once he was sick and Rose had to drive herself in their balky truck, but mostly her journeys to work were smooth and only her absence was notable.

Sonia found looking after Kate both familiar and strange. Her own children had never been so clingy or so vocal as Kate, who seemed to want solitude and companionship simultaneously. Sonia felt she was doing something wrong, but Rose said firmly, "Mum, she looks perfect to me."

One Saturday, Frances stayed home with Kate while Rose took Sonia into town, to show off where she worked. They left the truck behind the Island Telephone Company, in a parking lot Sonia had never noticed. Seeing the city through Rose's eyes, she thought, made it look brand new.

Rose opened a door in the back of the building and they climbed three flights of stairs. At the top, beside a dark, unlabelled door, Rose turned to smile at Sonia. Then she pushed the door open. "Ta-da!" she said, walking through.

Ta-da.

Together, they examined the high, dark room with its funny smell —dust on the mechanisms burning off?—and met the dozen women who sat together at the high boards lined with rows of button plugs and wires and heavy headphone sets and Bakelite switches. There was one sign in the stark room—Positively No Smoking—and a noise—part buzz, part hum — composed, it seemed, of the voices of hundreds of people talking all at once on the telephone lines.

The atmosphere, simultaneously electric and still, gave Sonia the jitters. "How claustrophobic," she remarked, and Rose frowned and pursed her lips. But she walked Sonia to the chair she used and encouraged her to sit down. "Try it, Mum," she said. "Who would you like to call?"

Rose produced not a local phone book but the big Island one and Sonia wondered where to begin.

She thought for a minute, then she opened the book.

Rose whipped plugs out of numbered holes and Sonia inserted them in others. "Hello, hello?" she said.

And then, like a miracle, it happened.

A woman in Borden who worked on the ferry said, "Yes, I seen her, dear. A lovely young woman. And didn't she have one walleye? She was going to Toronto."

TWENTY-EIGHT

Sonia made calls to Toronto until her voice went hoarse. Rose helped, expertly connecting and disconnecting the distant lines. Afterward they went together to the Purity Dairy counter, where Rose bought two chocolate shakes that they savoured while looking out at all the city people performing their lives along the unfamiliar little street.

Rose was quiet, and Sonia felt an exhilarating rush of certainty.

For weeks she'd spent entire evenings cloistered in her room, trying to imagine Stella's new life based on the fragments of stories she had told about Toronto. Now, as she looked out at the vibrant people on the street, she found she could picture Stella among the crowd.

When they got back home, Frances called out, "How was your shopping day?" and with Kate in her arms, came into the porch.

Rose glanced up. Then she shrieked, "What have you been doing?"

"Sitting on the kitchen couch, reading books," Frances said. "What's your problem?"

But Sonia saw it too: Kate had a bruise developing below one eye and a scrape across her cheek.

"Oh, heavens!" Frances said. "I didn't see!"

Rose narrowed her eyes. "I don't understand how you can fail to notice what's smack in front of you."

"Excuse me?"

"Do you actually watch Katie when you babysit?" Rose reached for her niece. She studied Kate's face for a moment, then set her down. "How did this *happen*, Frances? How did you *let* this happen?"

"It's not my fault! She ran into the cupboard door."

"You know Kate's clumsy. You're supposed to watch her."

Sonia couldn't imagine that Frances had neglected Kate. It was true Kate was clumsy.

But it was such a big bruise.

Instead of defending herself, Frances said, "If we knew Stella was unhappy and did nothing, does that mean we're to blame for what happened to her?"

Rose threw up her hands. "Frances, life is not deep or complicated. It's simple. And you'll be happier if you live it that way."

But Rose was wrong: life *was* complicated.

The next day, Dan brought the mail when he came in for tea, and he saw a bill from Island Telephones.

"You have to stop, Mum," he said. "These phone calls are costing too much money."

"We have to keep looking!"

"Mum, that woman in Borden was wrong. She told you what you wanted to hear. Remember, you talked about Stella to all those people who work on the ferry. They live in Borden too. This woman knew the story before you called. She probably just wanted you to feel better."

Sonia was silent, marvelling that Dan could be so harsh.

"Mum, Stella didn't run away. Think about it. She would never have left Kate."

Dan was so definite, so certain. But wasn't certainty the thing they'd all lost? Stella, whom they felt they knew, turned out to have done something utterly unpredictable. Now Dan was behaving like a stranger too. Gentle Dan, who had never spoken sternly to her before, sounded like Max or Evvie.

But Dan isn't cruel, she reminded herself, and he would hate to be characterized that way.

She turned to him. And he lowered his voice—though not enough to sound like the gentle son she thought she knew.

"Okay. Okay, Mum. She ran away. Let's say she did. Don't you think she'll come home when she's ready? Isn't it *her* decision? How are you going to help by chasing after her?"

Sonia felt rattled for hours.

But by mid-afternoon she was on the phone again, working her way from one Toronto ladies' rooming house to the next.

Rose's supervisor, Miss Annette Sauer, had given Sonia a Toronto telephone book. Only two years old, she'd said as she handed it over. She'd winked and promised, You ask for me, dear. I'll put those calls through.

Sonia was thinking about that wink and what she hoped it meant — free long-distance calls to Toronto. Could Annette Sauer really do that? How many calls would it be okay to make? — when she happened to glance down and see Kate walk into the table edge, for all the world as though it wasn't there.

My God, she thought, *I can't look after anyone!* She'd been staring right at Kate, and she hadn't seen what was about to happen.

Kate screamed, and Rose came running.

Sonia picked Kate up. "Mama!" Kate said, and burst into tears. She'd scratched her other cheek.

Rose put the facts together then: like her mother, it seemed Kate couldn't see.

Mama, Mama! Kate would cry — but if she bumped into Rose or Rob or Sonia she would correct herself immediately. Rose, Rob-Rob, Gram*ma*. She was all right once she figured out who was who. But she walked into things — chairs, table legs, door frames — and she tripped over toys she'd left scattered on the floor. She sat too close to the television. She rubbed her eyes continually. It added up.

"*Eye doctor*," Rose said. "I'll take care of this." She snatched the phone and wound the crank.

Later, Rose apologized to Sonia for her brusqueness. "I was just worried about Kate."

She had an idea, she said. "Why don't you come with me to work one day? There are usually two or three empty chairs. You could make as many calls to Toronto as you like."

For some reason this uncharacteristic kindness from Rose was worse than any of Dan's harsh directives.

She'd been a fool. What point was there in trying to find a daughter who'd run away from home? What if *she* was the person Stella didn't want to see?

Dan was right. The only way was to wait for Stella to decide.

TWENTY-NINE

The day of Kate's examination, Frances drove the truck and Rose held Kate. Sonia saw them off. Rose procrastinated in the lane, fussing over the truck in an attempt to redirect her worry that something serious was wrong with Kate's eyes. They all remembered Stella as a girl, stumbling around.

"Do you think the tires are low?" she said, kicking at each one.

But Frances would not be diverted. "Don't worry, Rose. Kate couldn't have congenital blindness because Stella wasn't born that way." Stella's eye was injured when the hay mower threw a bolt. "A definite accident," Frances said.

Rose and Frances pondered this bad fortune. Stella's injury hadn't carried down to Kate, but something had. Some curse.

Look at us, Sonia thought: staring at our feet, trying to outpace the bad luck of Stella's disappearance and failing to take proper care of the child she left behind.

She felt shamed.

She handed Rose a Thermos of tea to share with Frances, a box of crackers and a small bottle of milk for Kate. As she stepped back from the truck, Rose wound up the passenger side window and her earlier words came back to Sonia: *Life's not deep or complicated. It's simple. You'll be happier if—*

What did Rose know? She was barely out of childhood herself.

But Sonia resolved to pay attention.

Life's not deep or complicated.

Okay. Maybe Rose was right.

When they returned, Frances told the story:

The optometrist's office was shabbier than she'd imagined. In the waiting room a receptionist sat behind a narrow desk in a starkly empty room lit only by a weak bulb and a smudged window that looked out onto a parking lot. There was a picture on one wall, a filing cabinet with a dying plant on top and four hard chairs for patients. Two were occupied, so Rose held Kate in her lap, which made her squirm and whine. An older lady with a cane offered to give up her chair to Kate, but Frances stood to circumvent this. Kate leapt up and stood by Frances until Rose coaxed her to sit down. Then she leapt up again. In this way, half an hour passed.

In the examining room, Frances stood again while Rose held Kate. "You're a big, grown-up girl," Rose said, but Kate refused to sit by herself in the cushioned vinyl examination chair.

Anyone would have been afraid, Frances said. It was a sickly green and bristled all over with buttons and levers and complicated instruments attached to folding arms.

Kate cried and flopped dramatically to the floor.

Without hesitating, the doctor knelt beside her and whispered in her ear. He seemed to enfold Kate for a moment. When he stepped away, Kate climbed compliantly into the chair, transformed. The optometrist had performed a magic spell. In one hand Kate clutched a tiny teddy bear, in the other, a strand of licorice. A grin spread across her face.

After his examination, the optometrist offered Rose a well-worn card bearing, among others, the word *disease*, and a massive illuminated eye, to which he gestured with a pen.

"Here you can see the elongation I described. This is the reason she has trouble with her vision. It's a common problem. Perhaps it's unusually, hmmm... *acute*... in this case—"

Rose made a faint, sorrowful sound. For a moment Frances worried she was going to cry.

"However!" The optometrist sat up higher in his chair and looked carefully at them. "With *correction*," he said slowly, "I believe that Kate will see almost as well as you or me."

"Correction?" Rose said. "Are you going to *operate*?"

"No, dear! Nothing so drastic as that. We're going to make a pair of little glasses for her."

Rose sighed with relief. But almost right away she slumped again.

"She's barely even two. How will we convince her to keep them on?"

"I'm sure she'll want to wear them, when she realizes she can see."

In the truck all the way home, Frances said, they sang aloud, out of a sense of profound relief.

THIRTY

June 1965. Prospect, Prince Edward Island.

For what Rose insisted to Ray was their last date, he took her nowhere.

They sat together in the living room on an airless Saturday afternoon, watching television and drinking tea. This, Rose insisted, was what she wanted. She did not admit to Ray that his reckless driving frightened her. She'd been out with him four times. After her resolution, she kept giving in. But now she was determined to resist.

Rob sat with them for a while, Buddy wove in and out of the room, and while Sonia fretted and measured and boiled, and washed and filled jars with rhubarb jam, Frances spent those hours looking after Kate—playing hide-and-seek, giving her a bath, reading books, then lounging on her bed, singing lullabies until Kate fell asleep.

After Ray left, Rose tidied the living room and the kitchen, then went down to the root cellar with some of Sonia's finished jam. Sonia heard a shriek from the cellar, and a few minutes later Rose came up with a salamander in an old canning jar. She pressed the jar into Frances's hands. "You can study him," she said, "and then preserve him, like those frogs at school. Or," she said—seeing the look on her sister's face—"you could set him free out in the woods."

Sonia and Frances looked through the wavy glass, beyond the word *Jewel*, at the mucousy black and yellow creature sealed inside. An ordinary spotted salamander.

"*Ambystoma maculatum*," Frances said.

His name was Sammy, Sonia knew. Frances had been visiting him in the cellar for several years. As soon as Rose left the room, she went downstairs and released him back into the cold room, where he belonged.

Later that fall, Frances would be reminded of Sammy when for the first time she faced a frog cut open on a pan in a laboratory at the university. The creature's thin skin and damp, irregularly mottled look became conflated in her mind not only with Sammy but also with the friends in biology class who could not understand how a frog looked like a salamander, and why it might matter that either had died. For Frances, this visceral but undeniable response marked the end of her pursuit of science. Things die, someone said, and Frances lashed out at her friends, whom eventually she lost along with science. *Oh, Stella*, she'd cried, not understanding why.

Sonia knew it was a delayed reaction to all that had happened.

All along, she'd expected Frances to react emotionally. *Decide, Stella*, Sonia'd said, again and again. For your sister's sake, if not your own, *decide to come home.*

She did not know what to say to Frances herself.

THIRTY-ONE

July 1965. Prospect, Prince Edward Island.

Combing through boxes in the attic for old baby things that might fit Kate, Sonia came across some drawings and scraps of wool pictures she'd made in her youth. She'd forgotten they existed. Totems from her other life.

She took them down to the kitchen to look at, and became transfixed. The pictures were dense with colour and intricate pattern, mesmerizing. She felt proud to have made them, but deflated too. Something essential was missing.

"Mum," Frances said.

Sonia hadn't heard her come in.

"Oh, how beautiful!" Frances gestured toward the tiny, brightly coloured landscapes Sonia held in her hands.

Were they beautiful? Sonia couldn't imagine how she had accomplished such impossibly detailed work, yet the images would not come clear. It was hard to tell where one colour ended and another began. In her memory, she thought they had meant something more. She squinted and blinked.

"Mum!" Frances said. "Look at you! You're as bad as Kate! You need to have your eyes examined!"

Was that it? Just that her vision had become less acute?

She tried drawing clouds and some of her lines came back. The vividness of their shapes. The poignant vulnerability of their outer curves.

But only the darkest of lines worked. She found she couldn't render gradations. She couldn't draw subtlety. Were her eyes really that bad?

She moved on to objects around the house, vistas in the garden, the fields, the woods. She borrowed Kate's crayons so she could experiment with colour. But the wax shades were stubbornly dull, and impossible to blend.

She could imagine the pictures she wanted to draw, but she could not render on paper what she envisioned, never mind the emotion behind it.

Still, she kept trying, the days of summer blurring into a haze of meaningless black marks as they flew by.

August 1965. Prospect, Prince Edward Island.

And then the light changed, the season turned. Cool days, haying nearly over, the weather stable, the orchard quieter now in the early morning, a scent of honey wafting from the August apple trees.

One Saturday, Kate came into the kitchen while Sonia sat at the table peeling apples for a pie. "Mama," Kate said, though she could see Sonia perfectly well. She leaned over Sonia's leg, folding her body rag-doll fashion so that her head lolled upside down against Sonia's thigh. Her glasses fell off, and she let the cloth doll in her hand fall down after them. It was her nap time.

"Your glasses, Katie," Sonia said, and Kate slid to the floor so she could reach her glasses and put them on again, a procedure she practised a thousand times a day. The glasses were scratched because Kate treated them the same way she used her supple, springy two-year-old body — with perfect confidence and utter disregard.

Now she grabbed Sonia's waistband and hauled herself into Sonia's lap. Sonia helped.

"Gramma," she said. She'd left her doll on the floor, but she clutched her glasses in one sticky fist. She held them out to Sonia. She tried to press them onto Sonia's face, but was too tired to unfold the frames. Gently, Sonia took them from her, and Kate flopped against her chest and consented to be carried to bed for a nap.

The following Monday, Rose took the day off work to look after Kate, and Sonia dressed in her going-to-town blouse, her long black skirt and the low-heeled pumps she wore to weddings, wakes and funerals. In these clothes she felt taller, more confident — but impatient too. So often an unwelcome gloom descended when she dressed to go out. There seemed no way to combat this. Sometimes she regretted things she said under the influence of this mood, so the best thing was to remain silent as long as possible. She tried this now, getting into the truck with Dan, who normally practised silence like breath anyway.

Dan found the optometrist's office near the new Massey Ferguson dealer he planned to visit, on the edge of town, in a dismal single-storey building clad in siding stained red from blowing soil. Bleak windows, trash scattered in the parking lot. On the outer door a divided sign read *A. Llewellyn, Optometry* and *Royal Drugs*, just as Rose had said it would. Inside, a short hallway opened onto two more doors. One led into a little drugstore, the other into an almost empty waiting room: four chairs and a desk, behind which sat a woman doing figures in a ledger. Posters of giant red-veined eyeballs decorated the wall behind her. Sonia ducked outside, waved to Dan behind the wheel of their truck, returned, and gave her name to the woman at the desk.

Hours later, it seemed, Sonia was startled out of a daydream about wool fleece and tools with which to work it — a set of hand carders and a drop spindle made of birch or cherry wood.

"Mrs. MacAusland, you may go in."

She stood and walked in the direction of the receptionist's outstretched arm.

Even opened wide, the door to the optometrist's office did not admit enough light to illuminate the features of the darkened room. Sonia felt her way toward a metal office chair and lowered her body into it.

"Hello, Sonia."

He spoke so softly she wasn't sure at first that she'd heard her name correctly. *Sonia*, not Mrs. MacAusland. She peered toward the place the voice came from. But he wasn't there—he'd moved.

The room was utterly dark. He was beside her now. A small lamp came on.

First, a mannerism she recognized: the way he pushed his hair back from his forehead with the flat of his hand. Then, those penetrating eyes.

But what was he doing here?

He was looking at her. More than looking—studying.

She felt she didn't want him to.

Where was A. Llewellyn, whose name was on the sign?

But he must be the optometrist.

She shifted her eyes away.

His office was chaos, as messy as her own room in the weeks after Stella disappeared.

She hadn't imagined his life like this. In her mind, she now realized, he remained a twenty-three-year-old medical student, an aspiring surgeon, untroubled, ambitious and confident.

"Sonia?"

She looked at him again. How focused he was.

"I'm sorry about your daughter."

That snapped her back into the moment.

"I thought of calling you..."

All this time, they'd lived in separate worlds.

"I didn't know you'd moved back," she said.

"I came home after Angus Llewellyn died. A year ago. Listen, I know this is strange..."

What was strange were the feelings that came rushing back. How compelling he was. How abandoned she'd felt when he left.

She felt conflicted. At the same time, something in her calmed. Just by the fact of his presence.

Now she imagined his hands on her face.

He was asking her something. *What had he said?*

She was still angry with him. She could feel it. But she was not *only* angry. She closed her eyes.

He'd left her when she needed him. And all those years with Max, years of regret, imagining Pete was the one person who could have changed her life.

Experimentally, she remembered his hands on her face, and her own on his.

Her head began to spin.

"Will you look at me, Sonia?"

She opened her eyes, focused, saw the careless stacks of paper on his office floor and thought: This is not what he wanted to do with his life. He'd always insisted he wanted to perform surgery because it was the purest form of medicine. She'd been amused by this stubborn certainty, which seemed a vital part of his character. When they'd met on Cavendish Beach in 1943, he'd seemed lost. But she'd felt sure he'd find his way back to himself. Now she wondered if he ever did.

He touched her shoulder. Automatically, she recoiled. Who was he? Did she know who he was?

His expression hardened.

She read his face, which seemed to say, So that's how this is going to be.

He turned off the little lamp.

He made her look through a set of lenses at a faint, lighted point on the far wall. At the same time he leaned so close that she could feel his breath, as he peered at her eye through a ridiculously oversized magnifying glass. He lifted her eyelid with his fingertip. This hurt. "Do you mind?" he said. He gave her a stick with a big circle on it, like a large flat lollipop, and asked her to hold it in front of one eye and say whenever she could read the letters on a card he'd hung across the room.

He did not ask another personal question. He moved slowly around the room. He set his hand not on her back but on the back of her chair.

He gazed at her face. She looked away.

He said, *"Dear Sonia…"*

He said nothing.

He paced the room.

He left, not closing the door behind him. He did not turn on a light.

::::

She remembered how Frances and Rose had described Kate's *wonderful* optometrist, and his *fascinating* office, jam-packed with things. How smart he was, they said. His *complicated* instruments and machines. She'd put all that down to girlish hysteria.

She remembered the way Max had looked at him, the day they met. Pete standing too close to her, Max with his pulsing arm wrapped in a bloody pillowcase, humiliated and angry. She remembered Max's visits to the light. Pete gone by then — *yet undeniably present* — intruding, making Max seem insufficient.

He wore a rumpled soft shirt and his hair was the same, long and still dark, while her own had silvered like winter hay.

But he spoke more slowly and moved more carefully than he had then. He was, she realized, forty-eight years old. Mature, at least in years.

His eyes were grey, but in some lights, she remembered, they could look green or blue.

She remembered his unpredictability — arriving and disappearing according to his own mysterious schedule.

And she was startled by his familiarity. The way he touched his hand to his chin. The way he leaned forward when he spoke, his voice so soft, especially in the dark.

Did she know him, or not?

She heard the door opening, his footsteps, the squeak of his stool — he turned toward her — and then he was silent.

This was something she remembered, this courteous way of using silence to create space for her.

She thought, It was *him* I craved, not just some alternative to Max.

But she was older now. She did not want to be driven by any craving she could resist.

"Sonia?"

She opened her eyes.

"How long have you had difficulty seeing what's in front of you?"

Ha!

His eyes were as intensely alive with curiosity as she remembered.

156

"How long have you been unable to do close work?" He looked in her eyes. His own were bright, liquid, mobile.

"Is your vision blurred? Are things obscure?" Absently, he flicked through the lenses in his machine. "Do you close your eyes against bright light?" Again, he was studying her face.

It was hard to answer his questions because it was hard to look at him. What could she do but remain silent and nod her head?

Her throat felt dry.

"Do you have double vision? Do images recur after you've closed your eyes or turned away from them?" He lowered his voice to a whisper. "*Sonia?*" He touched her arm and this time, though she wanted to, she did not pull away.

"Do you suffer pain? Can you see in the dark?"

He said she needed two different kinds of glasses—one pair for close work and another for distance vision. He said, *It's time you saw the world around you!* He said this in a tone of evangelical zeal, gesturing with a practised flourish. A line he used on all his patients. He'd always liked lines.

He said he was going to take her somewhere when her distance glasses came in—an outing to test her new eyesight. He insisted that she agree. He extracted this promise before he allowed her to leave.

She agreed because she believed nothing would come of it. Too much time had passed to start up such an ambiguous friendship again.

THIRTY-TWO

After, Dan wanted to take her to Eaton's. He wanted to look at washers, he said.

She laughed. As if they could afford a new washing machine!

"With some of the Farm Credit money," he said. "When it comes in."

"Dan," she said reproachfully. She shook her head.

But then she had an idea. Since they'd come all the way to town, maybe she would like to call in at the wool shop—

He could not argue with this. He waited in the truck while she went in. But the wool shop carried no fleece or roving, only commercial yarns, too uniformly spun. Her hand hovered over one uninteresting skein after another. A clerk came up. "You're new to all this?" She tried to show Sonia scarf and mitten patterns. In the end Sonia felt she couldn't leave without purchasing something, so she settled for a skein of grey sheep's wool imported from the mainland.

She wasn't satisfied, but she could not say as much to Dan, who would not have understood.

The grey wool triggered something, though. Later, Frances would say, *Okay, Mum. I'm off. Dan said Lyman's looking for me,* and this would register with Sonia only faintly, more as a tangential worry than an immediate concern. Instead, Sonia wondered, could she get wool fleece somewhere? Might Cece or Eddie know a farmer who kept sheep? The colour swatches, pencil sketches and drawings in her hands were her only immediate concern.

Okay, Mum. I'm off. Lyman, Frances would say, and Sonia would hear only, *Okay, Mum*—would think only of her plans for work.

Eddie said, "Sheep's wool? Hmmm. We'll talk to Willie MacPherson on the Whim Road. Jump in." And he held open his truck door, ready to make the trip that instant.

They drove at his usual leisurely pace, Eddie chattering and gesturing all the while, other vehicles passing on the straights, the windows open for air and to let in the scents of other farmers' crops. That lad has quite a crop of sow thistle, Eddie would exclaim, slowing right down. Would you look at that!

Driving with Eddie was like taking a holiday. He made the world look new.

How she loved him.

He was the brother she never had, a sweet counterbalance to all those years with Max, who never chatted, never drove slowly, never dropped his work to address her smallest wish.

They sailed through Cardross corner, took the long way to Montague. Finally Eddie said, "We're here!" and pulled into a narrow, scratchily overgrown lane. Willie MacPherson was digging postholes when they arrived, a hot, tiring job. He stopped to greet Eddie, and Eddie easily charmed him into taking an hour to find Sonia the raw wool she needed and to make a pot of ferociously strong tea.

Come back any time, Willie MacPherson said when they handed him their empty mugs, and Eddie winked as if to say, I know it's weird, but she's dear to me. This sweetness, manifest so unselfishly in Eddie, ought to have kept Pete from her mind, but instead her memories of their visit intensified. Eddie talked all the way home, and shamefully she heard nothing, his voice no more than a soothing murmur in her ear. *Sonia*, Pete said. *Sonia, Sonia*...

The wool, when she handled it, released a wet, sweet odour like earth, or the woods after rain. She washed it and dried it and carded it as best she could with two old curry combs.

As her hands worked with the wool, her mind returned of its own accord to Pete. She remembered his observations about Stella.

"She would have seen everything you see," he said, "just less vividly."

He'd talked about Stella as he peered into Sonia's eyes. It was not a conversation, and he'd asked no questions, just delivered information. It was like he was speaking to himself.

"At first they would have concentrated on trying to repair the damaged eye, bandaging it so it would heal and treating it to prevent infection. They would have checked the other eye to see that it was good, and then corrected for any slight myopia and astigmatism, like your granddaughter Kate has. If her eye was damaged irreparably, of course there is an additional problem: the loss of an eye means the loss of depth perception."

The loss of depth perception. Was this his way of offering reassurance?

Later, as she wondered how to spin the carded wool, her dream of the wool shop came back, with its fantasy drop spindle made of cherry wood. Then Dan taking her to the real wool shop, with its unimaginative selection. Then Dan's voice, bright with what she'd thought of as foolhardy generosity, when he'd wanted to buy her a washing machine. How can we afford it! she'd scoffed.

Dan had said, We'll use some of the Farm Credit money, when it comes in.

Now she realized: if they could buy a washer with some of that Farm Credit money, they could buy a train ticket to Toronto, to look for Stella.

She knew what Dan would say, because he'd said it already. *She'll come home when she's ready. Don't go chasing after her.*

Damn you, she thought. She wasn't sure if she meant Dan or Stella. Or herself.

THIRTY-THREE

But the smell of the wool—its animal, foresty richness.

The *feel* of the wool. And the seductive whisper she could hear when she rubbed it between her fingers.

She thought of Mme Chevalier, and the sometimes funny, sometimes true things she'd said: *Never draw three lines when one will do! Colour is like seasoning—strive for clarity, do not blend. Live for art, don't expect art to live for you. Think with your heart, not your head.*

Mme Chevalier had said Sonia's pictures were like Berthe Morisot's, pretty but scalpel sharp. You have a gift, she'd said, never give it up. How disappointed Mme Chevalier would be, to see her now.

Sonia caressed her pliant carded wool. Why couldn't an artwork be more than a picture? Why couldn't it have fragrance too? And textures from the woods and the sea?

She thought of moss she'd gather, of pinning seaweed on her clothesline to dry, of spruce needles, and pine, and lichen and the barks of different trees. Cordgrass, rabbit wool, skeleton leaves. She could bind things into place, weave them through, work with raw fleece, leave out yarn entirely.

She put on her boots and jacket and emptied the canvas shoulder bag she stored clothespins in. She got scissors from the kitchen drawer and a small folding saw of Dan's from his tool kit in the barn. One day, she would find a word for what she sought—dimensionality. Now, she considered Pete's account of Stella's eyes.

What is depth perception? If it's what gives us a rounded, fleshed-out world—did that mean Stella saw a monotonous, paper-flat one? Is it the difference between life and the mere impression of a life? Sonia imagined it was flying compared to sitting still; outside compared to in; the difference between a garden and a seed in the hand; instead of a series of faded photographs, life itself.

Why did this, of all things, have to be what Stella lost?

She remembered now—Stella always did one thing at a time. How impatient Rose used to get with her slowness. She never combined chores as Rose so expertly did. In this way she was exactly like Max: ponderous, deliberate. What would you know of life, she wondered, taking it like that?

Stella could not really *see*. What must that have been like?

Sonia closed one eye and tried to imagine how the world might have looked to her daughter. The boring flatness of every surface.

She pictured Stella on the ice, *hearing* the sound of different thicknesses of ice under her feet, *smelling* open water. How sensuous this might have been, how exhilarating to apprehend the world so fully. Was this why Stella began to go around without her glasses?

Did she wish to be completely blind? When she closed her eyes, did she audition blindness the way some girls audition boys?

Sonia tried to imagine what Stella might have noticed. The smell of her house, the sound of big insects, such as bees, and smaller ones—a spider on a cobweb—the smell of mice in the walls, the way different objects felt to the touch. How to distinguish approaching people by their footsteps and to predict changes in the weather by scents on the air. How snow would muffle sound.

All of these were things to which Sonia too could pay attention. She could learn what Stella had learned that enabled her to get away.

She closed her eyes. It was the kind of day that encouraged speed—high cloud and a light breeze. Branches whipped by as she walked. She slowed down, noticed the crunch of dry leaves and twigs beneath her feet, felt the surprising give of mossy ground, resistance elsewhere. Scattered stone, the upbraiding feel of it against her toe. The sorrowful fragrance of the forest floor and the sharp, seductive tang of var and spruce. Rhythmic birdsong overhead, but everywhere the unevenness of the earth.

She put her hands out straight in front of her. She felt the canvas bag, with her scissors and Dan's little saw, bang against her hip. She heard the high, clear, strident voice of a jay.

And then she was on the ground. Something had tripped her up. A tree root? She felt the sting of a scrape on her ankle bone. She opened her eyes, drew her legs up, brushed leaf litter and dark, peaty earth from the palms of both hands. She closed her eyes again. She put a hand on each thigh to lever herself upright. Resumed her walk, slower this time.

The hardships Stella must have faced. And she was not completely blind. She'd had ten percent vision in one eye, forty or fifty in the other. But the criticism she took. Frances's impatience. Rose continually yelling at her over something spilled or knocked out of place. And always Stella drifting silently away.

Stella had paid closer attention to other people's emotional states than either Rose or Frances did. But criticism affected her more. Except for Evvie's, which she accepted, it seemed, as her due.

Sonia felt a flood of outrage at the thought of Evvie targeting Stella, cutting her down. *You idiot!* she heard him say. *You stupid cow!*

Where had this come from?

And then, without warning, Evvie grabbed her throat, and Sonia gagged and tripped.

What was that scratching, sharp instrument he'd used? Not his hands alone. A knife? From surprise, her strength failed, and she fell to her knees. *Stupid bitch!* she heard. *Get up!* The voice enraged.

But the voice was not Evvie, she realized. It was Max.

She put a hand to her throat.

And then she opened her eyes. She'd been attacked by a branch.

But now the idea was planted. And her feeling of helplessness when she'd felt attacked made her wonder, *What did Evvie do?*

She turned, her canvas satchel still empty except for her cutting tools, and ran east, across the stubble field.

THIRTY-FOUR

She found Eddie behind his barn, chopping wood. He seemed to listen carefully, but did he understand? When he said, "But do you have proof?" her knees began to liquefy. "Okay," he said. "You want me to, I'll show the bastard." Then he got in his truck and drove away fast and she thought, What now?

Marina gave her a square on a plate, and poured them each a cup of tea.

"Yes, of course it's possible Evvie harmed Stella," Marina said. "Even likely." She raised an eyebrow. "We all know that, don't we?"

But Sonia hadn't known. Not really. She hadn't allowed herself to know.

Marina said, "Have the police questioned him thoroughly?"

"They say they did. They say they have no evidence. Maybe they would have some, if I hadn't kept them at such a distance for so long." Sonia stretched her hands across Marina's table. Rubbed its scuffed, waxed surface. Pressed down, looked up. "Marina, what's wrong with me? In the woods just now, I imagined Evvie tried to hurt me. I heard his voice. He was as real to me as you are now. Then it wasn't him. It was Max."

Marina said, "Mmmm."

"Pardon?"

"Well, it would have been, wouldn't it?"

"What do you mean?"

"Come on, Sonia! You and your kids were over here for the night so many times."

Sonia felt her body go cold. She held it perfectly still.

"At least *three* times you were over here. I felt like wringing his neck myself."

Sonia shook her head. "No," she said. But then a thought arrived: Marina would never lie.

"Love, he hit you and he threatened you and you were scared to stay at home. You brought the kids here. How can you have *forgotten* all that?" The look on Marina's face now—deep concern, something seriously wrong.

Sonia tried to picture this. All of them in Marina's little house. Kids sleeping on wool puffs or blankets on the floor. The image did not make sense. "I don't remember. Are you sure?"

Marina sat back in her chair. She looked baffled now.

A moment came back. Max holding a two-by-four, screaming at her, the muscles in his arms quaking violently. Sonia frozen in place, baby Stella by her side. Had she imagined this? It seemed like a dream. But it must have been memory, real. She let out the breath she'd been holding. "Wait. I remember one time."

Marina nodded, rubbed her chin with her hand, a gesture that evoked Eddie Mack.

And that brought back a second thing: Max losing to Eddie at cards, chasing Eddie out of the house and screaming hoarsely after him, *You sonofabitch cheating bastard.*

Sonia felt her sense of balance let go. She grabbed the table. Her throat constricted and her chest would not expand. Her heart beat weakly but too fast. She pushed her cup of tea away and leaned her head against her hands.

Marina remained in her chair. They were quiet for a long time.

THIRTY-FIVE

Marina began to move about her kitchen. She said, "Would you like another cup of tea, dear?" She assembled the tea things, her back to Sonia, her movements slow and sure.

Sonia wondered, What other memories have I suppressed? *What's true, and what's not?*

That was the worst thing, the doubt she felt.

After a while Marina began to speak. "Remember the fence Max built when he and Eddie had that falling-out? Remember the way he used to hurl things around? The way he used to shout at people! There's never any need of that. Never."

Scenes came flooding back. Images like dreams. Max firing a wrench into the engine of their truck, the round and open ends of it turning over each other as it spiralled forward, the growl and smash when it hit home. A plate shattered on the floor and Rose kneeling immediately among the shards, sweeping scrambled eggs and china into a dustpan while overhead Max raged. Sonia pleading with him — *It's all right. It's all right* — and Rose stiff with fear.

Max didn't smile in anger in the disturbing way Evvie did. But the look he wore when he disagreed with something she or one of the boys had said: his face transformed by this ferocious hardening.

Sonia said, "But Marina, it was my fault —"

"*No!*" Marina set down her mug of tea, and it splashed across the table. "You let things go, sure. Max wanted his way, what could you do but give it to him? We all did it. I did, with Lyman's father. You never met George, but he was the same as Max, always expecting something done—*or else.* Woman! he'd say. I can still hear him. *Woman!* And then he'd wait. Whatever it was he wanted—supper on the table, a drink in his hand, sugar for his tea—he'd just roar and I'd jump right up. If he hadn't died like Max did, at an early age, I hope I would have boxed his ears and left by now."

Sonia pictured this, Marina with her hands in fists, raising them to her husband's ears.

Marina leaned forward over the spilt tea, her eyes focused and still. Her softness vanished. She spoke forcefully. "We have to stand up for ourselves, don't we? Or how will our daughters learn to? How will *your* daughters, Sonia? Have you thought about that?"

"I told Ed that I think Evvie did it. I think he pushed her."

"There now. That'll help." Marina grinned. "Eddie gets things done."

Sonia thought of a phrase she'd heard on the radio news, *vigilante justice.* She wasn't sure she understood its meaning, but she'd heard in the announcer's polished voice a tone of condemnation.

"There now," Marina said, beside her now. And Sonia realized she'd lost track of time, as in the days after Stella's disappearance.

But Stella hadn't disappeared. She was gone. Gone. Now and forever. *How could this have happened?* There was no sense in the world.

"There," Marina said, time swallowed up again.

THIRTY-SIX

Sonia took away what Marina had said. She stored it, then she retrieved and thought about one grain of information at a time. Max hitting her. The words he'd yelled. How she'd run away to Marina's with the kids.

Other memories came back—a child's voice, Dan's or Rob's, saying, Why is Dad mad? The relief she felt when he died, and her guilt and confusion over that. You're in shock, people said, but she wasn't. She knew shock, from other times: the move inland, leaving Surplus light. It wasn't shock she'd felt. It was elation.

THIRTY-SEVEN

Sonia walked toward home, entranced by the smell of the fields, by birdsong and insect sounds, distracted by the pleasure of sun on her skin and the liquid, bubbling voices of bobolinks undulating over the bright, cut hayfields.

She saw Evvie in his field before she noticed the RCMP cruiser parked in his lane. He looked like he was poised to take off. *Hey*, she almost shouted.

The officers walked through the muddy part of the headland in their good leather lace-up boots, lifting their feet like ladies and cursing as they came for him. Evvie looked toward the river.

Sonia could hear them. *Everett Corcoran?* they demanded as they approached. *Everett Corcoran?* The big one yanked a set of shiny handcuffs off his hip and flicked the bracelets open as he walked.

Why did they want him? Had they really listened to what Eddie told them?

"Aw, shit," Evvie said, and the officers led him like a sickly calf to their car.

Sonia could imagine his desperate thought: *Shoulda run.*

A cloud of effervescent birds flew by, their song following after, and she felt something light bubble in her own throat, a blockage dissolving.

THIRTY-EIGHT

It was Rose's idea to go through Stella's house while Evvie wasn't there. "Evvie has no right to Stella's things," Rose said. "And who knows what we might find." She seemed overeager, but Sonia didn't argue.

The house was dark. Rose went in first and Sonia followed, carrying boxes she'd brought from the Co-op. There was no place to set these down. The porch smelled of engine oil and dirt and the sweet funk of decay, as from apples kept warm too long. On the floor were muddy boots and coveralls, a crate filled with greasy tractor parts, piles of junk, including the broken back and legs of a kitchen chair, towers of empty beer bottle cases and bags of baby things that Evvie should have brought over for Kate. Rose opened one of the bags and lifted out a miniature wool sweater that might have fit Kate months ago but wouldn't now. Sonia ran a finger across the windowsill and gathered a pile of grime.

"*For the love of God!*" Rose stormed, snatching a newspaper off a toppling stack. "Here. We'll put our boots on this, over by the stove." It seemed a fruitless gesture. The paper was cleaner than the floor.

In the kitchen, Sonia opened curtains and turned on lights. She closed cupboard doors that stood ajar, their contents emptied in a jumble on the counter. Where to start? The sink was full of greasy plates smeared with beans and egg, the table a mass of newspapers, empty mugs, a shiny Massey Ferguson flyer and a pile of unopened mail. Rose began to go through this, sorting out the bills, stopping when she came across a letter addressed to Stella.

The house felt damp, so Rose built a fire in the stove and Sonia went through the rooms flinging curtains back and raising windows to let in air. There were dirty clothes in piles on the floor, empty liquor bottles underneath the bed — no food in the cupboards, no soap in the bathroom, no way to tell that anyone had cared for the place at all. It was a mercy Kate hadn't been there.

Rose said, "We have to find evidence. The Mounties will only hold him for so long without it."

They needed to find some fact or object that would establish *reasonable suspicion of guilt*. This was how an RCMP officer from Montague put the thing to Sonia when he phoned to say that Evvie had been charged. What? Sonia had said, confused by his insistence. But he would say no more.

After this exchange, she had felt to blame somehow. Why, and what for, she didn't know. She hadn't wanted to ask too many questions, so she tried to get Dan to probe for information, but Dan refused. "Let them do their job," he said. Evvie had been gone a week by then.

Rob, who'd been silent all along, spoke that day. He was delighted the police had picked Evvie up. "I *told* them," he said.

Rob had taken against Evvie back in the fall. When crop prices had been so low, Dan asked Evvie to join the farm — the family farm that was supposed to be Dan's and Rob's alone. Dan had argued they needed to expand — to take on more acreage or buy more animals. But expanding would require manpower. It was too much for Dan and Rob to handle by themselves.

"Dan thinks the farm belongs to him, so he just barrels ahead and makes decisions like Dad used to," Rob complained. "No one pays attention to me!"

This wasn't true, but Rob was away at school most days. It was understandable Dan didn't always consult with him.

Rob told the police that Evvie beat Stella. No, he hadn't actually witnessed this, he admitted, but he was certain it was true.

Sonia wondered if Rob had been paying attention where she had not.

Dan shook his head in disgust. "That was a dumb thing to do, Rob. The police are going to give him the benefit of the doubt—and they'll look at us like the guilty parties if we keep after them with speculation. We need evidence, real proof."

The way Rob flinched, it was clear he understood his mistake.

Dan narrowed his eyes. "What exactly did you say?"

Rob straightened up so he could look Dan in the eye. Dan was the solid one, but skinny Rob was just as tall. "I told them the way he treated her," Rob said. "I told them it didn't matter if he pushed her through the ice or not. The way he treated her, he drove her to it."

Dan said nothing for a moment. Then he shook his head again. He spoke sadly, softly. "That isn't proof."

But Rob's words, *He drove her to it*, were the ones that mattered. They echoed on the air like a hammered bell.

Sonia pulled clothes from drawers and began to fold them while Rose set out boxes to hold Stella's things.

"Rose," Sonia ventured, "why do you think Rob—"

But Rose did not want to talk. "Who knows why Rob does anything," she snapped.

Years ago Sonia would have reprimanded her daughter for this unkindness. But how could she now?

One day not long after Stella's disappearance, exhausted by Rose's constant bossing, Sonia had gone looking for her sons in the barn. Let me help you, she'd planned to say. But what she really wanted was some clue to their calm demeanour, some way to suppress the ache she felt. She heard them in the cow barn and sidled in.

"Would you look at that?" Rob said. Laughing, he plucked an egg from a bale of hay—he seemed carefree, buoyant.

One of the bantam hens must have gotten out. Rob held its little egg up to the light and grinned. Sonia thought, He's still so young. Oblivious and innocent as a girl.

But then, as Rob turned, his delicate features flattened out. "All right, Dan?" he said.

Dan was crying. Sonia hadn't noticed. He wiped a sleeve across his face. "Ummm," he said, nodding slowly.

Rob dipped his head in Dan's direction—a vague, unclassifiable gesture, not quite a nod—and resumed untying bales of hay. Alarmed by this display of reserve, Sonia moved to comfort Dan. He noticed her then—they both did, and startled like cats. Instead of moving forward, she slunk back.

It was understandable that they were skittish creatures, after all they'd been through.

"Mum!" Rose said now in her demanding voice. "*Look.*" She gestured at a gaping dresser drawer. Inside were Stella's things.

All the clothes Evvie brought over had come from Stella's closet. He'd insisted he brought all her things to the house yet he hadn't bothered to empty the dresser containing Stella's sweaters and socks. Now Sonia wondered why he had refused everyone access to her room, her things and any clues she might have left as to where she'd gone. Presumably the police had looked, but they hadn't been much good, had they?

From the lowest drawer, Rose had removed the makings of a quilt—scraps of old wool fabric cut into simple squares, a card of needles, a length of batting and a roll of muslin. Under this was Stella's diary and a bundle of letters.

Most of the letters were from a girl Stella had met in Toronto, now a wife and mother named Jane Czenzi.

The thought flashed in her mind: Stella must be staying with Jane! Then she remembered being tackled in the woods. *Again* she experienced the feeling of her body being smashed into and thrown down, by Evvie or by Max.

No, Stella had not run away. She had not left Kate.

"*Oh,*" Sonia said. She felt her body collapse. The certainty of what had happened getting through, a hard shove in the diaphragm.

Stella hadn't run away and she didn't throw herself into the river.

Leaving would not have occurred to her because she'd had no choice, not any more than Sonia ever had.

Rose said, "We didn't think to let Jane know."

The woods were dark. The ground was cold.

"Mum?"

Sonia willed herself to get up from where she lay, half on top of an angular rock. The woods swam all around.

"Mum!"

She willed herself back into Stella's bedroom with Rose.

Rose said, "The letter we found downstairs must be from Jane."

Sonia pictured the pile of mail on the kitchen table, the letter Rose had extracted from it. She nodded at her pragmatic daughter.

"I'll write to Jane," Rose volunteered.

They looked through the room again, but found nothing else. No evidence. No hint of what the police might need to establish "reasonable suspicion of guilt."

THIRTY-NINE

Then Sonia couldn't help but wonder, What else has he taken? What else has he kept? Stella's life a puzzle she felt desperate to solve.

He'd taken Stella's confidence as a mother; the peace of mind she deserved to have, but never did; that vibrancy she'd discovered in Toronto and then lost.

He'd taken Kate's entire childhood.

More difficult than the question of what he'd taken was why he'd done it. How could he? How could anyone?

But there was no way to make sense of the brutality of Evvie's mind, hard as she might try.

Perhaps if she'd tried earlier. Instead, she and everyone colluded with the fiction that Evvie was harmless. From the start they understood that so long as they appeased him, he'd stay calm. It became a reflex.

Sonia realized now that she had looked right past the most obvious things. Our compliance operates like a visual illusion, she decided, and the picture deceives unless we question it. The ease of status quo is seductive. And the mind is too accommodating, indulgent, untrustworthy.

All this, Evvie had in his favour.

FORTY

Sonia filled the firebox then sat in her rocking chair with Stella's diary in her lap.

Rose began to unpack the boxes of things they'd brought, sorting them into piles on the cot. She shook her head at the diary. "Don't even tell me, okay?"

But Sonia wanted to read it. She wanted to know what Stella had been thinking.

When she was a little girl, Stella wrote stories about the drawings she made. Sonia had marvelled at this. For her, the drawing was itself the point. But Stella appended to every picture she made its own vivid explanation, or a fantastic description, set down in line after line of earnest schoolgirl printing.

Just like those lines beneath her pictures, the diary was a living thing, a part of Stella, a trace she'd left behind.

Sonia opened it—and the sudden shock of her daughter's hand, alive on the page.

She closed it quickly.

Stella's diary offered privileged access to Stella's mind. Sonia felt simultaneously compelled and warned away, as by potentially scalding information. Until she read the diary, she was free to imagine what it held. The danger was that fantasy might be overtaken by reality.

It was an ordinary blank book like any you could buy at the grocery store. A cheap cover, embossed with the words *My Daily Journal*, enclosing a hundred wide-ruled pages. Stella would have picked it up on one of her weekly shopping trips, setting it in the cart beside her eggs and cans of beans. Sonia could see the diary in the cart, and Stella's hand reaching toward it, as though to wipe a film of dust from its lightly padded surface. She could see the diary in Stella's hand. She fanned it open in her own. There was no question — the handwriting was Stella's. Big looping letters wavered up and down the page; Stella had not been able to see the faint blue lines on the paper.

Rose held up a tiny knitted sweater and turned to Sonia. "Mum, do you remember when Katie was born?"

Stella's sadness had always distressed Sonia, but never so much as the day Stella gave birth to Kate. "I can't!" Stella had said, pushing newborn Kate away. "*I can't. I can't. I can't.*"

Sonia's irritation was with *herself*—that she couldn't help her daughter, that she didn't know how.

Rose had simply been baffled by Stella's behaviour.

Rose was astonished by the miracle of Kate, absent one minute, present the next. Her plum-shaped face more beautiful, Rose said, than anything she'd ever seen. She couldn't fathom Stella's despair.

"Do you remember, Mum," Rose said again, "how sad she was when Kate was born?"

Sonia remembered. But now she was thinking about what Evvie had said. *She doesn't even know how to look after it.*

And she was wondering about what else he might have said or done.

What she wondered was, Why didn't I see what was going on?

But what was there to see? Hiding bottles in the woodshed, yelling when someone poured them out — many men did this. The criticism, berating, insistence — these were familiar too.

It's only because she's gone that we care, Rose had said after the funeral. What this meant to Sonia now was that if Stella hadn't disappeared, no one would have thought twice about Evvie's behaviour.

Rose said, "*Mum?*"

Sonia nodded mechanically, sickened suddenly by this new idea.

It's only because she's gone that we care.

She turned to Rose. "Stella was a difficult person," she said. "Sometimes you could reach her, and sometimes you couldn't."

Rose sat on the couch among the piles of clothes. She said, "Remember the time Lil complained of tarnish on her 'silver photos'?"

Sonia had seen Lil's daguerreotypes, stiffly posed pictures of relatives on Lil's mother's side of the family, wealthy folk who lived in Boston and sent parcels back every Christmas for Lil's mother when she was a girl, an entire family of fairy godmothers.

Lil had worried aloud that the images were fading, and young Stella had offered brightly: I'll clean them for you.

Stella polished those pictures with silver cleaning paste, applying the thick, acrid stuff to all the pictures at once, efficient in the way Lil was when she cleaned her silver cutlery and tea service. Stella had watched Lil smear polishing paste on all her silver, rub the pieces with a scrap of flannel, rinse them in a pan of water, wash them all to remove the residue of the foul paste, and dry them carefully to make them shine. Stella loved to watch this operation, so different from the way it was conducted at home. Sonia used toothpaste or salt and half a lemon—neither of which really did the job, Stella complained.

Of course, when Stella "polished" them, Lil's pictures came as clean as brand new mirrors. Lil found Stella staring into them when she walked into the kitchen. All her precious images erased.

Sonia imagined Stella's feeling then as the sickening thrill of dropping down a narrow shaft—the dark strength of that guilt and failure.

Sonia opened Stella's diary at random. At the bottom of a page, under the heading *Other Mistakes I've Made*, Stella had written Evvie's name. Below this, a few indiscernible words had been repeatedly stroked out.

Sonia put her finger on the unreadable words, touched the pencilled gashes Stella had made.

"Well," she said, leaning away a little, rubbing her eyes, irritated from reading in the dim light.

"I guess we'd better get to work," Rose said. "Dan will be wanting his supper. And I have a blouse to iron for tomorrow." She stood and picked up one of the piles of Stella's clothes.

Evvie was worse for Stella than we realized, Sonia thought, but was he any different, really, than Ray or Dan or even Rob, who always believed that *they* were right and that life should proceed according to *their* plans? Maybe the only difference was that Evvie was angrier.

He wasn't different from Max, either. Max who insisted that they were going to do this or that thing, and when, and never imagined that Sonia might have another idea. Max who always convinced Sonia to disregard her own instincts and pile in with whatever scheme he'd cooked up. Moving to the Island. Starting a mixed farm.

And like a fool, she'd gone along.

Max had strong opinions about the world and how it worked. Opinions that were completely unlike Sonia's own and surprised her every time.

Why had she ever found this enthralling?

I was too easily swayed by what he said, she thought. Too ready to follow.

Pasted on one page, a clipping from the newspaper's Island History column:

> *Henry sick and cross last night, got no sleep, up half the night with him. What a blessing to have children when you come to think of it.*
> —Lemuel Vickerson, Aug. 11, 1868

And below this, in Stella's hand: *Kate is one year old today.*

On the next page Stella had written, *It's lucky Rose has so much time off school.*

But Rose had never had time off school. She'd been skipping school in order to look after Kate.

How had Stella never realized, all that time?

Rose has been a marvellous help with Kate the past few weeks.

Sonia turned the page.

Kate looks like Rose, but Kate is not extraordinary. Kate is exhausting to me. How I hate it that I feel this way.

Sonia understood how Stella felt.

The young are beautiful, Lil said once, because they have so few regrets.

Sonia thought, Lil was right: I am not beautiful; I am no longer young; and I feel tortured by regret.

Then, she'd said — too flippantly — Lil, you are so wise.

Lil had waved her away. I heard it on the radio, she said.

Rose was carrying boxes down the hall. She brushed by Sonia, pointedly ignoring both her mother and the diary.

Sonia thought, What Rose has that neither Frances nor I do is *certainty*. It lends a kind of glow.

Evidently Rose believed that secrets were incendiary, and none more so than whatever might be written in Stella's diary.

Rose maintained that people would say anything on the telephone. She complained that some days her work was a torrent of personal revelations. After all, she said, what is Switchboard but other people's secrets?

She hated that, she said.

Sonia wondered, What is it that Rose so desperately doesn't want to know?

FORTY-ONE

After supper, when the kitchen was empty, Sonia read farther:

What I love about my poor eyesight is the quiet. It's so restful without glasses. So much gets filtered out, so many distractions and demands.

It's true some things look strange. The lamp in the living room with its corset-shaped shade catches me off guard. It's like a person coming through the door. The gateleg table is a calf with knobbly knees. Several times I've caught myself wondering how it stands up on its own, why it doesn't collapse into a pile of fresh straw. The geraniums in the window wave to me. My pincushion is a fuzzy ball I want to pet. Evvie moves so fast he scares me. Kate is a romping dog.

But then I put my glasses on and the world transforms again.

Vision isn't everything. I smell bread long before I see it, hear the crackle of the crust when it cools, feel the sharp pain when I accidentally touch the oven rack or a hot pan on the stove. Laundry is the same—the bitter smell of soda and the sweet freshness of the soap. Sometimes sound and smell and touch are more important than a picture in the mind.

But when the picture's blurry is when it's most interesting anyway. Seeing light, shape, movement and colour is seeing possibility — it's seeing a flexible world that can become whatever you most need it to be.

I love it when the thing I want to see turns out to be the thing I really see. But that's so rare, it almost never happens. Once last winter, walking along the edge of the woods and hearing chickadees, I saw a blur on a hanging branch and wished it were a chickadee that'd stay until I reached her. It was, and she stayed! So I got to see a bird close up. Close enough, anyway.

More often I imagine things are other than they are and I am disappointed when I get close. Most things are ordinary, when you get right up to them.

Sonia thought, *Kate is a romping dog . . . vision is possibility*: my daughter was an artist. She saw what I struggle to see.

How could Stella see this way, Sonia wondered, and still believe that anything in life was mundane?

Stella saw only one blurry, off-centre version of everything. Sonia thought, No wonder she sometimes seemed confused.

People think that light's essential to good vision, but the opposite is true. Without my glasses, I see best in subdued light. Bright, glary light is too harsh, makes me want to turn away.

With perfect vision, I'd be trapped in the ordinary truth of the world, imprisoned in a banal reality I couldn't bear and wouldn't have the strength of character to change. This way, I can allow myself imagination, fantasy.

Rose and Frances did not remember Stella's accident, but Sonia knew they could remember what others had said about it, stories people told, and stories from Stella herself. What Sonia most remembered was the emptiness in those stories, which were always incomplete, their central incident left out.

How, exactly, had Stella been hurt? Who was to blame? Stella never said.

What Sonia wanted to remember was how Stella had reacted to her loss of sight.

How had she responded when her bandages were removed? To the months of healing and renegotiation?

She wanted to clarify for herself how Stella was different, after. Stella's own description of her experience was so different from Sonia's memory of it.

How little we understand each other, she thought.

Sonia covered her eyes with her hands. A quick panic rose. She fought it down.

She could hear the sounds of the house — the faint ticking of floor ties against wooden beams, an insubstantial sigh (wind caught indoors, like breath on a grand scale). There was the smell of clothes from the boxes Rose had unpacked, with their mingled burdens of soap and mustiness and wear, and there were the smells of the kitchen around her. The closeness and warmth of the enveloping dark (as if losing one's sight increased the ambient temperature).

She squeezed her eyes shut and put her hands out and began to move around the kitchen, aiming for the hall. She felt for something to grasp onto. She tripped on the fringed edge of the rug and stumbled down the hall, where the walls on either side were near enough to afford a sense of edge. Her hand caught something sharp, there was a scraping sound, and her eyes flew open. She'd hit the corner of a picture frame. She closed her eyes and pressed her hands against them.

Was this what Stella saw inside her damaged eye? The opposite of dark: a grey-red wall that refused to settle down, its surface frantic with exploding sparks and restless, floating blotches.

A senseless image of life, Sonia thought. At the same time, true.

FORTY-TWO

The way she started was by painting swaths of blue on a cut-open canvas bag she'd secured to strips of lath. The paint was left over from a metal fence Dan installed at the end of a marshy field. She'd thinned it with turpentine and now she applied it with big, broad strokes, sweeping her arm forward in an imitation of a wave. She wasn't sure yet what she'd do when the paint dried. But as she swept the wide-bristle brush across the nubbly canvas, she thought of sand and sun and all she'd lost. Evvie came to mind, the engineer of so much sorrow. She scrubbed harder with the brush. She dipped into the can of paint and pushed more blue into the canvas. She laid her brush down. She picked it up again and shook it hard toward the canvas. Lines of blue guttered out.

Rage, she thought. *Rage*. It was what he expressed. She said it, and the sound of the word embodied her own emotion. *I am enraged*.

She opened her mouth and screamed the place still.

So that was how it felt to act on a violent impulse.

But why bother? The act was briefly satisfying, then meaningless.

She'd asked Marina, Why did he do it? And Marina just shook her head. You will go crazy trying to answer that question.

She threw the brush at a wall.

FORTY-THREE

Over supper that night, Dan reported that while "you were swanning around" — here he nodded to indicate Frances frivolously at school, Rose frivolously at work, and Sonia doing God knows what, covered in spatters of blue — "meanwhile," he said, his voice tight with disapproval, "the RCMP let Evvie go."

You can make a telephone call, they'd said. Ask somebody to drive you home.

So Evvie had called Dan, since Dan was going to farm with him. This was what Evvie had said.

"Yeah, I'm gettin' out," he said. "Kin ya come and pick me up?"

Dan had told him: *No.* Now Dan glared around the table.

Rose said, "And this is our fault how?"

Dan shook his head, disgusted again.

Rose pursed her lips.

Then Dan did something rare. He said, "I'm sorry, Rose. Of course it's not your fault."

Sonia thought, *But why did they let Evvie go? Isn't he guilty? Was I wrong?*

After supper, Sonia washed dishes and watched through the open kitchen window as Dan set his fist down hard on the bonnet of Evvie's pickup. "Tell me what you did," he said. In a whiny, sarcastic voice — a cruel imitation of Evvie's — he said, *"That hole in the ice. Stupid bitch."* Then he slammed his fist again.

Dan roared at Evvie that he was going to farm alone but that Evvie would have to sign any forms that came from the Farm Credit because now that Dan was into this he had to keep on going.

Evvie stared, said nothing.

Dan kept on. "And if you think there's any effing way I'll farm with you, you're damn well Jesus fucking wrong!"

Evvie's scalded look seemed to give Dan pause for the briefest fraction of a second. Then he kept on. "Get out!" he roared. "Get the hell — " He waved his hand listlessly.

Evvie was still standing by his truck, as though by waiting there he might effect some change in Dan, and Dan would become himself again.

"Get out!" Dan warned again, and Sonia imagined Stella soothing Evvie the way she used to, calming him with her mild, thoughtfully inflected voice.

Evvie stumbled past Dan and climbed into his truck. Stella's voice was now an imaginary counterpoint in Sonia's mind: *Never mind, dear. It's not important. Never mind, never mind . . .*

Evvie mumbled, "Helluva kick in the guts." He put the truck in gear and turned to back out of the lane.

"Get the fuck — " Dan slammed his hand down on the hood of the truck.

Evvie wheeled around and slammed the transmission into park and got back out of the truck. He came at Dan, fists raised.

Dan was ready for him, icily calm now. "You *murdered* my sister," Dan said.

"The hell I did! Is that what you all think?" Evvie turned and glared at Sonia in the open window. "Stella wanted to fall through. You didn't live with her! She was a misery. I never saw anybody so miserable."

Dan said, "You made her unhappy."

"I never made her anything. She did it to herself." Evvie started to walk away, but then he turned around again. "I'll tell you something else. I miss her more than you all do!"

This remark was so unexpected, it silenced even Dan.

FORTY-FOUR

Frances could not remember Stella's face. "Mum," she said, "tell me what Stella looked like."

Sonia said faces were too complex for memory. "Who can remember what any person looks like? Would you remember my face, if I walked out of the room? You have to stop dwelling on this, Frances," she said. "You're going to make yourself sick."

Later, it dawned on Sonia that her response had been harsh. She went looking for Frances, and finally found her in the barn, sitting on a hay bale beside a litter of kittens that had just been born. Sonia reached under the sleeping barn cat and picked up one of her tiny babies.

"Stella had brown hair," she said. "Long, stringy hair that she let hang or pulled into an untidy knot. Her eyes were grey and her mouth was deeply red compared to the paleness of her skin. She wore her glasses on top of her head—so she didn't have to see, I think. Her one eye looked straight ahead."

This feature, the injured eye, was impossible to forget. But the rest —the hair, the colours—would not coalesce into an image in Sonia's mind. No wonder Frances couldn't conjure it.

Sonia said, "Remember how she always wore her clothes too big?"

Then she felt a sudden seepage of remorse and gratitude. Frances had been right in the first place—it was important to try—but faces were too complex for memory. At least, Stella's face was too complex. Or Stella herself was.

Surely this was something to be thankful for. Didn't it mean that Stella had lived a full life, brief and troubled as it was?

FORTY-FIVE

Then the heat of the late summer came on. Frances helped Rob and Dan bale the last of the hay, made jam or pickles with Sonia. Rose increased her hours at work, taking the truck when Dan didn't need it, catching a ride with one neighbour or another when she could. At night she sat with Kate and Sonia on the old swing in the grove, sipping cool tea with lemon and recounting the events of her day. For Sonia the surprise of these moments was their ease—Rose's relaxed state after work, Kate's calm and the feeling of normalcy this all brought. She longed for it to last. Of course it couldn't.

Rose was on her dinner break one sweltering late August day when she saw Ray with the woman from his wallet photo.

She'd heard about Chevette Gallant from Dan back in the spring. "Evvie's met her," Dan had said over supper, as though this fact would mean something to Rose.

Rose had decided not to believe in the existence of Chevette Gallant. But now here she was—an actual person—walking arm in arm with Ray along a downtown street.

"Chevette Gallant is Ray's ex-wife," Dan said. "She's Catholic, and she's divorced. You know that can't be good. A Catholic woman doesn't get divorced unless the man is really bad to her."

Recently, Dan had become more direct. "Rose, you need to drop this Ray. You need to do it now."

Rose had stopped calling Ray, but he persisted in telephoning her. This morning he had called to ask her out for a drink after work. She said no.

"But do you see," Rose marvelled to Frances and Sonia, "*he must have turned right around and called her.*"

On the street, Ray wrapped his arm around Chevette Gallant, who Rose could see was dressed beautifully and shod in swell new pumps, her glossy hair caught in an elegant upswept do. Even from the back Rose could tell the woman's sense of style was exceptionally fine. She had made herself look beautiful for Ray.

So why, she wondered, *does he keep calling* me?

Frances had shown Rose the photographs in Ray's wallet after she found it in the river. The automobile and the woman with the updo.

"Chevette *Vermeer*," Frances said when Dan brought her up. "That would have been her married name. Gallant must be the name she'd had before. Either that or she's gotten married again."

This Rose doubted, having watched Ray kiss her on the street.

"You should confront him," Frances said.

But Rose didn't want to.

"She had streaks in her hair like Holly Golightly," Rose said.

"*Breakfast at Tiffany's*," Frances explained for Sonia's benefit. Sonia had never seen Rose's favourite film.

"This takes the fun out of that movie," Rose complained.

Frances shook her head. "Rose, that movie was never fun. It was sad. What did you *think*?"

"Thank goodness I didn't agree to meet him," Rose said. "Serial marrier. No-good lech."

She would never see or speak to Ray Vermeer again, she said. She was determined now.

But Sonia could see from her face that there was something bitter in the knowledge that now she really was alone, and Sonia didn't know what to say or do to ease that ache.

FORTY-SIX

Marina said, "You have to let them make their own mistakes, but you have to know when to step in too. You're doing a good job. Sonia, do you hear me?"

Sonia nodded.

"This Ray Vermeer sounds like bad news, as the young people say. How can you help Rose see that? We women have to stick together."

Sonia nodded again, without looking at Marina. How could she help Rose see? She didn't have a clue.

"And how are *you* doing, dear?"

"Grain is good this year. The boys are pleased."

Marina levelled her cool, assessing gaze.

Sonia could not say that she felt most worried about Frances, who was passionate like her but in love with science rather than art. She could not admit that she was afraid Frances was lost. Not lost in the way Stella had been, in gloom, but profoundly lost in grief. What did you do, to help a child out of that?

Marina said, "Sonia, remember this: you are as mysterious to your children as they are to you. But you still have to solve your own life if you want to be of any help to them."

All that humid summer, Rose came and went like haze. Frances and Sonia looked after Kate. Rose's appearances at home were brief and insubstantial, and Sonia began to feel that she was fading from their lives. She seemed detached, as if she'd developed a protective carapace. After Ray she hardly spoke about herself, except in relation to her job at Island Telephones. With its rigid rules of conduct and electric buzz of energy, the sociability of the other operators and the fiercely solitary, mechanical focus required by the work itself, the job was a perfect fit for Rose.

The idea of connecting and reconnecting to that humming apparatus gave Sonia chills, but Frances said she envied Rose her smart new clothes and daily experience of urban life. She envied Rose the languid evenings she sometimes spent in town, staying over at another operator's apartment after work. She felt sure she'd never have a life like that.

When university started in September, Frances was supposed to live in town, in a room Dan had found, and her life at home would end. But Frances complained she didn't know how to begin. Sonia helped her pack her books and mend some of her clothes. None of this helped, Frances said. None of it made the move away more real.

Rose had gone, but something inside Frances would not let her leave.

In Rose's absence, Sonia began to notice how many things Rose knew that Frances and even Sonia herself did not: how to find a job, how to get to town every day, how to carry on.

From listening on the switchboard, Rose knew the true meaning of the things people were given to say, how they hurt each other, and how they made it up again. Rose was smart in ways that Sonia would never be. But her intelligence came packaged with an insidious form of misery: the sorrow that derives from understanding all too well how human beings fail each other.

Love plus knowledge added up to loss. Sonia understood how this calculation worked. What she wanted was to know how to add things up a different way.

FORTY-SEVEN

One day in the mailbox there was a paper-wrapped box with the label
P. Cope, O.D.

My glasses? Sonia thought. The woman from his office kept calling
to make appointments for her fitting, but Sonia had cancelled these
appointments twice.

She opened the parcel. It was not glasses. It was a little box of paints
and a tiny brush. Scrawled across the box, For Sonia. Love, Pete.

The paint set was impossible to resist. For days on end she did nothing
but draw pencil sketches and fill them in with colour.

My God, she'd say, and Pete's hand on her face, his lips on her own.
The little sketches piled up.

But the pictures would not behave as she wanted them to.

She squinted at them in the light, and the images were fine, but they
would not come alive.

She tried fields, woods, the bark of different trees, vistas of shorelines
drawn from memory.

She remembered from childhood the confidence she'd felt in her ability
to make art, even in the absence of objective proof. She remembered
restlessness—and certainty too.

She remembered how she felt when an image formed and how she felt
before that, when an inchoate emotion grabbed her by the throat.

She thought of letting the paint set go and adding wool to her blue
canvas, felting and fraying it, working in strips of an old silk tie of her

father's, a luminous, smoky grey like the sky on the shore before dawn. She could work with the silk's reflectivity. She knew how to manipulate its planes of light. But what would such a picture mean, if anything?

What she wanted was to convey emotion in an image. She wanted to make a picture that would come alive.

She laid out dinner—slices of ham with mustard relish, baked beans, brown bread—then impulsively she began again. She heaped a dinner plate, sketched it quickly, filling in the pattern on the plate, the multitude of beans, the bright chaos of the relish and the scratchy rectangle of toast. Max's plate had always been piled high like this. It was a habit, even now, to make her portion and her children's smaller. I work hard all day, he'd explained when Dan had challenged him as a child. *Why is Dad's supper bigger than mine?*

She picked up her paint set and a jar of water. No colour in the box was bright enough for the lurid relish.

She made it blue instead.

After the enforced regularity of meals with Max—five on the dot—she'd abandoned all sense of schedule for years. She'd had no choice. How busy they'd been! In agony on the couch one night, legs and arms throbbing from exhaustion, she'd raised her head to the touch of a hand on her shoulder—Eddie, over for a game of cards. This is too much for you, he'd said. I'm gonna come over tomorrow and get in the hay.

Despite the exhaustion of doing so many jobs at once through those first years alone, she'd felt a continual sense of relief. It's hard for you, him gone, Eddie had said. But it wasn't hard Max was gone: Max being gone was easy. Before, she'd put her life aside for Max, she'd shushed the kids and changed her own behaviour in a thousand different ways. Once, Dan complained that Sonia let Max bully her and why didn't she stand up to him? But how do you stand up to someone who smashes his fist through walls and screams and wrecks things? He was Jekyll and Hyde, destructive one night, charming the next. Sonia didn't want money wagered during card games, but he did it anyway. Grinning as he hid it and bringing it out when she left the room. Frances and Dan saw. Anyone can put something over on someone else if they want to. Anyone can betray another person's trust.

No, it wasn't hard that Max was gone. Only the physical work was hard.

All Max ever wanted was to escape the lightship. He hadn't known what he wanted to go to. And that wish to get away was not enough to make a life.

The dinner plate was glowing like a hot coal in her hand. This was not what she wanted. It was a painting with emotion, yes, but it was not emotion she wanted to revisit.

She threw it in the fire and took the others to the window. Sweet scenes of land and sky and shore. But flat. Every one blurry or out of focus.

The next eye appointment, the one she hadn't cancelled yet, was in mid-September. This time, she would have to go.

FORTY-EIGHT

Sonia bent to tuck Kate into bed and something leered at the window. Evvie's face.

She blinked away the image and bent to kiss Kate on the forehead. Then she stood, and there was Evvie, glaring.

She thought, *He's haunting us now?*

She had both expected and dreaded his appearance. But now that he was here, she understood how unprepared she was. She could do nothing, say nothing, felt frozen in place.

Frances came into the room and unlocked the moment.

How pathetic he was with his permanent sneer and unwashed hair, she said. She looked him in the eye as she moved toward the window and she closed the curtains in his face.

Evvie has no right, her ferocious whisper.

It struck Sonia that Evvie had been sleepwalking since Stella disappeared, and for some reason he wasn't anymore.

If he wanted Kate back, she would make it good and clear they would not give her to him.

She imagined a reunion, the father saying *Hi there, little baked potato.* And the daughter singing *Dadda!* She thought, two together, the storybook line Kate loved so much that went with a picture of a lion and a zebra holding hands.

He would catch her in his arms, or she would come running to him, pushing her new glasses up on her nose, like her mother whom Evvie claimed he missed, no matter what anyone else believed.

But none of this was ever going to happen.

Evvie was not that gentle father. Kate ran from the room whenever he appeared.

Later, Sonia would learn that Evvie had been drinking heavily for weeks.

The police refused to investigate further. "We questioned him," they said.

This seemed insane. Even kind-hearted Cece and Mae thought so. "I think Dan's right," Cece pronounced the next day, kicking at an imaginary clump of grass with his boot. "I think Evvie might have did it."

Still, there was no proof.

Rose stayed in town often now. Dan veered between rage and uncertainty. It was unsettling to see Dan doubt himself, and Sonia could not begin to make out what was wrong with Frances.

She called Marina, and Marina said, "It's hard to know what Evvie wants."

"He complained no one has any time for him. He said he misses her. *He* misses Stella."

"Hmmm. When was this?"

"Dan laid into him after he got out of jail, and that's how he responded. *What did he imagine it would be like without her?*"

"Now, Sonia, we don't know what happened. We don't know he *planned* to hurt her. Tell me again about him looking at Kate."

"I was putting Kate to bed in Rose's room. Evvie was at the window. But, Marina, he wasn't looking at Kate. He was looking at me."

"Oh." Marina was silent for a moment. Then, in her thoughtful way, she said, "Yes. That makes sense. Because you were closer to Stella than anyone."

This was what the police had said. *We can't prove anything, so you'll have to be vigilant, dear.* Now she understood what they'd meant: we can't charge him, so you have to watch out for what he might do.

"Be careful, dear," Marina said, but all Sonia could focus on was the softness in her voice as she'd explained, *You were closer to Stella than anyone.*

This was what Sonia so needed to hear. *You were closer to Stella than anyone.*

That Marina saw this meant everything.

FORTY-NINE

Lyman came by the next morning.

He refused to come in. From the doorstep he nodded at Sonia and said, "Come for a walk with me, Frances."

It was barely nine o'clock. Frances was tucking bread dough into buttered pans. She clapped her hands to get the flour off, looked them over, shook her head. No, she said. But Lyman took a step inside. "*Come on*, Frances. It's Saturday."

So she changed her mind. "Oh, all right. Mum, can I go?"

"Sure," Sonia said. Why not? A walk was an ordinary, harmless activity. Surely even Lyman couldn't turn a simple walk into trouble.

Frances told the story later.

Lyman led her toward the river. Our familiar haunt, as Frances used to think of it.

At first, she said, she'd felt glad to be out rambling with him. But when Lyman turned toward the river, she thought of Stella. The river wasn't theirs anymore.

No, she said when she realized where he was taking her. She stopped.

Lyman pulled her by the arm. He was angry, and for an instant, Frances said, she didn't recognize his voice. *Come on*, he said, and hauled on her arm. She dug in her heels. He hauled again, and then he let her go and began to cry.

Frances didn't want to go down to the river. She didn't want to see the river, or hear it move, or smell its rotting smell, she said.

But she couldn't stand to see Lyman cry.

He led her through the woods, along a narrow path only fishermen and hunters used. Frances had to wrestle branches out of her face and stretch to leap over swampy spots. Finally Lyman paused at a narrow opening where some willows had been trampled down. See there, he said, and he pointed to Stella's glasses, caught in the mud, amongst the trash at the river's edge.

Dan called the police, and Rose took a day off work to sit with Sonia and Frances while the RCMP sent a boat and dragger out, to search the river one last time. But they found nothing else, and in some important way that failure caused Stella's presence in Sonia's mind to become, for a time, not less but more intense.

FIFTY

Frances began tearing her room apart. Organizing, she called it. For university.

She pulled things out of drawers with a fury that troubled Sonia. She flung sweaters like an actor in a movie that had been speeded up.

Sonia said, "*I'll miss you, Frances,*" and Frances replied without turning around, "Will you really?"

Sweaters fell together on the bed like toppled blocks and Frances pulled blouses and skirts off their hangers and threw them into the pile.

Then without warning she sank to the floor of her messy room, folded her legs beneath her body and collapsed.

When Rose came home twenty minutes later, Frances was still crumpled in a ball, her face closed like a fist, the skin puffed and red and rubbed with grime.

"*Frances?*" Rose knelt on the floor. The glazed look in Frances's eyes was frightening. "Mum, what happened?"

Sonia left Frances with Rose and went to get a damp, warm washcloth to wipe her daughter's face. Then together she and Rose cleared off the bed and tucked Frances into it.

The next morning, Frances looked like herself. But she wanted to talk about Stella.

"I had a dream," she said. "Stella in a white skirt, twirling like the ballerina in a music box. She spun like this. She was going skating."

Rose said, "But we never went out when there was softness in the ice."

Frances frowned. "It was an *accident*," she said.

"*Okay*—" Rose said, her voice barely a whisper.

As children, they'd skated on the river every evening for weeks on end, Sonia with them. They soared, or believed they did.

The winter wind sandpapering our faces, Sonia remembered, and the river holding us up.

Every year they waited impatiently, from the day someone spotted the first skim of ice, or heard the music of its forming, a tinkling like chimes.

Sonia had seen this happen once, the current bringing to the riverbank small circles of ice—circles, and oddly shaped fragments that wished to be circles—delicate, glassy discs no larger than the palm of a child's hand. She thought of them as hands—a thousand hands joining to form the sturdy surface she and her children would skate on.

The sound was marvellous, more deliberate than chimes, less random —an aural artwork, if art could be a product of nature. Rose and Stella were with her, and heard the music too.

"Do you remember—" Rose said now. "*Frances*. Do you remember skating?"

But Frances was still in another world. "*She could soar.*"

It had been a day to soar. But instead Stella drowned. Was that what was wrong with Frances: she finally understood that Stella had drowned?

Sonia pictured Stella on the ice. She saw her glasses, caught in the mud, where Lyman had found them.

Rose sat thinking of what to say. Sonia knew Rose believed that she could gentle Frances out of this, as she had ordered the household and mothered Kate. This was the thing Rose was good at.

"*Frances*"—Rose took her hand—"*come with me.*"

But Frances would not let Rose lead her to a safer place.

Sonia thought, We are separating. All of us. We are spinning apart.

She could feel it happening.

FIFTY-ONE

Frances said, "Evvie said, *I done it and I'm not sorry.*"

Sonia thought, Yesterday it was an accident.

What Frances said could be true. But Frances still had that glazed look in her eyes. And as far as Sonia knew, she had not spoken to Evvie.

"Mum," Frances said.

Sonia nodded. She made her daughter a cup of tea.

Then, a week or so later, Eddie Mack came over with a pile of mail. He sat on the kitchen couch. His face was white.

"Everett isn't home," he said. "I don't think he's been there in a while." He set a small bundle of letters on the edge of the table. "This bunch was sticking out of the box." Then he held one out to Sonia. "I found this in the house."

It was an oil bill, still sealed into its envelope. Sonia turned it over. On the back, in Evvie's scrawl, three soul-destroying lines: *Kate. I didn't mean to hurt her. You be a good girl.*

Sonia kept reading the words until the envelope fell from her hand.

Eddie folded his body around hers.

Sonia said, "Kate can't ever see this."

It was an incomprehensible legacy.

Sonia and Dan took the oil bill in to the RCMP. A burly officer with a squint eye only gazed at Dan and said, "Would you like to report the disappearance?"

Dan got a fierce look on his face. "Do I want you to *find* him? *No!*"

Of course, the police couldn't charge Evvie if they couldn't find him.

On the drive home Dan said, "But they weren't going to charge him anyway."

They'd released him. It seemed the case was closed.

To Dan, it didn't matter whether Evvie pushed Stella or raged and shouted at her until she leapt. To the RCMP, it did. "We questioned him," they said, again and again. "There is no evidence he harmed her physically."

There was no evidence of Evvie himself, either. That was the one good thing: Evvie was gone.

FIFTY-TWO

September 1965. Prospect, Prince Edward Island.

The clouds had taken on a careless look. The fields were spent. The cellar and the woodshed full. Sonia had established a simple routine for Kate: breakfast at dawn, bedtime at dusk, a quiet time after main meals and a nap in between. Kate followed her, copying what she did, most of the day. With Rose's help, Frances had settled into a room in town and was attending classes at the university every day. Rose continued to travel back and forth so she could spend evenings and weekends with Kate. Dan handled a heroic portion of the farm work, arguing Rob needed to concentrate on school now he was in grade eleven. Rob was relieved to be released. To Sonia, Rob looked more confident and Dan serene, not overworked. Everyone seemed calmer.

One evening, Sonia watched from a distance as Dan began to build a fire. Beside him, a pile of brush he'd cleared in order to widen the headland of a field.

The sky behind Dan smouldered in layers of dusky colour, and the trees and the fields were grey. She watched as he piled stuff—layers of twigs and fine dry grass, birch twigs first and then mounds of brush. She imagined the sky as paint on canvas, small twigs and grass woven into the cloth.

Soon it would rain. The fire would burn hot briefly, and then the rain would put it out. The rain would wash the land. Wash things clean, and create a sense of starting over.

Sonia craved a sense of starting over.

Dan piled branches. Soon he would throw a match and watch the flames creep through the dry grass base he'd made, wait to ensure it caught, listen for the satisfying roar of ignition...

She watched him pat his pockets for a matchbox, and she could see her father in the gesture.

Beyond the old hedgerow, the stubble field began to glow.

When he was done watching his fire, Dan would look back at the house. He would see the yellow light, and maybe he would hear Kate laugh. There was a chill in the air, but a window would be open because of the heat from the stove.

As he got closer to the house, he would hear music from the radio, and a smell of biscuits and baking beans would take over from his brush fire.

The house would look warm and inviting. Kate would shriek and giggle, and Rose and Sonia would laugh the way they used to.

Dan would, too.

She watched Dan touch a match to the dry grass. His fire started. He stepped away from it.

She saw the bark of the trees (like raw fleece licked with wet black paint) and Dan's piled sticks, now so dark against his fire's leaping flames. She saw the lighted sky.

The strength of Dan's good fire and the glory of the world behind it: a vivid, unexpected benediction.

She thought of Rose, in the house with Kate, and of Rob and Frances. All they'd overcome.

She smelled the fire. The sky burned brighter. She thought to get Rose and Kate — they should see this spectacle —

But it was too late already. The light had begun to change.

She tried to focus on the meal they'd share when Dan came into the house and for a brief moment they were together — all except Frances, who was in town.

— and except Stella.

Dan was throwing fragments of paper into the fire. Glittering ribbons and shards turned in the uneven light. She walked toward him.

"Farm Credit application," he said as she approached.

He stirred the fire and Sonia realized what this meant. "But how will you expand?"

Cece and Grover Hurry and Eddie Mack would expand co-operatively with him, Dan said. That way they wouldn't need Farm Credit. "It was Eddie's idea."

"That's good, dear. That's good. Come in, now. Supper's ready."

Halfway back to the house, she turned to look at the fire, at the picture she'd seen or imagined.

But she couldn't focus. She told herself she would do better the next day, and then she shuttered her mind and went into the kitchen and blindly let Rose take over, as she knew Rose would.

FIFTY-THREE

The second time she found herself in Peter Cope's optometry office, Sonia was prepared. She had a bag of knitting, in case she had to wait. She was no longer bothered by the starkness of the place. She knew what lay behind the inner door. Pete wasn't going to catch her off guard. They didn't know each other anymore, if they ever had.

"*My dear,*" he said, opening the inner door.

She looked around. Apart from the inert and habitually silent woman who sat beside the telephone, the office was deserted. She picked up her bag.

"How are you?" he said.

She preceded him toward the examination room, his question a live thing between them. How *was* she? She couldn't tell. Good manners demanded an answer. But to Pete she could neither lie politely nor tell the truth: *I'm baffled. You baffle me. I've just lost one daughter and my other two are leaving home. Violent memories haunt me. I don't know what I think anymore...*

This time, the room was brightly lit. Blackout curtains had been drawn away from the windows. She sat in a chair he held out for her, positioned beside his impossibly cluttered desk. "I'm so glad to see you —" He bent and captured her face in both his hands.

She reared back in the chair.

He pulled away, but it was too late. His breach had destroyed her carefully constructed facade of calm.

"You know —" She stopped, unsure of what to say.

"Sonia, I'm sorry."

He didn't look sorry. But it didn't matter. She wasn't going to let him be in charge anymore. "You know," she said, "I just came here to get my glasses. I just want to see well enough to draw properly, that's all." The heat of his hands still burned her face. She rubbed her cheeks hard and the sensation fell away.

What had made her think she could get through this visit? What delusion?

"I'm sorry, Sonia. I keep thinking I remember you. I do remember your beautiful drawings. But I keep forgetting how much time has passed. Forgive me, please."

He held the glasses out to her and she put them on. Delicately, he touched the corners of the frames, then lifted the glasses clear away.

He took them into a corner of the room. She could hear the clink of metal. A tapping sound. A little hammer, maybe, or a percussive mechanism of some kind. The next moment he was leaning over her again, breathing sweetly, sweeping her hair aside in order to set the glasses in place, their unfamiliar weight pressing on her ears and across the bridge of her nose.

"How does that feel? Just take a moment to decide." He put a hand on her shoulder.

If there had been a way to run... but she wanted the glasses desperately. She wanted to see. She wanted to see as clearly as her children could.

Why did he imagine he knew her? The difference between his way of looking at the world and hers was profound.

Twenty-five years ago, he'd believed in observing one's commitments and she'd believed in taking leaps of faith. She could imagine following another path, and he, obviously, could not.

She had been willing to go to Montreal. He had not been able to imagine her in his life. Or, not her and Stella both.

On his face that last day at the station, she'd seen her future roll out before her, and it was lonely, full of bitterness and regret. You've made your bed, now lie in it, his expression said.

But why should *she* feel regret? The question tore at her. Regret arises from misguided choice, but she'd never had a choice.

She moved to the farm with Max *because* Pete left. Without her lighthouse posting, she could imagine nothing else.

He leaned forward again, peering into her eyes. "How does that feel?"

The way he leaned toward her, reaching for her glasses, urging her to speak, seemingly torn between wanting to take the glasses away to adjust them again and wanting to leave them with her.

How does that feel? She had no idea how the glasses felt. She could barely focus on the question, so startled was she by the weight of the frames on her face, his hand on her shoulder, his voice in her ear.

He waited.

She opened her eyes—all this time she'd had them closed!—and how fiercely sharp things were.

Complexity overwhelmed her. The room, which had been soft and harmless, full of rounded shapes and muted colour, now throbbed with detail. Angles grew from other angles, objects leered: clutter, books, machines, optometric tools, empty paper lunch bags, books on shelves, and photographs—so many photographs. One jumped out: that photo from the shore. Huh.

She looked away and saw her own lined hands.

She felt a pain.

Stella should have seen like this.

Her eyes blurred again.

She reached for the glasses, tore them off, swiped at her face.

Glasses wouldn't have helped Stella. Her eye had been destroyed.

Sonia could still see the blood, how it had welled up, the black look of it, and then how it remained caked in places on her face, even after Max brought her back from town. That accident had been Max's fault, the loose bolt a result of his carelessness with the mower. Or it had been her fault—the fight they'd had that morning all her doing, he said, and that fight the reason Max had started haying without looking over his machine. She'd tried to punish him, as she had so many mornings, for the way she woke—lonely, full of bitterness and regret.

So, what happened to Stella was not Max's fault. It was hers.

She put her glasses on again and the room came clear, all Pete's clutter and his machines. That photograph.

She hadn't seen it right away. But now it astonished her, her younger self suddenly more real than the person she'd become.

"So when your daughters were here—" He spoke in a whisper, hesitant, perhaps, to disrupt her visual exploration of the room, or to alarm her with talk when she was already so overwhelmed by what she saw.

"They're fine young women, Sonia. Beautiful and—"

He was still leaning toward her, clumsily trying to bridge the distance between them with this gift of words.

"Rose seems capable and clear-eyed, and Frances is exceptionally observant and bright...and your little granddaughter...so feisty! You should be proud."

Tentatively, he smiled.

Then—of course—there was more.

"Your oldest daughter—" he said, hesitating, leaving a deliberate conversational space for her to fill.

He wanted news of Stella. He was like Rose, who so often behaved more like her mother than her child—pushing, prying, saying ever so carefully in her relentless way, *Some people want to talk about the person they've lost.*

But she did not want to talk. Wasn't it enough she'd turned up here a second time?

FIFTY-FOUR

"Your daughter—" *What happened? Why?*

Pete's unasked questions had such power.

If there had been a way to go back in time, Sonia might have done it. She'd had no idea how to nurture the baby she'd been saddled with, as she thought of Stella then. Years later, watching Stella make mistakes with Kate, the missing thing had come to Sonia, unasked for, and she finally understood where she had failed. Stella was impatient—afraid, it seemed, that Kate would steal her days, suck up what little energy she had. Sonia tried to tell her to relax: *Sleep when she sleeps. Forget about the life you had before. Things will soon get easier.*

But Stella rejected this advice and turned aside just at the moment when, Sonia thought, she most needed help.

A scalding from the kettle one day frightened Stella, and finally she did call down to Sonia's house for help. Please, Mum, can you look after Kate this afternoon? I'm hurt, she'd said, and Sonia flew to her, afraid of God knows what.

The skin of Stella's forearm was pink and smooth, chafed by the steam so that it looked almost new, like Kate's.

Sonia wanted to help. But in Stella's eyes: nothing but reproach.

Stella winced when Sonia dressed the arm, and she went to bed without a word. Later, when the arm still hurt, Stella was angry—not grateful as Sonia thought she should be. Take another Aspirin, dear, Sonia had suggested, and was immediately sorry. From her earlier life she knew the magnitude of pain that could be caused by a burn.

September 1941. Surplus Island, Malpeque Bay, Prince Edward Island.

One cloudless Sunday, Sonia abandoned her lighthouse for the beach and lolled all afternoon among the marram-covered dunes. She felt she was being self-indulgent, but allowed herself to sleep for hours in the sun.

Pete was gone by then, and she was in a listless state, neglecting the light, ignoring as many of her duties as she could.

Soon Max would come to take her away, he'd said.

She was hardly awake when the air began to cool and an airplane buzzed overhead. She recognized the sound of it from her aircraft identification training just as it banked too steeply for its turn. A Harvard flight trainer out of Summerside.

The plane crashed behind the dunes, then exploded. Both the pilot and the flight instructor died. Sonia felt petrified with shame because she'd been sleeping on the sand instead of standing in her lighthouse when those men burned.

Of course, her being awake would not have changed the outcome.

Stella's burn was not Sonia's fault. Neither was that horrific crash. Why did she feel responsible? What failing did these moments stand for?

FIFTY-FIVE

August 1941. Surplus Island, Malpeque Bay, Prince Edward Island.

The letter arrived in late summer, when Sonia was busy with chores.
Her initial response was simple dismay at its predictably condescending
tone.

Your part in Canada's Home Front Detection Corps, she read. *Your
essential role.* As if she needed another. *Serve your country as you go about
your daily tasks.*

German submarines had been spotted in the Gulf, and German soldiers
might at that very moment be landing undetected in soundless rubber
boats. The threat was in the sky as well. *Look. Watch.*

As if this wasn't what she did all day.

They wanted her to be able to identify specific kinds of planes. *Proceed
to RCAF Station Summerside for instruction in aircraft identification. You will
see actual airplanes on the ground.* Of course the letter was addressed to Max,
but everyone around knew she was the keeper of Surplus Station. Also in
the envelope: a newsletter titled *The Observer* that offered a helpful column
of instructions on how to use the telephone. *You and Your Telephone*, it
read. *Make your report slowly and directly into the mouthpiece—your lips
not more than half an inch away.* There was more—a cardboard compass
she didn't need, a logbook with a place in it to indicate the type of engine
on each plane she saw. A list of names: Mosquito, Harvard, Anson...

⁙

At Identification Day, she met Grenfell Hillyard, fired up with enthusiasm over his own essential role.

"The military don't know what's out there, do they? Shells could be falling on us before they'd have a clue. But we fishermen know. We can tell the difference between a whale and a submarine. We can see a plane before it gets to land. Even in the fog, we can recognize a foreign boat by the sound it makes. Even in the dark!"

He cocked his head, leaned in to Sonia as though to impart an especially crucial fact. "It's dangerous at night, my dear. We have to open a hatch in the deck and shine a light out of it so our own boys can see who we are. But if Jerry's up there, he'll spot us just like that. Our only hope is to know the sound he makes."

He looked old, suddenly. She took his arm, patting it as they walked toward the lecture room.

The aircraft identification lessons were to be followed by a movie and a dance. "Stay," said Grenfell. "I'll buy you something cold to drink."

Sonia didn't need persuading. Marg Proffit would light the lamp, so she needn't be in any hurry to drive back. In fact, she'd rather never have to drive again—on the way, she'd almost rolled George's cantankerous truck on the Blue Shank Road.

Max! she'd cried when she'd got the truck stopped, her heart pounding in her ears—driving the one thing he was really good at—

The movie was *The Philadelphia Story.* Sonia sat beside Grenfell, drunk on one beer, and scenes swept over her in waves. Handsome Jimmy Stewart smirking like a fox, and Katharine Hepburn in her elegant, drape-y, mannish trousers.

After, on the dance floor, Sonia wished she looked like Hepburn. She'd changed out of her keeper's gear, but her faded and crumpled summer dress was the opposite of elegant.

It didn't matter. The airmen and the women from town were buoyant, and the room spun with life. Grenfell danced with her once then drifted away, saying she should dance with men her own age. "Smile, my dear. Those pilots have their eye on you." He winked, and she turned toward the sea of air force serge—but like a sailor lost for land, her eyes sought only the civilians in the room.

The nearest one was Pete.

"What are you doing here?" He gripped her arm, his mouth a hard, set line, his eyes a dark, saturated blue. She was instantly aware of his intensity, an aspect of the fiercely charged connection they had formed.

Momentarily unsure, she began to step away.

He took her hands. "I didn't think I'd see you again!"

Then there was a flash of light and she went blind. Someone had snapped a photo of a serviceman nearby. "*Hey!*" the man shouted.

It dawned on Sonia then that photographs record aspects of life she'd believed invisible to others, and for the first time she saw herself as an observer would.

Pete enfolding her and his shock giving way to something so gentle she could not give it a name.

This was the photograph she most wanted. That moment of realization, pure and untarnished.

FIFTY-SIX

September 1965. Route 6, Winsloe to Rustico, Prince Edward Island.

The drive from town grew kaleidoscopic as Pete increased their speed, but for Sonia the world transformed itself continuously even when the car slowed down. Seeing, finally, after so many years, was a revelation. She felt vertiginous and awed, overwhelmed, yet helpless to stop looking. She wanted to rip her glasses off her face—and to impress them on her skull. She wanted to laugh, to scream. Vistas like this were what she'd drawn and painted all those years ago.

With every mile, she felt more whole. A part of her that had been hollowed out grew full. Beside her, Pete drove and grinned, and she felt consumed by an urge she didn't understand—a product of joy or grief, or an amalgam of the two.

Laughter kept catching in her throat.

She didn't want the drive to stop. Pete was confident behind the wheel, not impatient like Dan and Rose. She gave herself over to the views unfolding beyond the windshield of the car—the colour of the trees, the clarity of the light, the pale blue sky with its wisps of pure white cloud (mares' tails, foretelling rain)—and to the intensity of the smooth new asphalt road, its deep blackness and the corresponding brilliance of its sunflower yellow central stripe. Oh, don't stop, she thought when the car began to slow.

Pete pulled over onto the edge of a narrow red shale road, resplendent woods all around.

He was asking her a question. She tore her eyes from the trees to look at him. "Thank you," she said, taking the bread and cheese he held out. "How delicious."

She chewed slowly. Never had such simple food tasted so complex. Store-bought bread and ordinary cheddar. Thick swipes of butter. He would have made this lunch that morning before he went to work. She tried to picture him slicing the cheese and spreading butter on the bread—performing this simple act of domesticity. Would he look at the bread? Would he see it? Or would he have his mind on other things? A patient whose care he'd attend to that day, perhaps, or a misty morning scene out his kitchen window?

Was there a window in his kitchen? Did he "camp," as a bachelor might, at a rented apartment in town—or did he live in a house outside of town, and care for it in a deliberate way? What she knew about him now could fit on the head of a pin.

And what she knew would be her downfall, or her saving grace. Because she was caught now, caught again: she could feel it.

"Do you remember when we came here?"

They were at the place where the road to Reilly's Shore began. Of course she remembered.

"Do you remember that long drive we took—it seemed like a long drive then!—on my bike?"

She remembered how they'd thrown the bicycle down at the end of the road and walked out to the beach, marvelling at the sugar sand and the whipped-up surf—as if they hadn't spent an entire summer looking at those same things.

"I remember lifting you up in my arms." He closed his eyes. "And setting you down at the edge of the surf..." He opened his eyes.

He was looking at her, but in a way it seemed he was looking through her—through her, to the girl she'd been when they met.

"I remember letting you go, and then running to catch up with you again..."

In some important way, he wasn't real. He'd made her see. But he wasn't real in the way Max had been real, simultaneously chaining himself to, and struggling against, the incessant demands of farm life and the needs of the children. She had hated Max's anger and ambivalence, but he was real.

Was Pete real?

Sometimes you could reach another person, she decided now, and sometimes you couldn't.

Pete had left her when she needed him. He couldn't be relied upon any more than those soap opera men Rose had briefly adored, whose promises fell apart from one Friday afternoon to the next.

"At school that fall," he said, "I slept for hours in the mornings. I couldn't figure out how to get up. It was as though I had a disease, but if I had to name it, it was just misery. Whenever I thought back to you, here on the Island…Well, I lost a year that way."

He reached for the wax paper wrapping from the sandwich he'd given her.

But I am better now, and I am over you. That was the subtext of this rehearsed-sounding speech, she decided.

He crumpled the paper. "But I'm better now." He actually smiled as he said it.

The drive began with scrubby woods, mostly alder with its dangling catkins and disordered willow. Then they came through an open area where a wooden bridge spanned the narrow space between two halves of an hourglass lake. Next, mature deciduous woods—a partridge sprang, panicked, in front of the car—then scrub again, with diverging tracks through woods and field. Finally, stunted spruce, wild rose, bayberry and rushes. And then the dunes themselves with their swaying, sword-sharp blanket of marram grass, waving silvery green in the weak fall light.

He parked the car and she tried to focus as he told the story of a recent patient, sent to Toronto for treatment—the success of the woman's surgery and the subsequent challenge of understanding what she saw. She'd been blind most of her life. Pete struggled to teach her how to see. She was like a child, he said, thrilled with each new discovery, but facing an impossibly long learning curve.

"Just think of things you've seen," he said. "How hard they would be to explain."

What had she seen? She couldn't think.

She closed her eyes, and unexpectedly Rose emerged, pinning ice-coated clothes to a line strung over the stove, frowning and complaining: *I thought it would be fine. Usually when they brag up a storm, it doesn't come to anything.*

Then, herself at the sink, filling a quart bottle with tea and wrapping it in layers of newspaper for the boys out digging potatoes in the unseasonable cold.

Taking their tea out to them. The clear, fluting call of a jay and a murder of crows massing on the dug-up field.

The digger going by: a dull roar and clatter over which a haphazard arrangement of squeaks and squeals rode like foam on waves. Max driving the tractor that hauled it. The awkward way he held his body, alert for a misplaced note in the seeming dissonance, any sign of breakdown.

Or Max beside the tractor, broken down, silence all around, and the explosion of his rage when he couldn't fix whatever had gone wrong.

Pete's still, patient silence beside her now, against these violent sounds that made such vivid pictures.

In the distance, the faint pop-pop of hunters' guns — like toys, harmless-sounding. But the next day all the water birds would be gone.

The look of light on water, spangled, glinting seaward.

Or water glassy calm, what Grenfell Hillyard called *all starched and ironed.*

Then her boys gobbling the squares and cheese biscuits she'd made. Unwrapping the bottle of tea from its insulating blanket of newspaper, laughing as they read a crazy headline: *Preacher talks to God, gets reply.*

In the hedgerow, all the leaves gone off the trees, next year's buds already formed at their tips — that expectant look.

The crows, that deceitful, gilded day, scolding from the porch roof while she hung clothes out on the line, insisting to her that something had gone awry. How she'd ignored their message out of selfishness; she'd felt so calm — for once — so contented, in that abnormal winter heat.

And then Evvie slamming in the door, indignant. *Isn't Stella here?*

Pete, looking at her now, an unfathomable expression on his face and his hands blanching on the steering wheel.

For a while he talked and she listened. His brother, Paul, had been killed eighteen months earlier in a fishing accident.

"One time when he was little he ran away," Pete said. "He was eight or nine, a skinny, sickly child, and too much babied by our mother. That was in the summer of '31, the night of that terrible storm — do you remember that storm? — three boats wrecked at Savage Harbour."

She didn't remember, but she nodded because he seemed to need her to.

"My mother'd heard him talk about the woods, and that was where we found him, curled up against the base of a sugar pine..."

Sugar pine. Her memory offered the smell of candy floss at the plowing match — the rides and the quilts and the aisles of beribboned flowers and pie and jam — and two-year-old Stella chattering to the laying hens in the poultry display barn.

"Afterward..." he drawled, hesitating, aware he'd lost her attention.

She tried to focus. He had to tell his story. *His little brother, Paul.*

"Afterward?" she said.

He took her hand, held it for a moment, gently let it go.

"He'd filled a sack with bread and apples. He had our father's Thermos, full of milk. He had his pocketknife and a blanket and a compass and he knew enough to tell the neighbours where he was headed. How incapable we thought he was and how well prepared he'd actually been! He planned his adventure like a four-star general. It was why we never worried later when he went out on the water..."

And then Stella alone by the exotic chicken cages, cooing and pushing her hand through the wire to pat their fancy feathered heads.

An interfering older lady tried to scoop her up. "This one has *no mother*," she complained, grabbing for Stella's minute starfish hand.

Several minutes passed in silence. Then something ordinary occurred to her: Pete was sad.

This felt like a revelation, though of course it was nothing of the kind. It was an observation she ought to have made earlier. He'd been paying attention to her. Why not she to him?

She had been too focused on her own persistent grief.

She forced herself to take his hand and she said the thing she now realized she felt. "I'm so sorry about your brother Paul."

At the shore, new after so many years away, sound exploded against Sonia's skin. Not only could she see as never before, she could smell and taste the sea. The moist, forgiving, fragrant air. The heaviness of the salt-laden water as it fell across her feet. The endless, swelling skin of the ocean. Its sonorous rhythm as it folded inward: a deep roar, a crash, a hiss and then the gentle sweeping sound as one fallen and flattened wave smoothed itself across another. Roar, crash, hiss, sweep... that simple, unvarying repetition. Necklaces of seaweed wrapped her bare feet. Bending, she gathered one to take back home. She opened her arms to the whipped-up spray, the settling, smattering waves.

Pete took her glasses off her face and dried them on his shirt. She didn't want to leave the water, but he was insistent. "You're getting the full tour." He led her to his car and turned it around, toward the paved shore road.

Out of nowhere — his voice too loud, overcompensating for the growl of rubber on asphalt, the rough-voiced engine, wind — he began to suggest that he could spend more time with her.

And her instant, instinctive response: a dismissive laugh. Was it really so easy? she wondered. Someone could just hand you a new life on a plate?

She felt amazed by the power and immediacy of her anger. And yet something in his gesture was captivating. This reaching toward her.

For a moment, imagining a return to that summer idyll they'd shared, she felt a weight in her body lift away. As though a bird had taken flight inside her chest.

And then the memory of how he'd left her, further anger, and the realization that she now had the power to affect his choice—his life.

How seductive it was, this feeling of being in control. She hadn't experienced it since those early days at her father's light, when for a morning or an afternoon Daniel would leave her in charge of the entire station.... It was tempting to grasp the opportunity. After a lifetime without choice, was it not her turn to be in charge?

Surely it was her turn. Resentment roiled up for a moment. But then he stopped the car—she turned to look at him—and when she looked, she saw *such concern.*

Again, that feeling like a lifting and her anger fell away.

He'd changed. She could see that now. He noticed more. His pretension was gone and that treasured sense of specialness because he was a medical student at McGill. Gone too the hurt she'd sensed that summer after he left medical school; apparently those wounds had healed. He was calmer. Certainly he seemed more compassionate, more attentive, more interested in other people. These were welcome developments.

All of this he must have learned from hardship or disappointment, just as she'd learned about life by living so unhappily with Max and from the constant work of raising their children and managing the farm after he was gone. She'd come to love her solitude, but she knew that to be alone after a long relationship was not the same as to be alone from the first. Shared experience changed a person.

Did they have anything in common anymore? Was there any point of connection, after all that had happened?

He drove without looking at her.

She looked around, marvelling first at the remarkable clarity of everything, then noticing where they were. He'd taken her to the light. At least, to where the light had been.

The tide road was gone. It was possible to see what remained of Surplus Island, but it would take a boat to get there now. Dredging for a harbour up the coast had caused a shift in currents that created a channel where the sandbar had been. Wave action had worn the land away.

She couldn't believe how much the lighthouse tower had broken down. The house and buildings were gone, hauled to Malpeque Harbour to be used as fishermen's sheds. The beacon had been decommissioned, replaced by a skeleton tower on a nearby cliff. There was a nest on the old gallery; Pete had seen a heron using it.

He held the door of his car open. She got in again, and as the air began to cool, they drove farther west.

"I want you to see the most beautiful place," he said.

This was what their friendship had been based on: Pete looked at her island and saw it for her. He looked at Max, and she saw her husband for the first time, his distance and lack of devotion.

Pete looked at her too. What did he see?

So this was the famous sandhills: bleak, nothing left of the community that had thrived so briefly, nothing now but sand and sea. How lonesome it felt. And yet, how tranquil.

Together, they surveyed the dunes and the ocean. Sonia looked without her glasses and then with them on. Laughing, they tried to count the layered lines that made up the sea, the sky, the land.

There were a hundred, or a thousand.

He said, "With those glasses, your pictures will be different now."

She thought of the hours — years, it sometimes seemed — she'd spent staring out of lighthouse towers at lines like these — at this same sea — willing a distant shadow, or a hint of a shadow, to resolve into a vessel of some kind.

FIFTY-SEVEN

Pete began to build a fire.

The lights from his car's high beams lit the marram grass on the bank and a stretch of sand, gilding Pete too as he worked.

A picnic supper and a bundle of wood in the trunk of the car testified to a certain premeditation. She didn't care. She couldn't remember the last time she'd been away from home like this. Had there ever been a time?

He tended their fire. He said, "Soon it will rain."

She said, "We should get back. My children will worry."

And he said, "No." He'd told Dan he'd drive her back, it didn't matter how late.

For the briefest moment, she felt betrayed by Dan for accepting this.

But the feeling of her feet in the cool, damp sand, and the contrasting heat of the fire Pete had built. Pete saying, It will keep us warm.

The night around them. That blanket of dark, enclosing what anyone could see was a ridiculously small portion of illumination and warmth.

In the parked car, gazing at the distant remains of the fire, she began to reconsider what had happened. His arms around her.

The last time she'd seen him at Surplus Station, she'd expected something. A commitment — not just yearning, not just a broken promise. How vast a gap there was between what she'd needed then — or what she'd thought she needed — and what he'd been able to provide.

"Tell me about her."

"Do you want to hear?"

He nodded, and the thought came: Stella had been preoccupied by something. With Sonia it had been wool, colour, luminosity, line and shape—the work that Max and her children took her away from. But for Stella it was something else. Some absence.

She saw Stella in her kitchen, holding newborn Kate. Evvie was there, his spirits high. *Do you like my baby girl? Isn't she something?* As though Kate were a prize he'd won. Kate cried inconsolably, and Stella stood by looking scalded, bereft, unsure of what to do.

You could hold her differently. Like this, Sonia thought of saying now. But what had she said then? What help had she been?

"My brother Paul," Pete said, and she realized he had not told as much of that story as he wanted to.

"My brother dying was the worst thing that ever happened to me," he said. He hesitated, wondering, Sonia understood, about the wisdom of telling a story that so closely echoed the pain of her own. She felt her mouth open, seemingly of its own accord, but there was nothing she could say.

"I don't mean to compare his death to Stella's," he said. "They're not the same."

Sonia nodded. They were not the same.

"But, you know, an interesting thing happens to your other relationships when someone close to you dies."

She looked at him, waited. What could he possibly say that would make any of this better? Why was he probing a wound that had not even begun to heal?

"I know they're not the same," he continued. "Because as hard as Paul's death was on me, it was a thousand times harder on my mother."

Sonia nodded, turned to gaze out at the sea. The idea that a mother might mourn a child was hardly profound. Or was he saying, even more obviously, that she and his mother had an experience in common?

"This might seem self-evident to you," he said, his voice now sharp, hard. "But it wasn't obvious to me. Until Paul's funeral, I hadn't seen my mother for almost twenty years."

She turned to look at him.

"I was angry with her," he said clearly.

She waited, curious, a little stunned. Pete so rarely expressed a negative emotion. She remembered how wild Max had been when he interrupted them in the lighthouse kitchen. And how tenderly Pete examined Max's weeping, damaged arm. How gentle he had been with Max, in spite of everything. How patient.

"You remember," he said. "She didn't want me to see you. She made me promise not to visit you, not to come between you and Max. She chased me back to Montreal a week before school went in, and she worried more about what the neighbours would say than what I wanted."

Sonia remembered what Cy and George had plainly told her: *He's leaving soon. You'll both get hurt.* She remembered Pete's discovery of her pregnancy, and his sudden distance, that instant chill.

"It was weak of me to give in to her," he said now. "*I should have given in to you.*"

Given in. But that wouldn't have been any better, would it?

Of course, there was no way it could have worked. He wasn't Stella's father; Max was.

So there was no way, was there?

A hateful sound—animal.

Weasels scream murder to distract their prey. She'd heard one once, around the time Buddy disappeared. Its cries were terrifying. If that's how they sound ordinarily, she'd wondered, what became of their voices when they themselves were trapped?

His arms were so tight. She could hardly breathe. She couldn't see. Everywhere was velvet blackness except that one faint pinpoint of flame-orange light.

Far away, it sounded like, some poor creature wept.

The louder the sound grew, the tighter his arms squeezed.

This *hurt*. She wanted to tell him. But she found she couldn't speak.

And she didn't want to be let go.

The realization calmed her, and she took a breath. She said, "It hurts."

"I know... Everything will be okay."

Okay? She tested the word in her mind.

It was meaningless.

She closed her eyes. His arms were still like bands around her chest, that tight.

Stella, she thought.

I'm so sorry.

And finally something taut inside her, something like a string, or a line, let go—

FIFTY-EIGHT

On the sandhills, the tender blue light that sometimes follows dusk sloped slowly into black before, eventually, it was replaced by the more stable blue that suffuses the sky at dawn. In the close dark, in the moments between their talk, Sonia began to wonder if she and Pete could replay what had happened and make it happen all a different way. In her sleep-deprived, exhilarated state, she wanted to believe that they could.

And that made all the difference. Because *belief* and *wanting*, it turned out, that combination, was what had been missing from her life all along.

FIFTY-NINE

After that hard year, everything changed. Rob and Dan expanded the farm and metamorphosed into serious businessmen. Kate lived with Sonia and Pete. Lyman got his electrical ticket and moved out west. The used car lot Ray Vermeer had been working at ballooned into something like a fairground, and somehow he bought into it. Someone built a Dairy Queen in town, the first fast-food joint on what eventually became a glittering, two-mile-long strip of grease. It would be another twenty years before the Purity Dairy counter closed as a result, but this was the beginning of the end of all that, too.

August 1986. Charlottetown, Prince Edward Island.

Stella reappeared the year Kate turned twenty-three. Not in some Toronto bedsit as — all those years ago — Sonia had hoped she would, but in Kate herself: stringy-haired, long-limbed, wan, intense, but mercifully not despairing in the way her mother had been.

Kate struggled some. At school she tried pure science, and for a while she floundered. But she was training now to be a large animal veterinarian, encouraged by Pete and Sonia, happily working with the creatures she had loved so dearly as a little girl.

Rose took Frances, Kate and Sonia out the day the Purity closed up shop. Rose was pregnant that summer, a scandalous single CA on the cusp of forty, but definitively in charge, and finally at ease. She wore a blue polyester maternity suit with a bow tie blouse—and a gentle smirk. With her good government job, she was easily able to afford this indiscretion of which no one had had the imagination to think her capable.

Reconciling Rose's new life with her old one required of Sonia an extraordinary mind shift: she had to accept that all along she'd had no idea who her middle daughter wanted to become. But she had no trouble admiring the result.

At the Purity counter on its last day, Sonia and her girls sipped chocolate shakes and reminisced. Kate was home from school in Calgary. Rose laughed at Frances's indecision: should she stay on the Island in the fall or finally move away?

While Rose and Kate nudged Frances along, Sonia silently hoped that Frances would find the courage to act. But she didn't interfere. Marina's voice echoed in her head: *All you can do is solve your own life.*

None of the women needed to speak the question branded on their brains: *What would Stella do?* Over the years they'd absorbed her story and fashioned from it something they could call their own. Their lives were made of Stella's life the way a wave is made of sea.

EPILOGUE

December 2000. Prospect, Prince Edward Island.

Christmas, and Frances claimed to experience a sense of peace unimaginable in the city. "No Sunday shopping! Thank God," she said.

"And get this," Kate cheered. "No Internet for twenty miles!"

Kate had brought her boyfriend, a man she met at a stable in Calgary. "He's a geologist, but he loves horses the way I do."

Kate missed her horse. "We should go coasting," she declared. "Let's *all* go!"

All meaning Kate and her guy, Rob, Dan and his wife Lisa, Rose and her daughter Lily, Sonia, Frances and Pete.

It was a ridiculous plan. Pete took medication for chronic arthritis. Physically, Sonia was slowing down. She was seventy-eight. But no one said boo.

Rose made a Thermos of tea. In the hayloft, Rob found the sleds they'd used as children and he waxed the runners.

Lily rubbed her mittens together as though to make sparks. "Oh!" she predicted, "we'll fly!"

As Sonia pushed off, she realized she'd forgotten the sensation of flying downhill. It was like submerging: being pulled down and borne up at the same time.

She watched her middle-aged sons coast like boys, decades falling from their faces, snow in their greying hair. The deep sound of their laughter and the gentle way they teased Kate's young guy.

When Dan said, "I guess we'd better head her home," Frances said she was carried straight to childhood, to the sensation of fingers and toes so cold they burned, to the comforting animal smell of mittens drying above the stove, to basins of warm water for chilblained feet, and to the silly, speculative games with which they passed the time as they waited for relief. *Where will you go? Whom will you marry? What do you want to be?*

How incredible to be reminded of that casual proximity, she said, that ease I never take for granted anymore.

Sonia looked at her children and grandchildren, alive with delight and sensitive to the vanishing moment. She looked at Pete. All she had.

For an instant, soaring down that hill, a powerful feeling had displaced her grief.

Lily raced to Sonia, skidded to a stop. "Grandma, *look!*" She clapped her mittens together, igniting sparklers of snow and ice that were bright and hot and cool at once.

Yes, thought Sonia, *look at this moment*. In Lily's eyes, it was ablaze with colour.

Notes and Acknowledgements

Most of the characters and settings in this novel are invented. But the summer community on the sandhills at Freeland, Prince Edward Island, was real, as were two of its inhabitants, Ace Walfield and Danny Adams. Alan Graham's historical essay "A Light on the Sandhills," published in *The Island Magazine* in 1981, inspired my imagined version of that place.

Lemuel Vickerson is also a historical person. Thank you to Fred Vickerson for permission to quote from Lemuel's diary.

Two books were especially helpful: *Lighthouse Legacies* by Chris Mills (Nimbus Publishing, 2006) and *B...was for Butter and Enemy Craft* by Evelyn M. Richardson (Petheric Press, 1976).

Excerpts from *Rules and Instructions for the Guidance of Lightkeepers and of Engineers in Charge of Fog Alarms in the Dominion of Canada* are from the fifth edition, published by the Government Printing Bureau in 1912. I am grateful to Dan Conlin of the Maritime Museum of the Atlantic for finding a copy of this document.

The epigraph is from *Against the Tide: The Battle for America's Beaches* by Cornelia Dean (Columbia University Press, 1999).

The title leapt out of the manuscript after I read Anne Compton's interview with Brent MacLaine in Meetings with Maritime Poets.

An early version of the novel's opening appeared in *Riddle Fence*. Thank you to Managing Editor Mark Callanan.

For essential support that sustained me and my children during the writing of this novel, I am grateful to the Canada Council for the Arts, the Prince Edward Island Council of the Arts and the Woodcock Fund of the Writers' Trust of Canada.

I am indebted to many individuals without whom this novel would not exist. Thank you to Chris Mills and Dr. Elizabeth Lai for sharing their expertise in lightkeeping and optometry. Thank you to Michael Cox, Mark Foss, Moyette Gibbons and Laura Kieley for feedback. Catherine Bush, Richard Cumyn and Margot Livesey set their own fine work aside in order to read mine and I am deeply grateful for their generosity and encouragement. Thank you to Denise Bukowski. Thank you to Goose Lane Editions, especially Susanne Alexander, Sabine Campbell, Akoulina Connell, Jaye Haworth, Corey Redekop, Julie Scriver and John Sweet. Bethany Gibson, Goose Lane's incisive and intuitive fiction editor, helped the novel become its best self, and I am grateful to her for a joyful and gratifying collaboration. For kindness in support of the novelist, as well as the novel, thank you to Greg Collins, Catherine Hennigar-Shuh and Anna-Lisa Jones. Thank you to my family, especially Anne Compton, Ben Compton, Judy Compton, Pamela Compton and Ralph Compton.

Photo: Anna-Lisa Jones

Born and raised on Prince Edward Island, VALERIE COMPTON
now lives in Halifax, where she writes and teaches fiction writing.
Her stories have appeared in numerous publications, including
The New Quarterly, *The Malahat Review* and *Riddle Fence*.
Her articles and reviews have appeared in *The Globe and Mail*,
The National Post, *Gourmet Magazine*, *The Ottawa Citizen* and
Quill & Quire.